"That was our brother: The Vampire God, the King of Petty Slights, the Monarch of Whining, the Narcissist in Charge... the child who was so, so very much like our father...."

GOD FORSAKEN

NORTHERN CREATURES BOOK SEVEN

KRIS AUSTEN RADCLIFFE

THE WORLDS OF
KRIS AUSTEN RADCLIFFE

Smart Urban Fantasy:

Northern Creatures

Monster Born

Vampire Cursed

Elf Raised

Wolf Hunted

Fae Touched

Death Kissed

God Forsaken

Magic Scorned

Witch Burned (*coming soon*)

* * *

Genre-bending Science Fiction about
love, family, and dragons:

WORLD ON FIRE

Series one

Fate Fire Shifter Dragon

Games of Fate

Flux of Skin

Fifth of Blood

Bonds Broken & Silent

All But Human

Men and Beasts

The Burning World

Dragon's Fate and Other Stories

* * *

Hot Contemporary Romance:

GOD FORSAKEN

NORTHERN CREATURES
Book Seven

By
Kris Austen Radcliffe

Six Talon Sign Fantasy & Futuristic Romance
Minneapolis

www.krisaustenradcliffe.com

Published by
Six Talon Sign Fantasy & Futuristic Romance

Edited by Annetta Ribken
Copyedited by Juli Lilly
"Northern Creatures" artwork created by Christina Rausch
Cover to be designed by Covers by Christian
Plus a special thanks to my Proofing Crew.

For requests, please e-mail: publisher@sixtalonsign.com.

First print edition, June 2021
Version: 10.19.2022

ISBN: 978-1-939730-80-0

GOD FORSAKEN

THE VAMPIRE

CHAPTER 1

He did not remember placing his hands on either side of Victor Frankenstein's head, nor the shifting movements of his own muscles as he completed his next actions. He did not remember the popping of tendons, the scraping of bones, or the wet smacking of meat that came with a beheading. He remembered nothing of the things in which a vampire should revel.

He remembered the lack of integration of his stitched-together body: The pressure difference between his left fang and his right as they descended through his also-unequal gums. The strange extra bluishness captured by his right eye, but not his left. The echoing caused by his mismatched ears. How one leg did not yet quite understand what his brain was telling it to do.

He'd been decanted into a new cathedral of a body, one built from parts taken from many demolished churches. Here, a foot from a Caribbean night lord. There, a knee from some sniveling Dark Forest vampire. Guts from The One. Elbows from an only recently turned Scotsman. Hand tendons from a strange mundane. An ear from a dumb American who had returned to the Old Country for a tour and had been bitten because he was too arrogant to understand the dangers of night travel.

And inside, where his soul should have been, he housed an equally unknown number of vampiric demons. Some parts spun their vampire hunger and rage so tightly that they'd become cords of power all to themselves. Some were only clouds of need floating inside his head, chest, liver. They all screamed internally, as vampires did. And they all kept him from seeing and understanding the world into which he'd just re-awoken.

There'd been a lab. Also a wooden table, one long and strong enough for his huge bulk. Rain. Thunder.

And old magic cutting through the fleshes that made his new body. Old magic knitting his pieces together because that was what it did, even for vampires.

He remembered some details beyond the uneven pressure as his fangs descended: The crackling white-hot pain of barely-harnessed electricity as it screamed through his body not once, not twice, but three distinguishable times. The rain leaking through the roof and the terror of the Bride as she stood in the doorway.

A woman, her eyes wide and her lips rounded. She, like him, carried scars from the old magic's cuts and connections.

Then his fangs were in Victor's neck and he remembered the slow, vicious beats—one, two, *three*—as the demons animating his flesh sucked every last drop from his reanimator's body.

It wasn't until he had his maker's blood flooding down his throat that his sense of the world turned on. He blinked, and the dingy lab— full of jars, knives, tongs, a spire of a lightning rod reaching into the storm—came into focus. Then the raven-haired woman in the white shift, who was gone in a blink of an eye.

He'd thought of chasing her, but his disparate parts were like puppies rolling around in the glee of killing Victor Frankenstein. What level of narcissism did a mundane need in order to think he could un-dead the undead without consequence? And now that narcissism had literally beheaded Victor's drained-dry corpse.

The vampire and all of his internal clouds and tornadoes of demonic power *were* consequences. They—*he*—was the personification of the raging violence held by the worthy against the unworthy. He was its flesh.

He would have what he deserved. He would control *everything*.

Solid memories only formed once he escaped into the streets of Edinburgh. He consumed rats, both human and rodent. Deer, also, and cattle he found in the Scottish countryside. He was giant, and grotesque, but he had his faculties, and he had the riches of his well-selected victims. He had the wherewithal to be careful with his corpses.

He managed to hide well enough to keep away both mundanes and Scotland's fae as he fed and forced his parts to coagulate into *him*— one being. One vampire.

He would become what he was meant to be—the one true god— even if it took him centuries.

His vampire pieces did not grow together so much as scab onto one another. Dissociations happened often as different personalities forced themselves to the surface, and he would lose significant amounts of time—hours, mostly. Sometimes weeks. Once, years.

He always regained control.

He blinked back into consciousness under a brilliant moon cresting over the sawtooth edges of unfamiliar mountains. The air was colder than it should have been, and drier. Snow drifted against the surrounding ragged scrub trees, all of which were shorter than his almost eight-foot height. But those mountains...

They were real peaks, not the rolling tall hills of the Highlands, which meant he'd returned to a continent. A dry, cold continent, and in the middle of winter.

He wore heavy boots meant for riding, unrefined brown britches, and a surprisingly soft undershirt over which suspenders held up the brownness on his legs. The fur of the coat topping his shirt and britches was a brilliantly soft grey and from an animal he did not immediately recognize. A soft and comfortable felted hat with large, folded brim sat on his head—a "cowboy hat" if he remembered correctly. Each hip carried a gun. Revolvers, from the looks of them.

He would have sneezed, if vampires sneezed, because of the dust carried on the breeze.

A woman stood at his side.

She was not the Bride. He'd mostly forgotten about the black-haired woman in Victor's laboratory. This new woman could have been her twin—tall, raven haired, with a roundness to her breasts that perfectly mirrored the roundness of her hips, and eyes so blue and bright they looked like the ice of a glacier.

She wore an emerald green dress so long that it skimmed the dirt, though its hem looked as fresh and new as if the dress had been made only hours before. She'd cinched her also-emerald fur coat with a sturdy leather belt. Unlike him, she wore leather gloves.

No, she was not the Bride. Nor was she human.

She picked her own cowboy hat off the ground and brushed off the dusty snow before placing it back onto her lovely midnight hair. "It happen again, darlin'?" she drawled in a very American way.

The accent sounded practiced, and not quite correct, as if some staunch Scottish refused to leave her voice.

It never would. A fae was always a fae. They carried their native land in their blood the same way he carried the parts of the many vampires that made up his body.

He looked around, and there, down the slope, saw an overturned stagecoach surrounded by many broken bodies. He touched his lip over one of his fangs. The socket felt fat and the spin of his demons had slowed.

"I fed," he said. He'd had his fill, too, from his body's satisfaction. He glanced at the woman. Had she fed as well? If she was the type of fae he suspected she was, she might have.

She dropped her hand to the revolver on her hip. "Definitely happened again." The gun, like his own, was steel. Hers, though, carried ornately carved silver plating.

She understood about his time lapses, which meant they'd traveled together. It also meant that at least some part of him trusted her enough to divulge such details.

He was not "some part." He was all his parts. He was the coagulated vampire son of Victor Frankenstein.

He pointed at her hand on her gun. "That won't help you." He'd snap her neck before she drew the revolver from its holster.

She laughed. "My dear, I know how to slow you down."

She was concerned, but not frightened. And yes, they'd been intimate. Quite intimate, actually, from the flashes of her breasts popping in and out of his mind.

Sometimes flashes happened after he reemerged. Mostly not. Flashes meant a long disassociation.

"Date and place," he said. If they were as intimate as the flashes suggested, then she would know how to handle grounding him in an unfamiliar world.

"It's 1885. December. You are in the newly formed Wyoming Territory of the United States of America. Green River is that way." She pointed southeast through the low growing scrub trees. "Rock Springs is that way." She pointed due south between two taller trees. "We had fun in Rock Springs two months ago."

She grinned with the iridescent malevolence only a dark fae could manifest.

A flash: Miners. Men from Europe and men from China. He'd "fit in" with the European miners. They hadn't understood what he was, or why he found them easy prey. It had taken nothing to spark the violence among his European brethren. The body count had been substantial. And filling.

Her grin vanished. "There's a reason you're with me, darlin'," she drawled. "Who do you think taught you to glamour?"

Yes, he thought. They'd crossed the ocean together. Which meant part of him knew how to glamour so his height would not draw attention.

She held out her arm and twitched her wrist. The green dress wavered as if alive. "Low-demons, love," she said. "Much better than making a new gown every year."

She had tamed a hive of low-demons and trained them to do her bidding?

He pointed. "Give them to me." Such a prize should be his.

She laughed. "You always say that when you come out of one of your happenings." She spun around and the green dress floated up, revealing her feet.

She wore boots on normal feet the same as he wore boots on his, even though he knew she didn't. Either she glamoured or the low-demons made her feet look human for her, because he was pretty sure this fae should be dancing on the hooved toes of a deer.

"*Heh,*" he said.

The woman took her hand off her revolver. She tipped her head to the side and continued to watch him as if all their intimacy had reinforced in her mind just how terrible he truly was.

Because he was terrible. He was a plague. He'd killed as many mundanes as the wars, famines, and diseases he used as cover.

"What's your name?" he asked.

She sashayed over, swinging her hips in a way which, if he were a mundane man, would have immediately clouded his mind.

She set a hand gently on his chest, barely touching, at just the correct pressure to cause a tickle to dance across his vampiric skin. "Evangeline," she purred.

Evangeline was not her name. This fae, like all fae, would not share her real name. Most likely she'd taken it when she came here, to the Wyoming Territory of the United States of America, after feeding well on stupid mundane male settlers, miners, and cowboys.

Like him, she sucked them dry.

The stories of her kind, when told by men, always cast the men as saints. They "yearned for their beloveds" and they "wished only for their wives." The *baobhan sith* knew better.

She was vengeance cast down on the cheating, his beautiful companion.

"My evil angel," he rumbled.

She smiled—a true smile, one that extended up to her eyes and down to loosened neck muscles. "We've been together two years." She nodded toward the stagecoach. "That was my anniversary gift to you."

She considered killing mundanes special enough to consider it a gift? Feeding was not special. Feeding was rote. His eyes narrowed as he looked between her and the carnage below. They'd ripped apart at least five mundanes. Parts littered the ground. Victor Frankenstein would have been proud.

She rolled her eyes and stepped back. "You can be such a bore when you get like this."

His fangs pushed against his gums as they always did when he found someone's attitude wanting.

She grabbed the crown of her hat and did a little two-step jig across their dusty hollow between the scrub trees. "Next it'll be 'I'm the vampire god! I got me Dracula's intestines!'" She patted at her belly, then slowly moved her hand downward. "Parts of you sure are kingly, darlin'."

She winked.

He had her by the waist and lifted so they were eye-to-eye before she finished her drawled out "darlin'."

She giggled and wrapped her arms around his head.

Dark fae like her weren't supposed to smell bright and alive. They smelled of raging waters mostly, plus small, hidden notes of other-worldly electricity. The smell was what gave them away. Mundanes always knew.

But his evil angel smelled of sweat and life and sage, too.

"Happy anniversary, my liege," she said as she placed a deep, intense kiss on his lips.

This is new, he thought. Though it wasn't. He was near a century old, and even if he did lose time, parts of him had felt the touches of a woman—this woman. The unafraid strokes. The kisses and the fingers running though his hair. This intimacy, even if it was between demons.

"*Hmmm*," he hummed. How many times had he flitted back into existence in the middle of a murder? While inflicting general mayhem? Or just existing next to a lake, or a stream, or in a ditch? And now, here, he got a treat for his troubles.

Her laughter turned to her own humming, which in turn became the bewitching song of a Highland fae.

And the King of Vampires, the Disassociating God, the son of Frankenstein, the Demon, the creature that would one day be called the last thing he was to anyone—Brother—carried his soothing, singing prize toward the scrub for the rest of the evening's anniversary fun.

CHAPTER 2

The scents of sweat and life and sage Evangeline carried? They did not come from her.

After the sex in the brush, he and his baobhan sith loaded up the spoils of their attack and rode to their homestead in the Sweetwater Mountains. He wouldn't call it making love—they were dark beings and love was not an emotion they felt. They circled around it with need and desire, fear of being alone, and parallel behaviors that united two, sometimes more, into covens. But they did not love.

Except maybe Evangeline. But that love was not for him.

Sunrise crept up the eastern horizon as they returned to the homestead. A fence surrounded a small house and a barn in a fully-cleared area with good visibility. The house looked comfortable for mundanes, or a vampire sized like a mundane. For him, the two rooms and the normal-height ceilings would mean stooping and knocking his forehead into beams.

Yet he'd lived here, with Evangeline, for at least a year.

They rode their horses to the barn. His was a massive draft beast, one capable of carrying his equally massive bulk, and hers a smaller yet still muscular mare. The two beasts were much too valuable to eat.

Horses rarely tolerated vampires, but these two calmly ate their hay and took a quick brushing.

"You brought us the horses," Evangeline said offhandedly as she nodded to the house.

He looked up just as a boy stepped out of the house. A boy that, like the house, clearly predated his relationship with Evangeline. A mop of thick black hair much like Evangeline's capped the boy's head. His shoulders were just beginning to fill out, and though he was gangly, he clearly did well with his body, and looked to be about thirteen years of age.

The boy stood in front of the door like he owned the place. His eyes flashed as they walked toward the house and were the same ice blue as Evangeline's, though without the preternatural fae glow.

Evangeline wrapped her arms around the boy. "You hold the fort for us?" she asked.

The boy smiled a real, genuine, mundane smile. "Yeah, Ma!" But he thought better of it and wiggled out of her grip, which she allowed.

His baobhan sith had a mundane-presenting son and she seemed quite proud of his small act of defiance.

Confusion set in first, then annoyance at both the low ceilings in the house he had yet to enter and the more-mundane-than-fae child with a beating heart and knowledge of vampires. Rapid fire emotions followed: Jealousy, fury, greed, bloodlust, envy.

He was all the deadly sins as he watched his beautiful predator lavish attention on a mostly *mundane*.

Yet he did not attack. He did not interfere. He watched them interact, the baobhan sith and the boy, as she sanitized their murder of the stagecoach occupants for his tender young mind.

The boy jogged over. "Sir!" he said. He blinked a few times. "You look taller."

"I'm not hiding anymore." He needed to figure out how to reengage his glamours.

The boy nodded approvingly, as if the vampire needed the approval of this mundane rival for the attentions of his evil angel.

"Good!" the boy said. "You shouldn't hide, sir."

Slippery fae enchantments hung off the boy like streamers of dark green moss.

Evangeline was hiding her son in the wild hills of Wyoming far away from other fae. Hiding him, the vampire was sure, because though he might present as a mundane, he was a half-breed, and all half-breeds were witches.

If there was one group the fae wished to control more than vampires, it was their own witches.

He clasped the boy's shoulder. Having a mundane-presenting witch around might be... valuable. Especially one who did not burn up with witch fire like so many of the other half-breeds.

Plus the kid loved his mother. And he seemed to respect the vampire giant he called sir.

"Let's go in," the vampire said, and ducked into the uncomfortable house and his life in the shadows under the Sweetwater Mountains.

CHAPTER 3

He built a new house with appropriate ceilings. The boy helped. He invested their acquired wealth into the local community. The boy helped with that, too.

They became a family, if a dark fae, her witch son, and a vampire could be a family.

He learned to harness many of Evangeline's enchantments so that he could wield them with his own magicks. Glamouring his height became second nature. He combined his vampire thrall with her ability to appear and disappear on command and taught himself how to change locations using his will alone. From the one low-demon she granted him for their tenth anniversary, he bred his own and filled them with ash to make his gray suit—and learned to prod his pets to shade his form so that he could walk in daylight.

And when it was time to move to a new stone manor in Rock Springs, the boy told his adopted vampire father that he was enlisting in the U.S. Army.

Soldiering knowledge would be helpful for the family, too.

Not once, through all this, had the boy asked to be turned, nor had he condemned his parents for being part of the darkness. The boy had always been pragmatic, and keen on understanding the true workings of the world. He grew, he learned, and he worked toward keeping the volatility of both mundanes and magicals smoothed and contained.

So the boy, now a man, left the new state of Wyoming to spend time with the Army in places all across the United States, but mostly in the state of Texas. Connections were made, and jobs granted. When he retired his commission, the vampire's son turned his security knowledge to his new role in the Pinkerton Agency.

The vampire and the baobhan sith settled into another decade of comfort. They found that the calmer their life was, the fewer lost times he had. The disassociations stopped altogether, and he found it much easier to pull knowledge—and refined magicks—out of his constituent parts.

He truly became the coagulated whole, unbothered by his bits and in control of his pieces no matter their origin—be they feral beasts, turned soldiers, The One Dracula, a chittering German thing, or a Castilian mundane.

Why the vampire parts of him had not fully consumed the mundane Spanish tendons of his hand, he never did figure. The small pieces of the man seemed simultaneously in The Land of the Dead and also inside the vampire, and were along for the ride, doing what tendons did. Without, it seemed, the same vampiric agenda as the rest of his parts. The tendons were as pragmatic as his son.

Wyoming continued to provide easy hunting, with its settler attitude and sparce population. Time pressed on. The other remaining territories became states. The nation grew. A new century dawned and the vampire began to wonder about love.

He'd spent a quarter century with Evangeline. Because of her, he'd learned to moderate his hungers, and to live amongst the mundanes. She sang away his rages and soothed the worst of his seethings all while helping to hide the bodies of their hunts. Without her, the mundanes would have destroyed him long ago, as they usually did with night feeders and murderers.

Victor Frankenstein might have stitched his body together, but it was a fae who made walking the mundane world viable.

He was a vampire—*the* vampire—yet he had a wife. A son. A family. That alone made him singular among the demons. Special.

So special he allowed himself to enjoy the mid-winter festivals the mundanes referred to as Christmas. The boy, now a leader in the Pinkerton Agency, had returned home.

The sun dropped fully behind the mountains. The vampire leaned against the thick granite column supporting his grand porch and watched tasty mundane children frolic in the snow like innocent lambs.

Behind him, on the other side of the great glass window separating the porch from the interior rooms, the boy sat in the front parlor in his customary well-tailored black trousers and jacket. Evangeline stood on the other side of the room, near the slightly ajar front door, and sang a Christian carol with just the correct amount of irony to bring a smile to her husband's and her son's lips.

It might not be the life of king, but better to exist and learn than to burn away because he could not control his impulses. Immortality allowed him the time he needed to take control of the world, and he would at his own pace.

Besides, the boy was poised to gain access to the power base that was the American democracy. Marauding could wait a bit longer.

An unknown magic hit the house.

Evangeline abruptly stopped singing.

The vampire moved, vanishing from his place on the porch step and reappearing instantly in the center of his parlor.

"Royal Guard!" The boy shouted, weapon drawn and pointed toward the threshold where his mother once sang. His bullets were steel, like the gun, and would do nothing to stop the fae now standing over Evangeline's fallen and lifeless body.

The fae who had found them in the middle of the American nowhere and taken his baobhan sith from him.

The fae who had killed his Evangeline.

"What have you done?" he roared.

The Royal Guard fae wore a gentleman's waistcoat on his human upper half and strong, dangerous-looking goat legs on his bottom. A set of large curved ram horns adorned his head. A mess of dark brown curls filled in between the horns and flopped disarmingly onto his forehead.

The fae looked more bored than attentive or annoyed. "Well, well," he said. "What do we have here?" He moved his hand.

The vampire's son dropped to the ground.

The boy who called him sir, who'd grown into an expert in security and spycraft, who'd helped the vampire build this house with his own hands, collapsed like a ragdoll onto the reds and blues of the rug under his feet.

He breathed still, but only barely.

The vampire lunged at the Royal Guard fae. The goat man danced to the side, twisted, and slammed a bolt of magic into the back of the vampire's neck.

He collapsed like his son, and dropped to the rug next to his dead baobhan sith. His fingers were less than an inch from her lifeless hand —from her low-demons and her lingering magic—but he could not move to call them to himself, nor could his low-demons suck their kin into his personal hive.

He tried anyway.

Goat feet appeared next to his eyes. Then the fae squatted just enough so that the vampire could see his face. He'd changed. His horns were bigger. Sharper. And his eyes had grown black and star-filled.

A fae of great power had come looking for his baobhan sith and her witch son.

The fae poked at the vampire. An eyebrow arched. "So this is where you've been hiding." He scratched at the side of his nose. "Why do vampires smell like spoiled vinegar?" He shook his head. "Does vinegar spoil? It's been a while since I've involved myself in anything domestic."

Had this fae come for *him*? "Who..." he mouthed. The stasis spell clamped his lips closed.

The fae leaned closer. "Are you asking one of those 'w' questions the mundanes love so much? *Why* did you kill the baobhan sith with the low-demons?" He squinted at the vampire. "*When* did you find us?" He closed one eye and moved back a little. "*What* will be left of me when this is over? *Who* are you?" He stood and stepped over Evangeline. "No *who* answers for you. You should know better than to ask a fae's name."

The Royal Guard fae kicked the vampire in the gut.

He did not feel pain the way a mundane did. He felt the damage done by the fae's toes—the splitting of his abdominal wall and the rupturing of his guts. But the damage wasn't anything a feeding could not heal.

He wiggled his fingers toward Evangeline's hand.

The fae nodded at his baobhan sith's cooling body. "Hiding a half-mundane child from the King isn't a capital offense." He leaned down again. "I've done it. We all do."

He pointed at the low-demons squirming over her body.

Without her reining them in, they were losing the emerald pigment they carried while in dress form. They would soon revert into a slithering mass that would drip through the floorboards in search of the darkest, dankest place available to hide.

Unless he pulled them into his suit first. He only needed another fraction of an inch and he could draw them to himself and maybe, perhaps, crack the Royal Guard fae's spell.

"She *defiled* her body." The finger pointing at the low-demons moved to pointing at him. "You're worse than a vampire. You're a re-animated corpse." He crouched again. "Are you cold in the morning, too? Like Death just *cannot* let go."

Too? Were there others like him?

Yes. The woman in the laboratory. The Bride.

The fae leaned closer. "Your brother lives with elves." He rolled his eyes and stood again. "Barbarians."

Brother? Victor Frankenstein built another before him?

The fae's hooves clicked along the wooden floor as he walked around the vampire and, he presumed, to the boy.

"This one has a wife and three children in Texas," the fae said.

The boy had a family? He'd never, not once, said anything about a wife or children.

"Oh!" The fae came back around and looked at the vampire's eyes again. "You did not know." He nodded toward the boy. "His daughter began manifesting magical sensitivity last week. That's how we found the baobhan sith." He looked back at the vampire. "You were a surprise, I'll tell you that." He stepped back and flicked the vampire's nose. "Surprise!"

He'd drain this fae dry of every drop of blood.

He pressed against the statis spell with all his vampire will. With all the strength baked into his giant body. He would not be contained by any fae. He would have his vengeance.

His fingertip touched the side of his beloved's hand.

The fae looked down just as the entirety of Evangeline's hive stiffened—and slammed against the stasis spell. They were unmoored, lost, angry. They'd lost their mistress. They needed their master. They needed their vampire.

The stasis spell shattered as his love's low-demons poured into his own.

He vanished and reappeared with his hand around the fae's neck. "Release my son," he said. They would kill this fae together. Then the boy would explain about his Texas family.

The fae's bored expression returned. He shrugged and released the stasis spell.

The boy gasped for air. "Stay..." he gasped. "Stay away from my children!"

He wasn't looking at the fae. He stared directly at the vampire.

His son meant *him*. "The goat fae killed your mother!" he bellowed.

The boy scrambled toward the settee. "She was a baobhan sith! You are a vampire! I'm not stupid. I understand how you work. You always escalate. Always! It was just a matter of time. Stay away from my family!"

Had it been a lie? All this time? The last quarter century? His family?

His family had been *a lie*.

His evil angel had belonged to *him*. She had not belonged to the fae, nor to the boy. And now she'd been taken away to The Land of the Dead on a *lie*.

They would all pay.

He vanished and reappeared directly in front of the boy. *"Witch,"* he hissed as he pressed his fangs into his son's neck.

Fae-touched blood poured down his throat. The low-demons rejoiced. He rejoiced, and the blood wove its way around his wounds as it filled every muscle and tendon of his body with the touch of fae magic.

He dropped the boy to the floor still breathing. He would drain the goat fae. Then he would slowly finish off the ungrateful brat. No need to allow him to turn and become a vampire himself.

The goat fae snickered, but his face and body were tight with anger. *"Else the Puck a liar call; So, good night unto you all,"* he said. "We're done here."

He vanished.

The rug under Evangeline's corpse burst into flames. The fire in the fireplace exploded outward into the room. The settee erupted, as did the end table and wall next to his son's dying body.

A wall of flame formed between the vampire and the room's exit. Another formed between the vampire and the window.

Viscous heat coiled around his giant body. The low-demons screamed and writhed. He pulled them in tight to his flesh and attempted to leave by moving, as Evangeline had taught him.

He could not. The fae had placed a holding spell on his home, to bind him here. To kill him in the one truly permanent way to kill a vampire, with fire.

His son coughed, then vomited the entire contents of his stomach into the flames. When he looked up at the vampire, his eyes had crystalized to the color of glaciers. "You *turned* me, you bastard." And then he was gone, through the flames, escaping through a binding spell that the fae had somehow made specific to the vampire and his home.

To the heat. The death. The ash.

He may have disassociated. Or maybe, perhaps, he wasn't the true coagulated personality of his body. Perhaps, maybe, his true personality would not shackle himself to family.

To love.

He was sure Death whispered to him at that moment, and struck a deal. *What do you want?* it asked.

Freedom, he thought.

Freedom, a part of him echoed, as if it had made a similar deal at a different time.

So freedom he was given.

CHAPTER 4

Now...

He sat in the corner booth of a neon-soaked Tokyo diner, cigarette hanging from his lip and a cooling cup of black coffee between his fingers. The mundanes saw a taller than average square-jawed man of Japanese descent in an impeccable ash gray suit, black loafers, and a pristine, perfectly pressed blood red tie. They did not see his dull, spade-like broken pike. It leaned against the corner between the booth's red vinyl back and the window, glamoured from mundane eyes both in the diner with him, and outside the wide expanse of window.

They found him unsettling—he was a vampire—but the yakuza glamour gave them an excuse for their gut-level unsettlement.

Beyond refilling his coffee, the mundanes left him alone. No one asked why he never ordered food, or why he never came in during the day. Nor did they make a scene about the occasional "associate" who would shuffle in and sit on the other side of the booth.

Japan had more yōkai than the Isles had fae. Tokyo alone teemed with magicals—hundreds of kami as beautiful as they were powerful, yūrei spirits, oni trolls, and an unending array of yōkai creatures of all shapes and sizes.

And like all magicals, some glamoured better than others.

The one sitting across from him wore a dusty beige trench coat and a wide-brimmed fedora as if it had stepped out of a random forties film noir detective movie. The vampire had not yet learned all the types of yōkai inhabiting the recesses and shadows of Tokyo, nor did he care to, and the small, hairy thing underneath the hat and coat did not inspire any new-found desire for such scholarship.

He extinguished his cigarette in the ashtray next to his coffee mug. Tokyo, like all civilized places on Earth, no longer liked the idea of tobacco. His puffs of bluish smoke were the only ones in the diner and were, he suspected, illegal.

Still, he smoked. It was his way of saging his barely perceptible— and unglamourable—hints of vampire decay.

The yōkai stared out the diner window at the bustle outside. Lovely women in short skirts and shouldering huge handbags darted by along the concrete walkway. Men in button-front shirts and sharply-creased trousers walked like robots. Young people with clothes and hair as bright as the flashing arcade lights laughed, hustled, and thumbed their phones.

So much had changed during his marooned century inside The Land of the Dead. He remembered less of how he ended up with the Dead than he did of removing Victor Frankenstein's head, and only that he'd been granted "freedom."

Such were the complications of his disassociations.

His time in the Land of the Dead had not been completely useless. He'd learned how to manipulate specific universal geometries to power his already substantial magicks, and how to glamour his low-demons into invisibility.

He'd never looked for Evangeline on the other side. There was no need. He'd been set free of love and family.

He'd found Victor Frankenstein, though.

The vampire blinked. He no longer disassociated, no matter what the wood blade in his shoulder wanted. It had taken him several hours

—and several sacrificed low-demons—to figure out how to isolate the Odin's Gallows wood stabbed into his flesh by his bumbling mostly-mundane brother, Frank Victorsson.

He hadn't been himself when the gate into Alfheim had opened. Close, yes, but that personality had not understood the need for calm.

Now, he had the bit of Norse magic mostly contained. The wound ached, but it would no longer prod disassociations. There would be no more appearances by Lord Dracula, though The One did have a seat at the council.

Every so often, he would remember he also carried a part of a mundane—a man called the Castilian. Then he would forget and go about his business as the whole, coagulated vampire he was.

That other vampire who had escaped with him from Dracula's little ash-filled node of reality—Anthea, the woman in the black dress —had had an affinity for the Castilian. The plump blonde vampire had spent their time together chatting words that had called up memory-bubbles of the Castilian's life. Nothing substantial. A prison, the smell of the sea, amorphous yearnings. Impressions, mostly.

Again, he blinked. He no longer concerned himself with his "father," or the Bride, or his brother who lived with barely-civilized bumpkin elves. There would be no more ever-so-subtle risings of the almost-him—almost capable of accessing all his magicks and memories—personality Frank Victorsson had called Brother.

His disassociations landed, on occasion, within common territories on the Venn diagram that was his consciousness. Memories and actions were shared, but not motivations.

None of which mattered. He was, he needed to remind himself, free of family.

And he was a god. *Kyūketsuki no kami*, as the yōkai called him. Vampire God.

Most of the yōkai were simple creatures and not all that different from their mundanes—lonely, overwhelmed, and hiding in plain sight in the middle of this huge city. It made them easy prey for a god.

He pushed at the cigarette butt hanging over the edge of the ash tray. He had eaten a yōkai when he'd emerged from that pocket hell in which Frank Victorsson's elves had trapped his body—yet another bit of evidence that Dracula should not be in charge. As his son had told him after taking on a command position with the Pinkertons, grandiose megalomania only served to get a vampire killed. Better to show some self-control and to build your empire slowly.

Was the boy still out in the wider world? Dracula carried no memories of him arriving in the pocket realm because of the Call.

More blinking. The vampire tapped his finger along the gray Formica of the booth's tabletop. These thoughts were not welcome, and he pushed them away.

"Are you okay, boss?" the yōkai asked.

One month in Japan was not enough to learn Japanese, even for him, so the yōkai spoke to him in English.

The vampire watched the little hairy beast twitch under his hat. He could reach across the table, yank the thing across, and drain him dry in less than a second. The yōkai's magic would stick with him for quite some time. Kami magic, unlike fae or elf, persisted for weeks instead of days. The magic of that nine-tailed kitsune he'd eaten when he arrived still clung to his bits and pieces and was a major reason the yōkai considered him a god.

Which, he suspected, was why yōkai blood was the gold standard on the vampire black market—and another reason why the Japanese vampires were formidable.

Yet they had all crossed over when the Call went out. Japan's three remaining vampires, who had somehow avoided permanent death at the hands of the kami, had fallen to Dracula's whims and traipsed through the gates into the pocket borderland Dracula had built—built with the pike and the blood of Frank Victorsson. The pike had broken the pocket's walls and allowed him to dig himself out.

The Japanese vampires had been turned mundanes. Not turned magicals, hence their weakness.

Turned yōkai would not fall to the whims of other vampires. Turned yōkai would wield more power than any turned witch.

He rubbed at his nose. He did not care about turned witches. He pushed aside that thought, also.

Turned yōkai would be unstoppable—as would their god. He would be free to take what he wanted when he wanted it, no empire needed. Just power and freedom.

Now, he granted wishes to underserved and underappreciated hairy yōkai. Now, he built his army with promises of respect and freedom.

"I am fine." He nodded to the creature that had, in the four weeks he'd walked the lands of the kami, become his Renfield. "What have you learned, my friend?"

The little hairy yōkai grinned. It was not pleasant, and sent a fascinating chill through a few of the vampire's parts. "The Emperor's taken more to sell to the kelpies."

Kelpies. Fae.

The vampire hated fae more than he hated elves, and it had been elves who had locked him in that pocket realm. The fae would be the first to fall to his new army.

And now he had angry yōkai looking to enlist. "He must be stopped." The vampire would say exactly what needed saying in order to close the deal.

The yōkai nodded vigorously. "Thank you, *Kyūketsuki no kami*. Thank you."

There was a balance to the flow of magic in Japan. The Emperor dealt out wrath and destruction. The kami contained his fun.

Time to throw a wrench into the works.

He ran his hand over the remains of Dracula's pike as he leaned back against the booth's cushioned vinyl. "Tell me more."

FRANK VICTORSSON

CHAPTER 1

Alfheim, Minnesota...

N ow was the time to talk about beginnings. About all those moments when you know something's started even if you don't know what. About the hairs standing up on the back of your neck, or your eyes narrowing, or for me, my elven tattoos tingling. When I sensed something starting, the silver treads of Yggdrasil coiling around my ear sang like the lines of magic they represented, and shimmered with power.

Or perhaps they called out from distant, deeply rooted waters.

Such a moment happened a little over a month ago, even though I didn't realize it at the time. A lot of my awareness had been subsumed under ghosts, and vampires, and the oozing magical manipulations laid down by a sibling also built by Victor Frankenstein.

The bits and pieces that had been stitched together to make me had suddenly all come to attention.

So you'd think I should be used to the chills and the tightenings. That I would heed them as portents, or signposts, or at least understand well enough to attend to the attention my body paid.

Because right here, right now, as I walked through the trees lining the path connecting Ellie's cottage to my home, one of those signposts stood alone on the steps of my deck.

Sophia Martinez shivered under the warming golden glow of an early November Minnesota morning sun. She stood on the step to the path in her pajamas, coat on but unzipped, no hat on her ten-year-old head, and pink unicorn slippers on her feet.

Behind her, the patio door leading into my home stood ever-so-slightly ajar and the curtains were rumpled. The smell of brewing coffee wafted from the house—the adults inside were awake. On the deck, toward the lake, one of my patio chairs had been flipped on its side and looked as out-of-sorts as the child in front of me.

Sophia Martinez, who was not an oracle, but who still knew way too damned much.

"Mr. Frank," she said. "Ms. Ellie."

Ellie Jones, my exquisite—and normally concealment-enchant-ment-hidden—fae-born love, blinked as if surprised under her yellow pompom-topped hat.

Sophia remembered Ellie. Again. We needed to figure out why, because something deep down told me that all this knowledge made Sophia a target.

And no child should be a target. Not now. Not ever.

Sophia held out her hand, palm up, on which sat a pile of twined, knotted leather and silver rings that could only be one thing.

Ellie gasped. "Where did you get that, honey?" she breathed.

Sophia looked down at the leather, then back at us. "My papa cut it off a kelpie."

She held a kelpie's bridle, which meant the Martinez family had interacted with a particularly nasty type of fae.

Target, I thought.

Salvation, who I held on my shoulder, flashed out the magical battle axe equivalent of a rage-filled roar. *Oberon will pay!* she bellowed in my head. She'd been yelling about the fae all morning. Nothing particularly coherent. Just a lot of anger.

Now I knew why.

"There was another kelpie?" I asked. We'd dealt with one last night.

Ellie had already hidden his bridle in her library, so there must have been a second kelpie in Alfheim.

Sophia pointed at Sal. "She has a sister, Mr. Frank," she said.

Then she pointed at me.

I knew what she was going to say. I didn't understand how I knew, or why, or what part of my piecemeal soul already understood the truth. Because I think I'd known since Brother took me on that trip down his Victor-forged memory lane. I think I knew during that time we were between The Lands of the Living and the Dead and he showed me Victor's lab in Edinburgh.

I think a deep part of me understood this particular beginning.

"She's alive, isn't she?" I whispered.

Sophia nodded *yes*. Ellie looked up at me surprised, shocked, hurt, frightened—I couldn't tell. They were all there, those pre-jealousy emotions that flip into existence when a mate tries to figure if her ire is needed.

I pulled Ellie close and squeezed her tightly against my chest. The pompom on her hat tickled the underside of my nose. "My sister?" I asked Sophia.

She nodded *yes* again. "Her name is Wrenn Goodfellow. She lives with the fae."

"What?" Ellie pushed away. "*Goodfellow?*"

Goodfellow? I thought. Then I remembered my Shakespeare.

Robin Goodfellow. Puck. The naughty fae who liked to cause problems.

"It's okay, Ms. Ellie," Sophia said. "Ms. Wrenn is nice. She helped Papa save us from the vampires." She sniffed. "The vampire in Texas had ice-colored eyes. I don't like vampires."

We had a kelpie *and* vampires in Alfheim last night while Ellie and I recovered from our own fae-caused ordeal?

All the ethereal control Sophia showed when she presented oracle information—the straight backbone and the tight jaw—vanished into a frightened ten-year-old's cinched up body.

Ellie's anger and confusion evaporated. She reached out for

31

Sophia. "Oh, honey. It's okay. There are no vampires here. You're safe. Right, Frank?"

I set Sal against the deck rail. "That's right." I knew I had messages but I hadn't looked at my phone yet. I'd wanted the few minutes it took to walk between my place and Ellie's to be with her without the complications of the world. Now I wondered if I'd done the right thing.

Sophia hugged Ellie. "Ms. Wrenn likes Ms. Benta best so you don't have to worry," she whisper-said next to Ellie's ear.

Ellie looked up at me, her blue-green eyes rounding in a new wave of bemusement. She blinked. "Okay, honey," she said.

Sophia frowned. "I'm supposed to give this to Mr. Frank so he can give it to you, but you're here." Sophia handed the leather and silver to Ellie. "Your home is the safest place in Alfheim for hiding it."

Ellie gingerly tucked the bridle into the pocket of her jacket. "I'll put it with the other one," she said to me.

Sophia looked up. "This one's special. There are three more like it."

This moment wasn't a beginning. Not like what I had with Ellie last night, when we anchored her cottage to Alfheim. Or the coming one when I would meet a long-lost sister. No, what unfolded between the ten-year-old shivering on my deck and the half-mundane, half-fae love of my life was something... else.

"Three more?" I asked. Kelpies. Vampires. Threats.

Targets.

And suddenly all the trees surrounding my lake—every single one of the massive birch, cedar, maple, and oak towering over my home, the water, the deck, and this child—felt silent and heavy. Crushing and crushed, like they knew something I did not.

Sophia sniffled. "The cold is making my nose run."

"Okay, sweetie." I lifted Sophia onto my hip. I was pretty much the only person in Alfheim physically large enough to carry the older kids with ease. Sometimes it offered them comfort.

I looked up at the naked winter branches overhead and thought we all needed some comfort right at that moment.

Sophia wrapped her arms around my neck.

Ellie squeezed my elbow. "I'll come back as soon as I've dealt with this."

"Thank you, Ms. Ellie," Sophia said.

Ellie jogged back toward the cottage. Sal yelled out into the magic around Alfheim a command—not a call, or an ask, or a polite request —that the elves come fetch her. She needed to attend to her sister.

I grabbed her handle with my free hand. "So Sal's got a sister, too, huh?" I set down Sophia so she could open the patio door.

"Yeah," she said. "She's a lot like Salvation." She pulled open the door and warm interior air washed over us. "But she keeps talking about Fenrir, Mr. Frank."

Fenrir.

All those moments that I suspected were beginnings, all those little puzzle pieces that I hadn't consciously attended to, clicked into place.

Yggdrasil sang, or shuddered, or yanked on magical lines of power.

It begins, I thought. *It began two hundred years ago. It might never end.*

But it would. I knew it would.

We all knew it would.

Sophia stepped through the patio door into my warm kitchen. She moved toward the dining table between the doors and the kitchen island. "You need to deal with the vampires first," she said.

I set Sal against the wall as my dog bounded across the kitchen to my legs. "What do you mean, honey?" I asked Sophia as I rubbed the golden fur of Marcus Aurelius's ears. "Hey, boy."

"Sophia?" My almost-ten-year-old fire elf niece, Akeyla, slid down the hallway and around the corner into the kitchen. Like Sophia, she still wore her pajamas. "Is Sal mad about the sword Mr. Magnus brought home from Texas?" She hugged Sophia. "Do you want to make pancakes?" Then she hugged me. "Uncle Frank's home!" she shouted. "I fed Marcus Aurelius already," she said.

I glanced over to his full food and water bowls. "Thank you," I said.

Sophia tossed her coat onto a chair.

Akeyla took her hand. "You're welcome, Uncle Frank," she said.

All the fae-generated horrors of last night and Akeyla still made sure that my dog was safe and fed. I scratched his ears again but I could tell he wanted to follow the girls. As long as she and her elven mother, Maura, continued to live with me, I wouldn't have to worry about my dog, or the house, either, for that matter.

The girls moved away from the patio doors and dining table into the kitchen proper, and I clearly wouldn't be getting more answers about vampires until after breakfast.

Lennart Thorsson, out of his glamour with his tall, pointed elf ears visible and wearing gray sweatpants and a t-shirt, skidded around the corner into the kitchen in very much the same way as Akeyla had earlier. Wave after wave of stormy, energy-rich, electric blue and violet magic rolled off him, and his big icy-black elven ponytail wiggled behind his head.

Someone was happy.

The girls giggled. Lennart grinned. "Did I hear someone say pancakes?"

I had a young, powerful Thor elf in full Dad mode in my kitchen while we had vampires, kelpies, and elven artifacts yelling about Fenrir.

"Frank!" Lennart clapped his hands together. "Where have you been? You missed a *lot*, my friend."

"Clearly." I opened my mouth to test if last night's changes with the cottage had also changed the overall effects of Ellie's concealment enchantments.

No words came out. I closed my mouth again. At least the enchantments had stopped messing with my thinking about Ellie, even if I still could not articulate to Lennart what happened with the tree and the cottage—and Titania—after I left Arne to chase our kelpie.

My sister calls to me!

Lennart squished his eyes closed. "No need to yell, Salvation." Like most of the elves, he could "hear" Salvation as well as I could.

"It'll be okay, Sal," Akeyla said. She slammed a cupboard door like nothing was wrong with the world. "Red is with grandpa and Mr. Magnus."

"Red?" I asked.

Lennart shrugged. "Redemption."

"Ah," I said. Why weren't they scrambling? We had Fenrir to worry about. And vampires.

Then I remembered I lived with elves. They *were* concerned. They also needed to eat breakfast.

"Lennart," I said. "I need you to catch me up." And to help me sort the situation.

He waved me to sit down while I stripped off my jacket. "Kelpies," he said.

"The one who took us smelled like dead seahorses," Sophia said nonchalantly as she set a mixing bowl on the kitchen counter.

So the bridle came from a stinky kelpie. "Sounds about right," I said.

Akeyla giggled.

Lennart's phone rang. "Hold on." He grabbed it off the counter next to the door. "It's Benta." He held it up to his ear. "Umm…I'll ask." He looked at me. "Do you want to meet your sister, Frank? She's come back to Alfheim."

CHAPTER 2

Turned out the other non-vampiric child of Victor Frankenstein went to live with the fae around the same time I walked out of the Arctic and into Alfheim. Now she was an official Paladin to King Oberon and a member of the Fae Royal Guard.

My long-lost sister worked for my girlfriend's wicked stepfather.

Not that I knew for sure that he was wicked, though the reaction of the elves and the look on Ellie's face when I broke the news made me strongly suspect that "works for Oberon" was not something anyone wanted to mess with right now.

"If she's like you, she'll be able to see me," Ellie said. She leaned against the wood rail of the fence surrounding her cottage and looked over her shoulder at her giant, now fully-rooted ash tree. The storm had stripped any remaining leaves, yet the massive tree still provided shade to Ellie's small cottage. "Banking on her forgetting me at night isn't wise."

I'd jogged back down the path to give Ellie an update. And, if I was honest with myself, to make sure she wouldn't be around at the same time as Benta the Nameless dropped off Wrenn Goodfellow.

Not that Benta would perceive Ellie. No highly magical creature could. Or interact with her. Yet I was sure they'd still generate drama.

Not that I blamed Ellie. Or Benta. I just didn't want to navigate Ellie versus the ex-girlfriend elf at the same time my unknown sister came for a visit.

Ellie tucked her hands into the pockets of her jacket. "I still need new boots," she muttered.

She did. "We'll go shopping," I said. I tugged my hat tighter down over my ears and rubbed at the part of Yggdrasil on the side of my neck. *Later*, I thought.

I had no idea what to think about all this. I had a sister. Was this good? Bad? Ed's kids vouched for her, so unless she was hiding also-wickedness, I didn't think she was evil.

Misguided, obviously, having spent two hundred years with the fae, but not evil. Not like Brother.

Was this my chance to have a family beyond the elven one I'd built over the centuries? And why did I have this deep, uncomfortable twinge that my gathered family here in Alfheim wasn't as real as some woman who had been equally abused by the same narcissistic "father" as me?

It wasn't as if my genetics—all of my genetics, from all the different men whose body parts became mine—had anything more in common with this Wrenn Goodfellow than they did with any of the elves or wolves in Alfheim.

Victor had promised me a companion. A friend. *He* had decided to build a woman. *He* had ranted about a master race. I had naively wanted someone who wouldn't run away screaming every time they laid eyes on me.

A few centuries removed from Victor's yelling and snarling and I was pretty sure he'd wanted a superior woman who wouldn't die and leave him the way his mother had—a realization that had made me hate him that much more.

It also meant that Wrenn Goodfellow was probably perfect and strong and gorgeous to behold.

Ellie sighed. "Frank," she said.

I pulled my attention back to where I should have been in the first place. "Yes?"

Mate magic flared around her shoulders and head, which was new. The cottage must have decided not to siphon it off anymore. Or more likely, Sal had taught it how to fine-grain what it drew from Ellie.

The magical artifacts of Alfheim were very quickly escalating into a sentient community of their own. I wondered what that would mean for Sal's sister sword.

We had a lot to figure out, and my sister was only a part of it. All those feelings about beginnings I'd had earlier? They were quickly being washed out to sea by an "in the thick of it" tsunami.

"I want you to go back up that path," Ellie pointed around my arm, "and I want you to sit down with this Wrenn Goodfellow. I want you to hash out what you two need to hash out, because I'm sure she has as many questions about you as you do about her."

Probably. I shrugged.

Ellie reached up and cupped my cheeks. "Don't tell her about me," she said. "Don't tell her about the tree, either, or the cottage. Not until the elves make sure she's not carrying spy-and-report magicks."

The fae, it seemed, were particularly good at intricate space and time warping magicks, and down through the centuries, they'd figured out how to use their inherent talents to their advantage.

They were surprisingly inventive, too. But then again, they lived for drama, and drama required innovation. Otherwise it's all status quo all the time.

Of all the horrors of my life, I thanked the universe every day for dropping me into good old boring Alfheim, where if I wanted to be inventive and innovative, I could do it on my own terms. Nothing exhausted me faster than having to protect myself from someone else being innovative and inventive with my business.

"There's no way to spook the cottage into moving again," I said. The cottage used to move from location to location as part of its mandate to keep Ellie hidden from the world. It had almost moved last night, but Sal and I—and the tree—figured out how to root it in Alfheim.

Little sparks of bright blue danced around my shoulders. Fae magic wouldn't steal my love from me, which made my mate magic visibly happy.

Ellie frowned. "The cottage is not the point, Frank. Neither is your sister."

Or my mate magic. "Oberon is," I said. "And your mother."

She nodded.

Her concealment enchantments had morphed somewhat since last night, but were still functioning in basically the same form they had been when Ellie and I met—still hiding her from the sight of magicals, keeping me from talking about her, probably making everyone forget about her every night except for me, who the cottage and her mother had accepted. And Sophia, for some unknown reason.

All of which meant Titania might have helped us and the elves, but she was still the Queen of the Fae, and she still had a vested interest in keeping Ellie and the cottage behind protective concealments.

So I couldn't introduce my girlfriend to my fae-employed sister. I couldn't tell Wrenn Goodfellow much of anything about my current life.

"Ask her about Brother," Ellie said. "And Victor."

I didn't want to talk about Brother. Or Victor. And I doubted Wrenn did, either. But they were our common ground.

The worst vampire in existence and a bad father made us family.

I kissed Ellie's forehead.

"And Fenrir," Ellie said. "And if she'll talk about the fae, see if you can get her to tell you what Sophia meant by there being three more bridles like the one I just put in the library."

I inhaled deeply, and exhaled slowly. "I don't want her to think I'm shaking her down for information."

Ellie pinched the bridge of her nose. "Robin Goodfellow is messing with us," she said. "He's messing with *her*." She pointed down the path. "If I had to choose between Robin Goodfellow or Hrokr Lokisson, I'd choose Hrokr every time, Frank. Every. Single. Time."

"Who?" Did we have a Loki elf in Alfheim I didn't know about? We did. I knew we did. I could feel memories just below the surface.

"Concealments aren't just for the fae," Ellie said. "I'll explain later."

I nodded.

"Do *not* mention Hrokr, either." She looked up at the sky. "Why did the woman Victor Frankenstein built to be your perfect mate and companion have to show up now?" She bit her lip. "And with the name Goodfellow?" She threw her arms wide. "Of all the fae in all the realms, the one who takes her under his wing had to be Robin Goodfellow, didn't it? Oberon's Second in Command is the very definition of the trickster fae."

I had no idea what comfort I should offer. "I'll be careful about what I say."

She sniffled and stood up straight. "I'll stay here. Make some tea." She waved me away. "Please come back before sunset, okay? Don't make me sleep without you tonight. I need to know you're safe."

And not with Wrenn, the set of her face said.

"The mate magic's got me locked down, love," I said.

Ellie laughed nervously. "You should sit down with Gerard Geroux and ask him exactly how mate magic works when there's fae magic involved."

I blinked. My stomach did a tiny little jump as if a part of me believed Ellie just broke up with me. Or was planning on breaking up with me if Wrenn Goodfellow turned out to be an option and not a sister.

Damned Victor Frankenstein planted all sorts of stupid notions in me and Wrenn being a mate was the worst of them, especially since no other part of me entertained that thought. Yet here it was rearing up specifically to harass Ellie.

"Sophia said she likes Benta best." My lip twitched and I was pretty sure I pouted just a little.

Ellie grinned. "Benta *is* hot."

I chuckled. "She's an elf. They're all gorgeous."

Ellie tapped my chest. "She is Earth-shatteringly, gloriously-perfect, volcanically hot."

Benta really was beautiful. "Magnus is objectively the most glorious elf in Alfheim."

Now she laughed. "He's terrifying, Frank." She sighed. "Benta the Nameless is just as terrifying under that supermodel glamour of hers."

"They're aspects of fertility gods," I said.

Ellie squeezed my hand. "All the Norse gods are war gods. Even Freya and Freyr." She kissed my cheek. "Go on. Talk to your sister. Just don't make any kissy faces."

I chuckled. "Do you have any idea how much I love you?"

She kissed me again and pointed at the barely visible seam in the bark of the ash tree where I'd slammed Sal so we could siphon off Titania's magic in order to move the cottage. "Yep." Then she sent me on my way.

CHAPTER 3

I rounded the bend and passed between the two oaks framing the path between Ellie's world and mine.

Dryads had appeared here. Dryads come to invade the elves' privacy—my privacy—and report back to Oberon. Or Robin Goodfellow. Or both.

I stopped and looked up through the naked branches at the bright blue November sky. *Breathe*, I thought. Ellie was safe. The Martinez family was also safe—I needed to call Ed once I had a moment. Sounded as if little Grace had been born last night too, on top of the issues with the other kelpie.

No one had died. No one had been hurt. Dagrun continued to heal from her wounds.

Wounds that had not come from the World Wolf.

But had been caused by a very powerful wolf.

A wolf who did not like elves.

Not a genie, as that rich mundane blowhard St. Martin had claimed. Not the World Wolf, but close. Queen Titania hinting at terrible things to come. And Salvation's sister sword yelling about Fenrir.

The sky became the most brilliant of blues. Jays cackled. And the voices of arguing women in front of my home carried through the trees. Because such eureka moments were like magic, in a way. They clarified everything.

Everyone knew what happened when Fenrir got loose.

Bastien-Laurent St. Martin—the man who'd brought the "genie's" power to Alfheim—had been working for Fenrir.

Fenrir. I closed my eyes. What did that even mean? Just exactly what kind of magic came with the name Fenrir?

Besides Ragnarok. *Damn it,* I thought.

Maura's voice rang out between the trees, as clear as if she stood next to me. "If I catch even a whiff of fae magic I don't like, I'll take off your head. Understand? No warning. No questions. Lennart says you can be trusted but my gut says anyone who calls themselves Good-fellow should have their ass kicked all the way back to the fae realms."

My elf sister must be threatening my fae sister.

I rubbed my forehead. How did my life get so complicated? But then again, it had always been complicated in some way or another. After two hundred years, it looked as if I was about to experience a whole new kind of family drama.

And the end of the world.

"It's your right to think that," said a woman I did not know. "I don't blame you."

I looked up at the sky again, and as I watched a lone puffy cloud pass overhead, my brain made the pettiest, most obnoxious thought it could.

At least I got to go into the end of my world surrounded by a king-dom's worth of extraordinary elf and fae women who loved me.

Unlike my father.

I *hmphed* as I continued down the path, thinking I should definitely keep that thought to myself. We had other issues to deal with first.

I rounded the last tree and my house came into view.

A woman stood on my deck just a few feet from the break in the railing and the step to the path, but she wasn't looking at me. She watched the lake.

She was tall like an elf with thick black hair she wore loose. She had some width to her shoulders that said she could easily wield Sal's sister sword. But she was also as perfectly proportioned as I suspected Victor would have desired in a perfect woman—that width in her shoulders was mirrored exactly by the width of her hips. And between the two, lovely breasts and a strong, center-of-the-hourglass core.

Her clothes and boots were also black, and looked both modern and not at the same time. Like her, they had an ethereal air to them, as if they'd been manufactured by magical artisans. The black leather jacket in particular looked fae-made.

Something in the lake made her flinch. "Are you okay?" I asked.

She turned toward me. No scars. No tattoos, either, to accent her sharp Anglo Saxon features and dark fire-lit irises—irises much like my own. Other than the wisps of green and red fae magic lifting off her forearms and wrists, she didn't carry any overt spells I saw.

I extended my hand. "Frank," I said as I stepped up onto the deck. "You must be Wrenn."

She blinked and looked me up and down. I clearly wasn't what she expected. Not that I had any idea what she would have expected. Though I could guess at what Victor had probably told her, if he'd told her anything.

I smiled and put my hands in my pockets to be as nonthreatening as possible. "Is this as awkward for you as it is for me?" I looked at the lake. "Two hundred years and I had no idea you'd survived."

When I looked back, she was peering at my shoulders as if ghosts danced on my back. Did this have something to do with our father?

"Victor told you I was a monster, didn't he?" I asked.

She inhaled. Her lips thinned as if she was trying to decide what to say. "He told me you tried to drown me to force him to make me your mate," she said.

No sugarcoating, there. Right into the terrible lies of our father. Honestly, I would have been more surprised if she'd said Victor spoke lovingly about his long-lost son.

"I saved that young girl from drowning," I said. Victor knew. I'd told him. I suspected that's where he got the idea for the lie he told

Wrenn. "He blamed me for his friend's death." Henry had been his name, if I remembered correctly. "There was a boat."

I looked up at the sky. We'd dived right in, hadn't we?

"He told me that I didn't deserve a companion." I might as well dive in, too. "That I was unlovable and horrific. Then he showed me... parts... that were supposed to be you."

"Your mate." She said it as if expecting me to throw her over my shoulder and run off with her, my made-to-order bride.

"What?" Then it dawned on me why she had been looking at my shoulders. "Oh! You see the mate magic, don't you?" She was definitely my sister. She saw magic, like me. "Don't worry. It's not for you."

That mate magic was all for Ellie.

Wrenn's face and neck visibly loosened.

"You look relieved. It'd be weird, anyway. It's been two hundred years. Besides, I've always thought of you as the sister I never had, no matter what Victor thought."

Out front, a truck started up.

"Benta's leaving?" Wrenn said. She glanced around at the walkway leading along the side of the house to the front and all the automobiles that had to be crowding in front of my home.

Part of me wondered why Benta hadn't come around back with Wrenn just to watch me squirm, but it was only a small part. Benta and I had our issues, but she was an elder elf, and as an elder elf, she had duties.

"She's taking Sal in," I said. Lennart had said everyone agreed to separate the angry war axe from all things fae for a while. "The elves need her to see if they can crack the fae enchantments on that sword the kelpie left behind. Sal went crazy this morning. Started yelling 'How dare they!' and about how she would 'take care of the fae threat.' We figured it would be best to keep her away from you for now."

"Is Sal another elf?"

I chuckled. "She's an axe." I scratched at the back of my head. "And a bit possessive."

Wrenn nodded. She looked at the lake again, and stood in front of

KRIS AUSTEN RADCLIFFE

me, her own hands in her own pockets, obviously not knowing what to do any more than I did.

"Victor Frankenstein had a lot of romantic stupidity in his head," I said. "He thought he was entitled to dance along the threshold between the living and the dead." I swept my hand at the horizon. "He got angry when he came face to face with the consequences of his actions." I sighed. "That anger turned to madness, didn't it?"

It had turned into madness long before I left him in the Arctic, but I suppose I was grasping at the one lone straw that he'd left her out of his misery.

She nodded *yes*.

He probably laid it on her so thickly it should have broken her back. That was what narcissistic men did to their victims. Yet here she stood on my deck, a free woman who had moved on with her life. She was Fae Royal Guard.

"The only information we found were letters written by a ship captain," I said. "We all thought he'd died shortly after I left him on the ice. I didn't learn otherwise until last month."

She blinked a couple of times.

"We're not his only creations," I said gently.

Her cheek twitched. "I watched him behead Victor," she said.

She hadn't only been terrorized by Victor. Brother terrorized her, too.

"I am sorry." I rubbed at the top of my hat. "If I'd known, I would have come back." Though going back to Europe two hundred years ago would have been nearly impossible.

I would have found a way, though.

"We have a lot to talk about, don't we?" She peered at my face again.

"Yes, we do." I motioned her toward the house. We walked up the steps to the large table by the patio door and I pulled out a chair. "Here," I said.

"Thank you," she said.

"You're welcome." I didn't have any real proof that she was who she said she was. No evidence beyond her height and her strength

46

described by the elves. And the fact that the sword had been talking to her. And the bits of fire dancing in her eyes. And how much she knew about Victor Frankenstein.

And the fact that, like me, she saw magic.

"Sister," I said before I realized that saying it out loud would probably make this awkward situation even more awkward.

Wrenn took my hand. "Brother."

She didn't reject me. "Welcome to Alfheim," I said. "Where do we start?"

CHAPTER 4

We talked until the kids came back from the Martinez house with their clothes and homework. The sun crested over the house and warmed the deck nicely. We stayed at the table, coffee in hand, warming ourselves in the last bit of autumn before winter fully charged into Minnesota.

I learned about the realm Wrenn called home. Turned out that the fae, for all their primal magic, were not primitive, and had built the equivalent of a fae metropolis they called Oberon's Castle. They'd teched-up, too. Much more so than the elves.

All because about a decade or so ago, Oberon had declared that the fae needed a hand in the digital future of their mundanes.

I also learned about how the fae collected all their witches. They had some sort of spellwork in the realms that siphoned off witch fire and allowed them to live real and productive lives.

Which meant the siphoning spellwork embedded in Ellie's cottage was off-the-shelf, so to speak. I'd have to ask her about that tonight.

I talked to Wrenn about not exchanging too much information. She agreed, and held most of her talk about the fae to a little about how the Royal Guard functioned, and about Oberon's Castle, but not a lot. I got the impression that the sharing of such facts might not be a good idea, and that they might cause "an incident."

The fae were all about slights and tricks, and secrets were the currency that fed their theatrics. So it was best for her not to talk too much about life with the fae unless she could do so in the presence of an elder elf.

Like, say, Benta the Nameless.

"Maybe Benta will give you a tour of Alfheim Wildcat Sanctuary." I took a pull on the coffee the girls had brought out to us earlier and looked out at the light dancing along the surface of the lake.

Wrenn leaned forward. "Ranger," she said.

The kelpie who had abducted the Martinez kids had called himself Ranger, which we were both sure wasn't his real name. Dark fae did not use their real names. Seemed the whole "naming the demon allows you to control it" wasn't simply a good metaphor for life. The strongest of fae containment spells—fae prison—relied on knowing the true name of the fae involved.

"He kept saying that he was in love with Benta." Wrenn took another sip of her coffee. "I know she can protect herself." She set down the cup. "But elves are... stubborn, aren't they? Overconfident too, in that once they decide something will be the way they think it will be, they ignore the unlikely?"

I set down my cup. "The elves have their own brand of arrogance." I'd seen it in action with Dagrun when she didn't think the "genie" that came after Axlam was a real threat. And now she was in the hospital. "Though I think it might be more of a Minnesota thing than an elf thing."

Wrenn raised an eyebrow. "The rest of the world sees Americans as loud barbarians."

I chuckled. "This is Minnesota. The entire state prides itself on knowing that we're the best in the Union and that we don't crow about it. The not-crowing part is important because it's why we're the best."

Wrenn laughed. "But *is* this place the best?"

Now I laughed. "If the elves like you, yes." I waved my hand at greater Alfheim.

"You all are as arrogant as the fae." She shook her head. "That's why I'm concerned. The elves here can handle Ranger, especially an elder elf, but there's always that possibility. Ranger's smart. If there's one kelpie out there who might be able to harass—or worse—Benta the Nameless, it's Ranger."

Wrenn sat back.

So we had a stalker kelpie to worry about, too. "But Ed controls his bridle." I didn't say anything about where the bridle was now.

Wrenn sighed. "Yes. But there are always contingencies with the fae. If Ranger is motivated enough."

"I'll talk to her." *Great*, I thought.

Wrenn watched my face. "You don't seem excited about a conversation with Benta."

I tapped my finger along the rim of my cup. "We did not have a good break-up." I rubbed my neck. "Break-ups."

"Ah." She sat back and morning light shimmering on the lake. "I'll talk to her. I just wanted you to know in case I need backup."

I nodded and sipped my coffee. "Whatever you need," I said. Benta deserved to be safe.

Wrenn watched me for a moment until a hint of a grin appeared at the corner of her mouth. "So the mate magic's not for an elf?"

I set down my cup as I pinched my lips together. Most of the time, Ellie's concealment enchantments kept me quiet. I actually needed to use my willpower this time.

Wrenn chuckled. "Dark magicals rarely manifest mate magic," she said. "It requires a level of selflessness that's not compatible with evil." She shrugged. "Or naughtiness. Or immaturity."

I don't blush. My steady-state body doesn't usually produce such obvious physiological responses.

I looked away anyway.

Wrenn rubbed her cheek. "Victor was not a man who would have produced mate magic."

When I looked back, she was staring at the lake.

She blinked a few times. "Anyway. Kelpies."

My neck muscles did a little dance as I processed the rapid—though welcome—whiplash of our subject change.

I nodded, partly to loosen those muscles. "Sophia said Ranger's bridle was special. That there are three more like it."

Her brow furrowed. "She didn't say anything about it being special in Texas. Or there being more like it." She tapped her finger on the rim of her coffee cup. "Though Ranger manifested some weird and honestly terrifying changes on the beach." Her eyes rounded for a split second, and a wave of disgust washed over her face. "This need to cover my nose and mouth came over me even though he didn't smell strange. Like he was diseased or something." She blinked a few times. "He was speaking some form of Spanish." She shook her head.

"Spanish?" I asked. Spanish wasn't a language I'd expect from a Scottish kelpie.

"It lasted less than a minute. His eyes turned white, too, like he was possessed."

"A demon?" I asked. We did not need more demons. The vampires were bad enough.

Wrenn shook her head again. "I don't think so. It stopped the moment Ed cut off his bridle." She tapped at her coffee mug. "It looked like something... repressed." She looked out over the lake. "I'll investigate when I get home."

"I'll talk to Ed. He might have some insight." Especially if he'd picked up anything Ranger had been babbling. Ed had a gift for communication, something I'd found out after he'd yelled several languages' worth of church words at Brother when he first manifested. Ed said knowing a little of everything helped him with his work as Sheriff. I suspected that more than anything he just enjoyed learning new things.

After a moment, Wrenn stretched her back. "That house across the lake is quite the monstrosity. Is it one place or three? I can't tell."

I chuckled again. "Three interconnected units. The Carlsons are lawyers up from The Cities and I suspect they were thinking about renting part of it out or something, now that they've had to rebuild.

They know about the town magicals. They've been helpful." I pointed at the lower level door in the middle unit. "That's where Akeyla set Brother on fire."

Wrenn leaned forward again. "I've been using all the resources of the Royal Guard to look for that demon for two centuries and him showing up here last month is literally the first time he's manifested since the night he ripped off Victor's head." She shook her head. "I want to know why. And how."

I nodded. "I do, as well." I suspected it had something to do with his ability to transit in and out of The Land of the Dead.

The patio door curtain moved. Akeyla appeared first, then Sophia and little Ella Martinez, who waved.

I waved back.

Wrenn smiled. "Do you always have a house full of children?"

I sat back in my chair. "Maura and Akeyla are living with me until they find a place of their own. The Martinez kids I'm sure won't be here all that long. The place isn't that big."

Wrenn watched my face for a long moment. "You like it."

I grinned. I did. "Living well is the best revenge."

She snorted. "You do not seem to me to be a man who would shape his life around showing up Victor Frankenstein."

The patio door rattled. Someone was about to step outside. "It's a nice bow on the gift that is my life here in Alfheim," I responded.

She turned to look at the house. "True."

Ed's oldest, Gabe, burst through the doors, phone in hand and a smile on his face.

"Ms. Wrenn!" he said as he closed the door. "Mr. Frank! Papa sent pictures of Grace." He held out the phone.

She looked like every newborn everywhere—a wrinkly little human who resembled other babies more than she resembled her parents. She was also adorable, as was her father's expression as he held her up for the camera.

"I bet your dad made that same exact face the first time he held each of you, didn't he?" Wrenn asked Gabe.

Gabe's birthday was coming up. He was about to turn thirteen and had just started his major growth spurt. He was taller than the last time I'd seen him in person, probably about an inch or so, and seemed to be handling the changes pretty well.

He smiled. "It's *so* embarrassing."

I stood and gathered the coffee cups. "So, are you all staying here again tonight?" I asked.

His lip twitched ever so slightly. "I don't know, Mr. Frank," he said.

Did he think I was kicking them out? "Your entire family is always welcome," I said. "I'm wondering if we need to go into town to buy air mattresses. You have schoolwork and we can't have you sleeping on the floor."

"Oh," he said.

Wrenn squeezed his shoulder. "I was telling Frank earlier about how well you handled Queen Titania."

He looked up at her. "I live with elves, ma'am."

She looked impressed. "That you do." She peered into the house. "Is Benta back? I think it's time I made my way to Applebottom."

She'd been on her way to visit the troupe of a murdered sprite when Raven hijacked her trip.

Which was something else we needed to talk about. "I can give you a ride to Raven's Gaze," I said. "Maybe Raven will talk to me. I'd like to know why she hijacked you like that."

Wrenn raised an eyebrow. "She said, 'That was easier than I expected,' which seemed odd." She absently rubbed at her wrist. "Nothing about what she did triggered the Heartway or any of my tokens, so I'd like to know, too."

Raven taking up residence at Raven's Gaze Brewery and Pub—and from what Lennart said, mostly banning Bjorn and him from entering the restaurant proper, all while messing with some sort of gate-slash-doorway-slash-transit system—was not another brick I wanted to add to the load I carried.

And then there was the question of Dag's interactions with Raven, of which I knew nothing.

"You have the World Raven living in Alfheim," Wrenn said as if she, too, was just digesting the true extent of what having a World Spirit in Alfheim actually meant.

"Betsy and Ross are neat, though," Gabe said as he pushed through the door and disappeared into the kitchen.

Wrenn looked at me quizzically.

"Two ravens that showed up around the same time as Raven," I said.

"Ah." She nodded. "The Huginn and Muninn I saw when I arrived?"

I scoffed. "They were at the restaurant?" Somehow, I figured they would have followed Lennart here, or gone to the hospital with Dagrun.

"Bopping and chittering up in the oak tree," Wrenn said as she moved toward the door. "I need my satchel. It has a police report in it." She nodded toward the kids watching through the door. "The worst thing about living with the fae is that I can't bring the kids gifts when I visit." she said.

I balanced the mugs and walked toward the house. My sister was talking about visiting again. "Yeah," I said. "Probably best not to risk it." Make no deals. Take no gifts. These were the rules with the fae.

I ushered her into the pandemonium inside. Akeyla and Sophia helped the little kids color at the table. Maura and Lennart fussed around with blankets and sleeping bags in the living room. Gabe raided my fridge. And Wrenn stood in the middle of it all with her eyes wide like she'd never heard so much noise in her two hundred years.

"You're always welcome here," I said. Even with her fae-adjacent work.

She smiled up at me. "Thank you."

"Let's find your satchel and get you home."

CHAPTER 5

Maura stood in the entryway, between Wrenn and the door, with a beautifully tooled leather bag in her hand. Not nearly as beautiful as what Lennart made for my notebook, but nice enough.

Maura handed it over. "Dad found spy spells on Ed's shotgun," she said.

Wrenn stood still, her face motionless and her posture identical to Ed's when he thought a situation was about to start.

Wrenn had dealt with angry magicals a lot in her life and must have fallen into the mode without thinking about it.

I was pretty sure the flat affect was making Maura angrier.

"That's why I gave it to you," Wrenn said. "Robin *not* adding spy spells would have been the oddity here, not the other way around."

"Why did you take *his* name, huh?" Maura said. "He's the fae's Loki."

Wrenn's posture stiffened into full cop. "I told Frank the story," she said. "He has my permission to share."

Maura's nostrils flared. "I don't like fae hanging around my daughter's favorite uncle," she said.

Why were the women in my life so possessive? "If we have to drive out to Paul Bunyan, we need to leave now," I said, in case Raven didn't cooperate.

Maura stared at Wrenn long enough to make it clear she'd roll up her sleeves and start a fight if she felt Wrenn was a threat to her family. "I'll check Bloodyhood when you get home," she said.

Wrenn looked over her shoulder at me.

"My truck," I said. "Magnus bought it for me after Brother ruined my other one."

"Ah," Wrenn said.

"Because elven gifts aren't a problem," Maura said.

"Mommy!" Akeyla burst out of the kitchen. "Can I go to the forest with Uncle Frank and Ms. Wrenn?"

Maura closed her eyes. "You have guests, honey."

"Sophia can come, too. There's room in Bloodyhood."

Wrenn moved around Maura and opened the door. She looked back at me and walked outside.

"Ms. Wrenn and I need to talk some more, pumpkin," I said.

Akeyla frowned.

Sophia appeared at her side. "We need to stay here." She tugged on Akeyla's arm. "They have work."

Maura inhaled. She looked at me, then Sophia, then back to me. "What do you mean, sweetie?"

Sophia turned on her heels. "Why does everyone keep asking me that?"

Maura squeezed my arm as she walked by. "I'll call you if our oracle says something you need to know."

"Not an oracle!" Sophia yelled from the kitchen.

I shook my head, pulled my keys out of my pocket, and walked outside into the lovely early-afternoon warmth. "I'm sorry about that," I said.

Wrenn squeezed my arm in much the same way Maura just had. "It's okay."

I unlocked Bloodyhood and we got in.

"I saw Bjorn Thorsson do something similar when Ranger held the kids in Ed's garage." She hooked her seatbelt. "They're protective of their own, aren't they? The elves."

I started the truck. "They are."

"Must be nice," she said. "I mean, to have a family like that."

It was. Most of the time. Maura's anti-fae attitude was going to be a problem, though. "We'll need protocols for when you visit. Who to call, who needs to come by and check you for spy spells, etc."

She watched the trees as we drove toward Raven's Gaze. "Like entering a prison."

She wasn't wrong. "More like crossing a border into a new country."

Wrenn pulled out her phone and unlocked the screen. "Why don't you give me your number. I'll call you—oh, no."

"What?" Did she get an alert? "Vampires?" Sophia did say something about dealing with vampires.

I did not want to have to deal with vampires. I wanted to see Wrenn off safely and without complication, then go home, tell Maura not to worry about sleeping in my room, and make my way down the path to Ellie.

A calm evening in the cottage's new sunroom cuddling with my girlfriend sounded like perfection.

But the universe had a different idea. Because the universe always had different ideas.

"I think Ed needs to have an elf check his phone." She tucked hers away without taking my number. "Two elves. Maybe three."

We pulled into the Raven's Gaze lot and I parked my big truck in the back of the lot out of habit. Several spots up front were filled with people waiting for takeout, anyway. "Why?"

Wrenn bounced her fingers against the dash. "Robin came to collect me." She closed her eyes and pressed the middle of her forehead with her ring finger. "He..." She clamped her mouth shut.

I waited. Best to allow her to sort what information was sharable and what wasn't.

She inhaled and turned toward me. She held up her phone. "My phone is fae-built."

I stared at the device. No magic wafted off it. Nothing about it or its case made it look like it wasn't a standard smartphone like everyone else's smartphones.

"When in the mundane world, the fae circuitry folds in on itself. All the magic is, right now, condensed down into a tiny ball inside." She popped it out of the case, flipped it over, and held it up on its edge. "Look along the edge and focus your eyes about a third of the way down the phone, in the middle. That's where the fae chip sits."

I took the phone and held it up, as she said. And there, right where she said it would be, was the outer rim of a small but intense ball of magic.

"When it's in its case, you can't see the magic at all."

I handed the phone back to her.

"Because I'm Royal Guard, I have a few... special... apps. Spells, really. Stuff that allows me to fully clone and unlock mundane phones."

What were the fae up to? Elves didn't run around with hardware that could do such things. Certainly not something that could invade privacy so intensely.

Except, of course, for the mind-reading axes and swords.

"You cloned Ed's phone," I said. Cloned it and took that clone back into the fae realms.

"I did it so I could access the tracker he had on the van." She popped her phone back into its case. "I used the location info to get us to Texas and find the kids."

Maybe no one realized she had a copy of the Sheriff of Alfheim County's phone with all his logins. And contacts. And access to the trackers he had on his children. And their phone numbers. And access to the games they play.

Target, popped into my head again. "This is bad," I said. Robin Goodfellow did not seem to be a fae who would miss an opportunity to spy on Alfheim.

Wrenn stared out the windshield. "The clone folded up with the mundane interface and I forgot." Now she slapped the dash.

What had Ellie said? *Robin Goodfellow is playing her.* From Wrenn's reaction, I was pretty sure she suspected as much.

I got out and rounded the truck.

"I'll check when I get home," she said as she closed her door.

"It let you find the kids, though, correct?" I asked.

Her cheek twitched. "It did."

"Okay," I said. "The kids were most important." I looked out at Raven's Gaze. "I'll talk to Arne."

Wrenn watched me silently. Then she strode across the parking lot toward the wide concrete walk leading to the restaurant's door.

The restaurant, a squat, rustic building with "Raven's Gaze Brewery and Pub, est. 1062" painted across its front in a huge blocky font, still had some outdoor seating out even though all of the umbrellas had been taken down. The brewery building was around back, along with Bjorn's loft, and was not open to the public.

The snow had stripped the last of the leaves off all the trees except for the big red oak in front of the restaurant. Red oaks usually kept their leaves until spring, and this one wasn't any different. The leaves had mostly dried out in the sun today, and had taken on the leathery rich-ness and crinkly rustling they'd have until the flowers bloomed again.

Two ravens flapped down from the oak's branches and landed on the walk between us and the door.

Wrenn stopped ten feet from the birds, hand on her satchel and her posture back in full cop form. "I see your magic, Huginn and Muninn," she said to the birds. "I know you're not regular ravens."

The smaller of the two honked.

I wanted to say they weren't actually Huginn and Muninn in the same way that Magnus wasn't actually Freyr, and Arne wasn't Odin, and Oberon wasn't... I didn't know. But like so many pedantic differ-entiations in the world, such distinctions mattered only a fraction of the time.

We *did* have a Huginn and a Muninn living here. We also had a World magical who had decided she wanted both of the non-vampiric children of Victor Frankenstein in one place.

Wrenn crouched and held out her hand. "You two are *beautiful*," she cooed.

The birds bounced toward her hand and stopped just outside of touch range, chittered, then hopped backward. "Have you two decided which one of you is Thought and which is Memory?" she asked.

Both of the birds preened their chest feathers as if ignoring the question.

Wrenn chuckled. "Several of the fae queens are also fond of ravens," she said.

Both birds took wing. A small gust fluttered Wrenn's hair and she watched the birds land in the oak tree.

Wrenn stood. She looked around at the trees, tables, and parking lot of Raven's Gaze Brewery and Pub as if this was the first time she'd seen a mundane restaurant. Mostly, though, I suspected this was the first time she'd seen Alfheim without an elf watching her watch their world.

Part of me wondered if her bright-eyed wonder—I was pretty sure she did a better job of keeping her emotions off her face than I did, but sometimes that control cracked—was because this was the first time in her two hundred years that she had looked at a magical place without that place having some sort of ulterior motive.

Because from what she had said, and from what Ellie had told me, the realms of the fae all seemed to reflect the motives of their magicals.

"There's an interesting landmark here." I pointed through the brush at the church hidden in the trees. "If you'd like to see it before you go."

She peered through the brambles but didn't say anything.

"One of the first things the Norwegian and Swedish immigrants did when they arrived in Alfheim was to build Bjorn a church."

She looked back at me. "Of their own free will?"

I stuck my hands in my jacket pocket. "They had no overt knowledge of the elves. But subconsciously? They were drawn to the aspects of their old gods."

Wrenn stood on the walk to Raven's Gaze holding her satchel and dressed head-to-toe in fae textiles and leatherwork, clearly wondering about this elven world into which she'd stumbled.

I didn't say anything. Best to let her process on her own.

After several breaths and cheek twitches, she looked up at me. "How powerful *are* the elves?" she breathed.

I opened my mouth to respond. *They're elves*, I wanted to say, but that response did not answer the question. Like the mundanes of Minnesota, they lived their lives and ignored everything about the world they didn't like and couldn't fix immediately with a snow-blower or a plate of lefse.

I'd also watched Arne and Magnus go toe-to-toe with Titania. I'd seen them isolate Vampland from the rest of reality. Wrenn had been on the receiving end of a blast of Bjorn's magic strong enough to send Ed and her into the Heartway.

But I'd also seen the elves battle each other to a standstill. I'd seen Dag taken down by Fenrir's magic. And I'd watched them confounded by Brother.

So I honestly didn't know.

"It's not a glamour," I said. That, at least, I did know. I'd glimpsed Arne through a crack in his glamours and was pretty certain I could tell the difference between true reality and magically-hidden reality. "The magic here. It's not slight-of-hand, like the fae."

Wrenn stood in the center of the walk as she took in the bucolic splendor that was this little elf-owned small town restaurant. Or the glamour of it.

I opened my mouth to ask her a question about the fae. Something half-formed and vague that was solidifying as my lips prepped for the words of it.

But magic had a different idea.

She appeared directly behind Wrenn, the last magical I'd ever expected to see again, especially in front of a restaurant owned by a Thor elder elf.

One of the two magicals who were nothing but trouble, and who gave any Loki elf—or Goodfellow fae—a run for Best Trickster in Show.

"Kitsune!" Wrenn yelled as she whipped around.

Lollipop, now in a bright yellow puffy jacket instead of her polo shirt, stared at us wide-eyed, and pulled from her mouth a throbbing, heart-shaped candy.

CHAPTER 6

The kitsune bounced a little in her oversized, unlaced winter hiking boots. She stood on the walk between Wrenn and me and the restaurant door looking small, beautiful, and utterly absurd in the boots, the puffy yellow jacket, and a tight pair of silver lamé booty shorts. She still had the exaggerated curve to her hips and breasts, the same gleaming black hair—this time in pigtails— and the same big, ever-changing magical lollipop.

A candy lollipop that literally throbbed like a cartoon heart.

My mate magic flared outward like a swarm of homicidal fireflies. How *dare* Lollipop come to my town and question my bond to Ellie. I *knew* she was questioning my bond. I *felt* it.

Lollipop blinked as if she had no idea at all what she'd just triggered.

"Wrenn's my sister!" I bellowed.

She blinked a few more times, wide-eyed and pouting like a frightened child, and slid her boots backward just enough to make herself look put-upon.

Several people sitting in their cars in the parking lot looked up from their phones even though most of them had their windows rolled up.

I'd attracted an audience. Which the kitsune probably wanted. She did like to make a spectacle of things. And she was definitely feeding the show.

"There are mundanes here!" I nodded toward the parking lot.

Lollipop stuck the candy heart back into her mouth and looked at the six or seven cars.

"You know a kitsune?" Wrenn asked, clearly more concerned about the magical than my mate magic. Which was wise.

Yet Lollipop *dared*.

"Why are you here?" I asked. *How* was she here? "Is this another of Raven's interventions?" I looked around. Why would Raven care? Unless this was another trickster moment. I jabbed my finger at Lollipop. "You need to leave."

Wrenn dropped into her cop stance again. "Was that candy heart in reference to your...?" She waved her hand at the air around my shoulders.

I nodded *yes*.

Wrenn pushed the satchel's strap higher on her shoulder and stood her ground between me and the kitsune. "Do not provoke a diplomatic incident by manipulating Frank's mate magic, kitsune. Do you understand?"

Lollipop rolled her eyes.

Wrenn took a step toward the trickster fox. "You have, what, three tails? So you're a messenger. Who do you work for?"

Lollipop stuck out her tongue.

Wrenn was not deterred. "Why are you in elf territory?"

Lollipop continued to suck on her candy.

"She doesn't talk," I said. The last time I'd dealt with Lollipop and her partner Chip, that candy had been Lollipop's way of communicating—commenting, really—about my circumstances.

Lollipop pulled a shrugging-emoji candy from her mouth.

Wrenn looked from me, to the kitsune, then back. "A *silent* kitsune?"

"Sort of," I said as I looked around. "Where's your sidekick?" I asked the kitsune.

I took a step toward her. "Is this about Las Vegas?" I asked. I'd gone to Vegas looking for a dark magical to help Arne with a political problem and ended up with all sorts of "promises of service" hanging over my head because I apparently didn't know when to shut up when someone needed help.

I pointed at the restaurant. "About Raven?"

Lollipop shook her head *no*.

Which meant it was the *other* offer of service I'd gotten myself into.

Fear burst across Lollipop's features as if she'd just realized her lollipop was poison. Then she pulled the one shape from her mouth that my gut did not want to see right now.

A set of vampire fangs.

I'd offered the kitsune help dealing with vampires in exchange for information about Ellie.

Wrenn took a step closer to Lollipop, but it wasn't an authoritative cop step. She was offering comfort. "Vampires?" she asked.

Lollipop nodded vigorously.

Wrenn inhaled. "Are there kelpies involved?" she asked.

The syndicate she'd been investigating was run by kelpies. They were trafficking low-powered fae to the vampire clans.

But they might not be the only magicals involved. The kami had a lot of dark magicals—yōkai, oni, yūrei, a few other types, too. The kami arguably had more than the fae, and most definitely more than the elves.

Lollipop's lip quivered. Her arm tightened as if she was about to pull her candy from her mouth again.

Huginn and Muninn appeared directly over her head.

One second they were in the oak tree, the next they were squawking and cawing and ripping at the kitsune with flapping wings and big raven talons.

Lollipop pulled an almost-full-sized flaming candy katana from between her lips and swatted at the birds in wide swirls.

Wrenn, still between the kitsune and me, did not move back away from all the squawking and attacking. "Hey!" she yelled as she, too, swatted at the birds. "She might be a witness!"

The door of Raven's Gaze Brewery and Pub blasted open with an angry jingle and a puff of warm air. We all turned to look.

Raven stood on the walk in her white t-shirt and motorcycle jacket, hands clasped behind her back as she watched her birds peck and slash at the kitsune. "Leave the fox alone, loves," she said.

Huginn and Muninn rose away from Lollipop as fast as they'd attacked.

Wrenn watched the birds flap their way back to the tree before she returned her attention to the door. She silently stared down Raven like someone who knew a whole lot more about how to deal with tricksters than I did.

Raven's eyes narrowed. An eyebrow rose. "All of you. Inside. Now."

Lollipop pulled a bright red *NO!* out of her mouth. She backed toward Wrenn.

"Listen to Raven," I said. "No more antics in front of the townspeople." I glanced up at Raven. "We'll get this sorted."

Lollipop blinked. Her cheeks tightened. Then she nodded.

Raven pointed at the door. "Inside, now, before the wolves show up."

The Alfheim Pack was on the way? "Wolves don't much appreciate foxes," I said. Not in their territory. Not in front of their favorite restaurant.

"You didn't think about that, did you, kitsune?" Raven licked her finger and held it up to the slight breeze moving through the November air. "You've left your fox scent all over Alfheim."

Wrenn sniffed as if she'd smelled the fox stink too.

An eerie silence fell over not only our small group of angry magicals, but also the oak tree and the restaurant. The parking lot, too, and the road beyond, as if the entire area stopped making the noise of life just to highlight the World Raven's displeasure.

Lollipop quickly stepped behind Wrenn as if she also wanted a jotunn between herself and the World Raven. She looked back at me, blinking like a sad lost fox from behind my sister's elbow, and vanished.

I threw my arms into the air. "Why do they do that?" Especially in front of the local mundanes.

She reappeared, now inside the restaurant and waving to us from underneath the "Open for takeout" painted on the window.

"Nobody notices in Japan," Wrenn said. "Fae do it all the time too, popping in and out of situations all over Europe." As we walked toward Raven's Gaze, she continued, "They're not supposed to anymore. Too many cell phone cameras that *do* notice."

She nodded to Raven as she stepped inside.

I walked toward the entrance and reached to catch the door.

Raven placed her hand on my bicep to stop me. "One moment."

I looked down at her, then back at the dark cave mouth that was the door into the restaurant. "Did you know Lollipop was going to show up?" I asked.

She shrugged.

I watched Wrenn move toward Lollipop like a detective about to grill a witness. "Chip might be missing, Raven," I said.

"Yes," she answered.

"I promised them help with a vampire problem." I rubbed at my cheek.

Wrenn set her bag on a table and bent over so she could look Lollipop in the eye.

"Is that why you hijacked Wrenn?" Why would Raven pull my sister into this? "Because the fae blood syndicate might be involved?" There might be another reason. Another vampire. One Raven did not —or should not—know anything about. "Is my brother involved?" I asked anyway.

Because if he was, we needed to know. Now.

She lifted her hand off my bicep. "Your services are required."

The way she said it made me think she wasn't talking about my promise to the kitsune. "I thought you released me from my offers of service." That's what she'd told me, in that bar in Las Vegas.

She grinned. "*I* did."

But she'd also said that she'd traded my offer to the Las Vegas Wolf. For what, I did not know.

67

She sniffed. "The elves say you're a jotunn." Then she reached up to touch the tattoo of Yggdrasil on the side of my face. "You've been accepted by the World Tree, I see."

This had nothing to do with Wrenn or the kitsune. "...Yes," I said. Best to let the trickster talk.

"Odin was the son of a jotunn," she said. "As was Loki."

The jotnar were a big part of Norse mythology. "Yes, they were." I peered into the restaurant to make sure Wrenn was dealing with Lollipop, but the sun's brightness threw the interior into dark shadow and I couldn't see.

Raven also looked into the restaurant. "Do you know what the jotnar are?" she asked.

Jotnar weren't "giants" in the big-and-tall sense. That much I knew. But I've never been able to get a straight answer out of the elves. After a while, I'd begun to wonder if they even understood themselves.

Not that this situation had anything to do with the jotnar.

"Please tell me if this has anything to do with Brother," I said. "He's dangerous, Raven. He might even be dangerous to you."

Car-alarm kitsune gekkering came from inside the restaurant.

Raven nodded into the restaurant. "Go on, Son of Wood and Rage."

"What?" I looked down at her.

Just before the blizzard, I'd seen Arne's glamour crack. Not his middle-aged boxer, town father, everyday glamour, but his elf glamour.

I'd gotten a glimpse of what's underneath.

And if I wanted to be honest about it—if I wanted to take a quiet moment and consider what I saw and what Ellie saw—I'd admit that I wasn't so sure the elves were simply elves. And that magic worked the way I thought it did.

What I saw when I looked at the World Raven wasn't human. It had learned how to use the human container into which it had been poured—but something told me that Raven's humanity was not her choice.

I felt it in my gut. In my soul. In the rustling of leaves and the flit-

tering of the wind. In the need for space, for life, for acknowledgement that there were more things in heaven and earth than my
philosophy held.

Clever, clever Raven of thought and memory. The bringer of light
to the world. The bird who released the stars into the heavens. The
trickster creator. The bird who pulled the tufts of fur from the World
Wolf and tail feathers from the World Raptor.

The god who cawed from the branches of the World Tree.

Then she was Raven again, a woman of all the tribes, strong, tall,
brilliant, beautiful.

She flashed a sly grin and pushed me across the threshold.

CHAPTER 7

C risp winter air slapped me full in the face and I inhaled sharply. Raven had flicked us out of Alfheim like bugs on the edge of a seat—no warning, no acknowledgement, no anything. Only a magical "be gone, insect."

Wrenn grabbed my arm. She, too, inhaled sharply.

We stood outside in a heavily forested area. The ground under my feet was rough and uneven, and I needed to pay attention so I didn't twist an ankle. Only slivers of moonlight made it through the thick, though leafless, tree canopy over our heads. The air smelled as fresh as it did in Alfheim, but different. Thinner, perhaps, as if we were at a higher elevation.

I could barely see in the darkness even though my night vision is better than most mundanes.

I blinked a few times, to let my eyes adjust.

Wrenn's arms shimmered with the green and red fae magic she carried. Around me, coming off my elven scalp tattoos, the faintest glow of violets and blues, as well as the bright blue buzz of my mate magic. But this place carried neither the leaf-claw of fae magic, nor the ice of elven.

Pink and silver danced along the bark of the trees and rocks on either side of us, giving stem and leaf a soft, glowing outline. The mosses clinging to the roots of the trees also shimmered, but in earthy greens and browns, and looked a lot like fae magic. But not quite.

The magic tinkled, too, like little bells. Except that the trees and plants were so eerily quiet that my brain was probably making up sounds for what I saw.

The extraordinary level of background magic here gave me the equivalent of a good pair of night vision goggles. I could see, but not in real light. The world looked as if I'd stepped into one of Ellie's photographs.

My mate magic flared upward like a flame licking at the sky—or looking for its reason for being. For its core. Its reality.

Its soul.

I sucked in my breath.

I was too distant from Ellie.

Wrenn watched the magic rise off me. She grinned and looked away, then sniffed at the air as if she was Pack. "It's colder here," she said. "About twenty degrees Fahrenheit lower than Alfheim."

I was too far away from my beloved in a place I did not know. I bent over, sucking in my breath again.

"You're going to need to breathe through it," Wrenn said.

I looked up at her.

"It's the mate magic linking. Everything I've heard is that it's at best annoying and at worst debilitating." She stepped closer and rubbed my back as if she was the older sibling. Or my mom. "Can you imagine having generalized anxiety, or attention problems, or memory issues *and* a swarm of needy magic swirling around you all the time? At least you see it and know what it is."

"I suppose," I said. We had other worries, anyway.

Yet my heart and soul only wanted to find a way home.

She shrugged. "Honestly, what use is the linking in the modern world?" She pulled out her phone. "Just call."

For the first time in my two-hundred-plus years, I'd fallen in love with someone who loved me as much as I loved her—and it seemed for our troubles, our connection had decided to manifest separation anxiety as if it was a magical baby. Or puppy.

I breathed, like Wrenn said. "It hasn't been annoying until now," I said.

"That's good." She patted my back again. "Honestly, from what I've heard about mate magic, that's excellent. *Not* annoying signals something. I don't know what. You'll need to ask a werewolf."

Not like I could call up Gerard right now and ask him to stop by for a beer. Which Ellie had told me to do. Because fae magic was involved. Which meant *complicated*.

And I was too far away.

I breathed in, counted to five, and breathed out. I could not let my swarm of bright blue tiny whining mate-magic puppies distract me. I wouldn't get home to Ellie anyway if I couldn't figure out how to get out of this pitch black silent forest.

Wrenn pointed at the closest tree. "Do you see the magic wiggling on the bark?"

"Yeah, I do. Silver and pink." Longing yanked at my soul. "Where are we?"

"Pink and silver is what I see, too." Wrenn held up her phone. "This place is as magical as Glastonbury." Her screen lit up. "I've got a strong mundane signal." She tapped the screen. "Looks like we're on the west side of Lake Saiko, at the base of Mount Fuji." She looked up at the tree canopy. "We're in Aokigahara Forest. That explains the ambient magic."

Japan.

Raven had kicked us into *Japan*. And not just any part of Japan, either. We were in a haunted place under one of the most magical locations on Earth.

I looked around. "Where's Lollipop?" My mate magic was like candy to kitsune. "I'm surprised she's not here basking in the glow of my panicking heartstrings."

Never in my life had I been so distracted by my own emotions. No, that wasn't true. Never since I came to Alfheim, at least.

Wrenn shook her head. "I don't think she's here." She peered through the trees. "She's part of a duo? The other one you called Chip, correct?"

I rolled my shoulders to help me focus on the trees. "I met them in Las Vegas. Chip would eat potato chips from a magical fanny pack of ever-changing and utterly-nauseating flavors."

Wrenn chuckled. "Sounds about right for two kitsune messing with an American." She glanced at me. "What did they want in Las Vegas?"

"They stole my phone." I inhaled. "And... helped me with something."

She flipped her own phone around and turned on the flashlight. "So you owe them?"

I owed them. "I promised them help, Wrenn," I said. "With vampires."

She nodded as if not surprised. No admonishment about promises to tricksters, either. From the way she stood, I was pretty sure she would have done exactly the same thing.

She swung the light around looking for a path. "Why did Alfheim's King and Queen allow those two vampires into town? The ones that showed up during the Cold War?" She pointed. "Look."

She'd found what looked like a trail.

"Tony and Ivan?" I asked. "Arne wanted to see if he could help dark magicals not be so dark."

Wrenn picked her way over the smooth rocks and fallen branches toward the trail. "Did he make progress? Because if he did, you have no idea how valuable such magic would be to the fae."

"They were fine for seventy years." I shook my head as I followed. "It's not that simple." It wasn't. Every magical, like every mundane, had good and bad in them. The real issue wasn't the good and the bad, but how that good and bad sorted itself in the real world. And how the real world allowed that sorting to happen.

And Chip might be missing.

Wrenn pointed up the path. "I don't think we're alone."

About twenty feet ahead, a magical woman sat atop a large boulder in what had to be the only shaft of moonlight in the entire forest.

Her magic wafted off her in sheets of golds and silvers with hints of violet-reds. Her hair was as black as the night around her but somehow also as blood red as a vampire's kiss, as if the red had twisted the night around her into fine silk strands. The effect gave her severe asymmetric cut a sense of geometry more than a pop of color.

She wore loose black pants, a white silk blouse, and a long golden coat that flowed around her equally long legs, now crossed where she sat on the rock a good five or six feet above the forest floor.

And she sang.

I didn't understand her words. I didn't need to. I understood—*felt* —who she sang for, and why: Other magicals. *Dark* magicals.

Wrenn grabbed my arm. She pointed off to the side, into the trees across from the boulder.

I knew the names of some of Japan's yōkai—mostly the ones that pop up in Western media, like the turtle-like kappa and the spider-woman jorōgumo.

What giggled in the trees was unfamiliar.

There were *heads* up there—giant human heads, heads on fire, heads in wheels, heads ready to drop from the trees. Bird-like things, too, with red piercing eyes. Something that looked like a weasel with knife-like paws. One-eyed humanoid creatures. Things that looked more like walking corpses than any yōkai.

"There have to be at least a hundred of them," I whispered.

Wrenn pulled us back behind the tree cover. "It's the beginning of a Night Parade," she said.

It took me a moment to remember the horror of what a "Night Parade" meant when it involved yōkai. "They dance through the streets looking for victims, don't they?" I asked.

She nodded. "It's like a festival, but evil."

Weren't most traveling festivals evil? "They just need a clown or two," I said.

Wrenn pointed back through the trees. "Vampires have made their way into Japanese magic. Why not clowns?" She leaned against the tree. "Night Parades are supposed to happen in towns, not hidden forests."

Yet here we were in the deepest part of the night in a black forest with a parade of yōkai. I inched far enough to the side to see around the tree.

The horde of yōkai in the branches dropped, rolled, shuffled, ran, sauntered, snapped, crackled, popped—they were as varied in their locomotion as they were in their shapes—out of the trees and formed up as a stream of malevolent weirdness flowing around the magical woman's boulder.

She watched them move by, peering at one, then another, until she dropped her hand down and yanked a yōkai out of the parade.

"Wrenn," I said.

My sister inched closer and also looked around the tree.

The magical in the golden coat lifted a yōkai out of the parade the way she would have lifted a kitten out of a litter—by the back of her neck. She'd grabbed a lovely porcelain-skinned yōkai in a kimono and with upswept hair held in place with sticks and combs.

A man walked out of the shadows and around the side of the rock.

A white man with a strong jaw and a mop of curly black hair. He wore a black polo shirt with a small-yet-visible sea-green stallion emblem over his left pec. And a black kilt.

He stopped behind the held yōkai, at her back, where she couldn't see him. We could, though.

"A kelpie," Wrenn said.

"Ranger?" I asked, because part of me expected Ranger to manifest himself everywhere Wrenn walked, at this point.

"No," she said. "I don't recognize him. He's new to me."

So he was a random kelpie who also didn't know us, which might be useful.

A long serpent-like tongue snaked out of the back of the lifted yōkai's hair and snapped at the man. He laughed and pointed. The woman on the rock—the one in the golden coat—frowned but did not set down her captured yōkai.

The kelpie shrugged. Then he pulled a black hood out of a pocket in his kilt and threw it over the captured yōkai's head.

"The magical on the rock must have called a Night Parade so she could sell victims to the kelpie," Wrenn whispered. "I need to follow him." She stood up. "If there are kelpies operating here, I need to know."

She was right. But I had a feeling that Raven wouldn't do something as straightforwardly simple as dropping us someplace with immediate, concrete evidence of a problem we could rectify.

I looked back at the trees from which the parade erupted. The shadows wiggled in the dark branches—shadows that looked darker than the ones around the first group to dance out toward the magical on the rock. Different. Oilier. Angry and venomous.

Malevolently green-black.

I pointed. "Low-demons."

Wrenn peered toward the branches. "Where?"

A month ago, I'd been infected with low-demons I couldn't see and the elves could not read. Then a vampire's ghost made them as visible as the auroras of magic I see around magicals.

At the time, I had no idea where the slimy, angry dark magic had come from, or why it had attached itself to me.

But I knew now.

I was up and running toward the magical in the golden coat before I figured out what I was doing.

CHAPTER 8

"Frank!" Wrenn grabbed for my arm. "Wait!"

I was already several paces down the path and out of her reach. I skidded to a stop. "Do you see the dark magic?" She probably didn't. She hadn't had Ivan's non-vampiric soul turn up the gain on Brother's evil enough to make it visible.

"Do *not* mess with yōkai." She followed me out of her hiding place and into the shadows around an open area which, if we weren't careful, would be visible to the woman on the rock.

The kelpie sniffed the air.

"He smells us, Frank," Wrenn said as she motioned to my shoulders.

She meant he smelled my mate magic, my yearnings, my need to go home to Ellie. Even over the parade of yōkai, and the magic of the forest, a kelpie was still a kelpie. And still dangerous.

The kelpie alone was a threat that might need both of us to take down. Add on an unknown power level of the yōkai Night Parade, and the magical sitting in the beam of moonlight on the rock.

Then spice it with the green-black slimy low-demon magic with which I was all too familiar. The magic that meant Wrenn and I—and the entire nation of Japan—were at a tsunami-level of danger.

Brother was here, somewhere.

I wasn't sure, but I suspected Brother had "domesticated" the low-demons. When he was Dracula, they'd contracted down into an undergarment of sorts under his ash-made armor. How much of his ash-sucking and manipulating abilities were actually fueled by his symbiosis with the low-demons, I didn't know. But I suspected at least some.

And those low-demons were here, now, in a haunted forest in Japan.

Which meant the body that was both Brother and Dracula—and Odin knew what else—had escaped from Vampland.

We had a literal open can of worms on our hands.

"Stay back." I held up my arm to signal her to stay where she was. I'd dealt with the low-demons before. She hadn't.

Wrenn yanked on my arm to pull me back into the shadows, but I didn't move. "I can handle a kelpie."

A kelpie, yes. Better than I could. But not a kelpie *and* yōkai *and* Brother.

I pointed at the trees and the slimy darkness. "It's not just the kelpie. Some of those yōkai have been touched by Brother," I said. No playing around or drilling her on what she could and could not see, magic-wise. She needed to know what we were dealing with here. "They're carrying his magic."

"What?" She stepped to the side and peered at the yōkai teeming in the shadows. Her brow furrowed.

She did not see what I saw.

"You are sure?" she asked.

"Yes," I said. "A vampire's human ghost made sure I could see his magic."

She squeezed her eyes closed in surprise. "Alfheim isn't the sleepy little town it pretends to be, is it?"

I shrugged. "Probably not." I pointed toward the yōkai. "The low-demon hive operates like an extraordinarily well-trained pet."

"All right," she said. No playing around or drilling me about how I saw what I saw for her, either. "I have jurisdiction to arrest the kelpie and hold any Japanese magicals involved in the syndicate. But we're going to need to keep the infected separate from the non-infected."

I nodded. I had no authority here, no understanding of the culture or the magicals beyond seeing their magic, and no way on my own to get across to any local kami that I wasn't a threat.

Or that Brother was a threat beyond anything they dealt with internally.

Wrenn patted at her waist, then frowned. "I should have worn my star." Then she stepped into the center of the open area and into a spot visible from the rock.

"Kelpie!" she called. "I am Fae Royal Guard! Stand down! You and your friend are in danger. My name is Wrenn Goodfell—"

The air whistled.

Something burst from the trees and slammed into Wrenn so hard that she—and it—flew into the brush on the other side. A trunk cracked with a snap that echoed off the rock and down the path.

"Wrenn!"

The woman on the rock looked at us.

A spider web of golden magic manifested around her. Her eyes turned black. And... and for a split second, for just a short moment, I counted eight long, black-shrouded legs.

"She's a jorōgumo," I muttered. We'd gotten the attention of an inherently malevolent and particularly dangerous yōkai: a jorōgumo, a spider demon. From the magic she threw around, a powerful one, too.

But none of Brother's oily evil magic touched her. Were we looking at a magical we might be able to count as an enemy of my enemy?

I thought so, until the gray of the boulder lifted off the rock like smoke rising from a flame.

Or ash from the cold entropy of The Land of the Dead.

CHAPTER 9

Shrieks rose from the Night Parade moving around the rock. Panic blossomed through the mass of malevolent magicals. The stream of bodies bowed out from the rock as if pressed away by an invisible force.

The fog around the base of the boulder shifted and roiled.

The kelpie sniffed the cold air again. His face turned wrathful but his shoulders tightened and rose toward his ears as if he couldn't tell his terror from his rage. He cinched the hood around his victim yōkai head and backed toward a shadowed tree next to the rock.

The jorōgumo, who still sat on top of the massive, tall boulder, scrambled up to kneeling. She flared out her hands.

A golden web of magic appeared between her and the fog.

He's here, I thought. I reflectively pulled up my arms to block a punch. He liked to pop in and out of situations, attacking each time he manifested. Lollipop popped in and out to annoy; Brother did so to kill.

The fog coiled around the boulder. Nothing hit me. I dropped my hands a little, to peer into the shadows.

A yōkai deep in the trees released a harsh, piercing banshee-like shriek—a scream that cut through the golden loveliness of the jorōgumo, the dark of the forest, my mate magic's need to return home, my confusion...

I yelped and covered my ears but it didn't matter. The deep, silent night turned as loud and bright as a midday filled with booming, burning echoes. Storms. Electricity. Blue strikes and... Germany, not Japan. Germany, where Victor stitched together the multiplicity of my body.

Dark German forests. Dark German castles. And an even more darkly German narcissistic psychopath of a father.

For a split second, I *became* that past, as if I wasn't recalling memories but was instead a walking, talking container of those moments' energy. The memories themselves blurred. The years I spent orbiting Victor become a second, a moment, an ethos. I was alone, and I was as terrified as the terror I stirred in others. And that terror shifted the spectrum of my rage. I burned bluer; I vibrated faster.

The yōkai's shriek harmonized with what I had been and drew it into my consciousness.

Brother had done something similar when he dragged me into The Land of the Dead to visit Victor's Edinburgh lab. A similar abrupt disassociation of my sense of place and time. A similar disruption of my understanding of *me*.

I didn't understand what he'd done that first time. I understood now.

I sucked in my breath. Was he slamming me into a different realm again? I had to hold it together and not allow him to gain control.

I wasn't in Europe. I wasn't home, either. I was in the Aokigahara Forest at the foot of Mount Fuji. In Japan. In the home of ghosts, demons, and kami.

Not elves. Not fae. Not in the lands of any of the spirits or monsters or ghosts that dwell in the shadowed places between the cities and towns I recognized.

I concentrated on the closest tree. *Blink,* I thought. *See what's in front of you.*

Send the flashback away.

A yōkai manifested directly above me—or the head of a yōkai. Or the yōkai was a head. A huge head as tall as me snickered and snuffled as if it was allergic to the ghostly flames encircling it scalp to chin.

It dropped out of the treetops.

I jumped back along the uneven ground and it missed landing on me by only a few inches.

Huge, wet black eyes stared unblinkingly at me. An equally black eyebrow arched. Razor-sharp teeth peeked out from behind red lips.

I've seen a great and terrible fae rip through Confederate forces. I've seen the real god face of an elf. I've been to The Land of the Dead and I've stepped into places infected with low-demons.

But I'd never before dealt with a vomit-inducing, disembodied demon head. "You are exactly what I would expect from my brother," I said.

It snickered.

I punched it in the nose.

It blinked, sniffed, and then fell over onto its back, if a bodiless head could have a back.

The kelpie, still holding the trapped yōkai by the neck, scowled. He snapped his fingers at the jorōgumo. She kicked at his head. He yelled something I did not understand and backed into the shadows.

Something in the trees banshee-screamed again. I looked over my shoulder.

A different yōkai flew out of the hole where Wrenn had vanished and smashed into another tree, this time not hard enough to crack the trunk, only shake it and drop crackling ice onto the path.

The yōkai chattered its many teeth and ran back into the hollow— and directly into Wrenn. She stepped out with yet another small, moderately human-shaped yōkai firmly gripping her shoulders and back. She reached over her head, her hands glowing with fae magic, grabbed the writhing hairy thing, and slammed it down hard into the frozen path.

The yōkai vanished.

The slimy dark low-demon magic that had been coating the yōkai did not.

I snatched Wrenn away before it had a chance to attach to her arm.

82

"Don't step in it." I pointed at her hands. "Whatever spell you're working seems to be acting like gloves."

Wrenn flicked her hand and the spell around her hands expanded up her arms and across her chest.

"He's here." I pointed at the rock. "See the fog? He controls a witch's ashes," I said. The ash of Rose's charred and destroyed life.

I'd told Wrenn some about Rose. Not a lot. Rose, the witch child I'd carried back from the bayou and raised as my daughter. Because I wasn't a monster like that damned kelpie. Or my father.

She peered at me as if looking for oily stains. "It's making you angry." Not a question. A statement.

I tried to stop those old embers from reigniting but the oily dark low-demon magic wormed its way in. I held down my bright electrical anger, but my sister saw how I held my face and body as if I had my own personal rage magic.

Wrenn peered at my face, then my shoulders. Her eyes rounded. "*You* need to stay back, Frank," she said.

"Why?" I would not prostrate myself to our brother.

Wrenn inhaled sharply as if holding back a chastising. She gave the head I'd knocked over a shove and it rolled into the trees. "Focus on kicking the yōkai attacking us. But that one," she pointed at the rock, "is obviously powerful. I need info and that kelpie."

A roar pushed up from my core. This jorōgumo fed *demons*.

Wrenn grabbed my arm. "Frank! Stop!"

I knew my body was about to charge toward the rock. I also knew, back behind the blue wall of rage, that I was not acting as me.

Yet I was. This was me. Deeply buried me. The part of me the elves had helped place in hospice. The part that I had allowed to pass on so I could leave it behind.

Yet here it was, rising from its grave like a ghoul.

Like a vampire, come to suck away my soul.

My muscles tightened. That jorōgumo was *part of this*.

The fog congealed.

He was there, *right there*, between the boulder and the Night Parade. The vampire made by the same overly-creative semi-scientist with mommy-issues as Wrenn and I. The creature made from just enough of Dracula to be the worst monster on Earth. My brother— our brother, the terror I had so unceremoniously named Brother because I was just a big dumb lug living in rural Minnesota and I don't have a creative bone in my reconstituted body.

He'd returned to wearing his well-tailored ash-made suit. The lightning bolt scar still darted along the side of his face. He wiggled his shoulders arrogantly, and took a moment to adjust his blood-red tie.

He loomed over the Night Parade, and at eight feet, was tall enough he could have snagged the jorōgumo around the waist.

The wall of golden magic between him and the jorōgumo grew so bright it became opaque.

The vampire called Brother snarled and slapped the magic wall with one of his big hands. "You sell your own?" He slapped the wall again, then held out his arms for all the yōkai to see. "I will *never* sell you to the *fae!*"

He spit the word fae as if it left a sour metal taste on his tongue.

"That's *him*," Wrenn breathed.

"Yes," I said.

Wrenn stared at our vampire sibling. We were both frozen in place, on the path, in the open area close enough that he could see us, but too far away for us to do anything useful.

Frozen not because he'd locked us in place, but because neither of us knew what to do. We'd known he was here. He'd been messing with my head and throwing yōkai at both of us. The fog around the boulder had been there for a good long moment before he manifested.

But the concrete reality of a monster who should be contained in a pocket realm of his own making was too shocking. Seeing his face was too much. Hearing him bellow in support of the yōkai was too much to parse. For both of us.

"We have to kill him," Wrenn said.

"Yes," I said. "Yes, we do." We agreed on that, at least. The children of Frankenstein needed to commit fratricide. Otherwise the world would never be safe.

Brother leaned forward. He reached like a father looking to pick up a child.

A small, feathered yōkai jumped into his arms and gave him a real, if brief, hug before falling back into the Parade.

"What the hell did I just see?" Wrenn asked.

A second yōkai did the same thing. This one pointed, though—first up at the golden magic on top of the boulder, then toward the shadowed tree where the kelpie stood.

Brother set down the yōkai and vanished.

He manifested directly in front of the kelpie. He had one hand on the fae's neck and the other on the wrist holding the captured victim before the fae could respond.

"Only a kelpie would be so stupid as to stick around when a vampire showed up," Wrenn muttered.

Brother moved his hand. The kelpie's wrist snapped. The victim yōkai dropped back into the Parade.

The gold magic on top of the boulder abruptly vanished. The jorōgumo, unlike the kelpie, was smart enough to run.

Brother strong-armed the kelpie out in front of his chest. He cocked his head to one side, then the other, then turned again.

He looked directly at us.

It no longer mattered if we hid. I didn't know if it had ever mattered—he controlled a good number of the yōkai constituting the Parade. His low-demons had sniffed me out. He knew exactly who was here, where we stood, and the entirety of our words, deeds, and emotions.

Fangs emerged from behind his lips.

He grinned.

"Vampire!" Wrenn yelled. "I am Fae Royal Guard! That kelpie falls under my jurisdiction!"

Brother's grin turned to a hard, sinister death's head snarl. The look he gave us was one full of hatred and chaos. And also somehow grudges, as if Victor's worst child blamed us for all the misery he himself inflicted on the world.

"That's not Dracula." Wrenn couldn't keep her surprise from making her cheek twitch.

No, that was family. Yet I didn't think we were looking at the combined personality I called Brother, either.

Whoever this vampire was—whatever he was—sunk his fangs into the kelpie's neck.

The kelpie jerked as the monster vacuumed his blood and his magic. I counted one, two, three...

Brother tossed the drained and dead kelpie into the Night Parade as if offering his dogs a bone on which to gnaw—and gnaw they did.

A yōkai scrambled up the side of the boulder backward, face and body toward us but fingers and toes moving it up the vertical side of the rock like a gecko. It stopped near the top, but did not crest over onto the flat surface.

Brother gently touched its shoulder and cheek until it grinned. Then he looked directly at us again and winked.

He pointed.

The entire Night Parade stopped flowing by the boulder and every one of the yōkai turned toward us—the ones carrying Brother's magic and the ones not.

"Run!" Wrenn said, and turned to dart up the path.

A pure-white seven-tailed fox manifested on me—feet braced against my hips and hands gripping my shoulders.

And the last thing I remembered was the full-force knockout-level kitsune headbutt right to the middle of my forehead.

CHAPTER 10

I wasn't quite conscious enough to realize that the swinging, too-bright, buzzing environmental stimulus over my head was a naked lightbulb. The light swung to the right and burned a brilliant trail onto my retinas. Then it swung back to the left, burning the other direction, as if I should be rocking. But I wasn't. An annoying light swung over my head.

I lay on something cold and not quite sturdy enough for my almost seven-foot height and three-hundred pounds. Nor was it long enough —my knees were bent and leaned against something that felt like a wall. One of my arms had been folded over my chest toward that wall, as if someone wanted to make sure I didn't roll off my hard, creaking bed.

I opened my eyes just as the light swung back toward my metal bunk.

Blue-white hit my pupils. I closed my eyes again and rubbed my scalp as I sat up.

The bunk was attached to the wall and entirely too narrow for my frame, hence the folding. The wall from which the bunk hung had been painted a matte black. The rest of the room, a flat gray. A wall jutting out of one corner offered a bit of privacy for a small bathroom.

The only light was the swinging bulb. I had no idea what time it was.

Wrenn sat on top of a crate in the far corner. She leaned back with her shoulders against one of the gray walls and her feet up on the edge of the crate, watching me. "They knocked me out, too," she said. "I woke up about ten minutes ago." She also sat up. "At least they gave you the cot."

I shook my hands. The air here was chilly, but I hadn't cooled down like I usually do when I'm unconscious. "We couldn't have been out all that long. I'm not cold."

Wrenn watched my hands. "So it happens to you, too?" she asked softly. "Getting too cold when you sleep?"

She rubbed the back of one hand with her other as if to test if she, too, had made it through this without the corpse-cold settling into her flesh.

I couldn't tell from her face what she found more upsetting: waking up cold, or the fact that she woke up cold because of Victor. Or both.

I set my hands on my thighs. "I sleep like the dead," I said.

A low, sad chuckle erupted from her throat. She looked down at her own hands, then tapped the side of her head. "Well, that silences any remaining voices claiming Victor 'saved' me from drowning."

I had never gone through what she was going through, in terms of accepting what I was. At least she was able to articulate what he did to us. And she had me to help explain what little I could.

"I knew the moment I woke up on that table what he'd done," I said. "It took me a few weeks before I could talk again. But I knew."

She looked up at the ceiling. After a moment, her shoulders settled. "I don't have scars," she said, as if those voices really hadn't been silenced.

She *did* have scars. Victor had just done a better job with her cosmetically.

Now she shrugged. "I can see exactly what you're thinking in your expressions."

"So you know what I'm thinking is true." I was easy to read. Some people could read me better than others.

She shook her head. "He made me for *him*, not you." Her hands tightened as if she wanted to smack the crate. "I'm sure of it."

I suspected she was correct. Should I offer comfort? We'd just met, even if we had just fought Brother and yōkai together. "My home and hot chocolate are always available to you, if you want to talk more about it."

She rubbed at the tip of her nose. "When we get out of here."

"When we get out of here," I patted at my jacket pocket. No phone. No wallet, either. Still had my winter coat and boots, which was good, since the room was cold.

"They took my phone, too," she said.

I sighed and stretched my shoulders.

"I've seen him several times. In the Heartway." Wrenn sat forward. "The Demon. Brother." She closed her eyes. "Not *him*, but a phantom memory of him."

She'd already told me about the flashbacks and the version of him called up by the demanding magic of the fae Heartway. The Heartway seemed to find the memory of him ripping Victor's head from his body particularly tasty.

Fae magic tended toward the vindictive.

She rubbed her hands together. "And now he's adopting yōkai."

I knew exactly what she was thinking: What little we thought we understood about how that vampiric body operated had just been tossed out the window. This was a personality neither of us had met before.

"A vampire is still a vampire," I said. Still a creature with two souls —one the demon vampire and the other what remained of its human personality.

Except with Brother, we were dealing with bits and pieces of not only human personalities, but also the many vampires whose parts made the whole.

Wrenn looked up at the ceiling. After a moment, she looked at me again. "Do you feel better? You don't seem to be raging anymore." She jumped down, walked over, and sat on the bunk next to me.

"He did the same thing in Alfheim," I said. "Attached low-demon magic to me to dredge up the rage." I'd had no idea what was happening to me the first time. I knew now.

I did a quick check of my visible skin. "I don't see any of his magic." I couldn't see my back, though, and Wrenn hadn't been able to see the oily magic in the woods, so she wouldn't be able to check for me.

Her shoulders tensed up even though I could see that she was trying keep her body loose. "You know what that means, right?"

I pulled off one of my boots to make sure it hadn't gotten into my socks like a swarm of slimy wood ticks. "What?" I asked.

"He might not be Brother, but he has access to all of Brother's magicks and enough of his memories to be able to use them."

There was also another alternative. "Or he's Brother accessing memories of a part he hadn't used when he was in Alfheim. He was Dracula when the elves sealed up Vampland, though he did seem to be disassociating at the time."

She glanced around my head. "Your mate magic's back."

It had left?

It had. I'd lost my connection to Ellie when Brother's magic touched me in the forest. I'd lost Ellie.

My heart thumped in my chest. My core jittered. I blinked too frequently, and the deep parts of my brain tossed out flash after flash of that lovely spot on Ellie's neck just below her ear, and the hollow of her throat, and the V between her breasts.

I'd pretty much had my fill of losing Ellie.

My mate magic flared so high it fanned out against the cold ceiling of our cell like a rolling cloud of firefly-filled smoke.

Wrenn grinned. "It disappeared when you started raging, as if hiding from something I couldn't see." She patted my shoulder. "I saw *absence*, so I figured you were onto something."

It swarmed my head now.

"I need to go home," I said. I was too far away from my beloved.

She watched me with concerned eyes. "Is this the first time you've been apart since the magic clicked on?"

"Yes," I said, but that wasn't quite true. Except for my time in Las Vegas, we were both in Alfheim the entire time we were apart. "No." I rubbed at my head again. I just wanted to snuggle with my woman.

Snuggle, because big me wasn't much better than a puppy.

I looked up at the swarm above my head. "Is it as distracting for you as it is for me?" I asked my sister.

She patted my shoulder again. "Like I said, only the good amongst us manifest mate magic." She grinned again. "It does give you a halo."

I leaned back against the wall. "I punched a yōkai," I said. A yōkai doused in Brother's magic.

Now she laughed. "And landed us in kami jail."

I sat up again. "The kitsune who headbutted me was white. Had seven tails, too, so not Lollipop." I watched my puppy love swirl in the air in front of my face. "Or Chip."

She watched me check my other ankle. "Brother did not appreciate that jorōgumo selling off yōkai to the syndicate." She exhaled. "For what purpose?"

The answer seemed obvious. "He's building a local army instead of calling all the vampires to him the way Dracula did."

She frowned. "And I bet you that kitsune thought we were somehow here to help him." She waved her hand at our jail. "Why else drop us here?"

I suspected she was correct.

Wrenn tugged on her sleeves as if unconsciously mimicking my own checking of my clothes for Brother's magic.

"White foxes are messengers of Inari." She stood and smoothed her jacket. "Inari aspects pretty much run things among the kami. They act like Odin aspects."

So we had the attention of the local Arne. "And the jorōgumo?"

Wrenn pulled the crate over so she could get a better look at our one swinging lightbulb. "There's a shadow magical organized crime syndicate in Japan." She jumped up on the box. "One that leans more into human trafficking than most of the yakuza."

"Which explains the kelpie," I said.

Wrenn nodded as if she'd read my mind. "They're run by a spirit manifestation of a particularly nasty and malevolent emperor." Wrenn let go and the bulb started swinging again. "They're legit, too, and run a distribution company called Central Kobayashi Shipping and Transportation. Cen-Ko for English speakers. They've never come anywhere near fae territory, so we only keep tabs on them. But now I have proof they're dealing with kelpies."

Nothing works better for human trafficking than legitimate access to shipping and transportation operations.

I stretched my shoulders again to get out some of the metal slab kinks. "The elves don't run syndicates," I said.

Wrenn laughed. "The Elf Emperor has an iron grip on the Nordic enclaves and your American elves seem to value a low profile more than riches and rewards. The same cannot be said for the enclaves in Normandy and Russia."

"The Siberians?" Why was I not surprised that the Siberians were up to no good?

"Mostly the satellite enclave outside of Moscow." Wrenn poked at the lightbulb. "There's an Odin elf there who goes back and forth between the urbanized elves and the main group in the Arctic." She touched the lightbulb's cord. "He's not as old—or as powerful—as your Odinsson. I think that's why he likes to win at all costs." She squinted at the cord. "Odin elves are as likely to be warmongering narcissists as they are to be good chieftains." She stopped the light from swinging. "So no, the elves are not as pure as their driven Norwegian snow, even when they have their Loki elves under control."

She had to be talking about Niklas der Nord, the Siberian who'd caused all the problems in Las Vegas. "I think I've met him." No wonder Dag divorced him.

Wrenn stopped the light from swinging again. "Do you feel any motion?" she asked.

I held out my hands. Nothing touched my balance, or annoyed my inner ears. "No."

She watched the light. "Me, neither." She jumped down off the box. "If you had non-local magicals you'd like to keep separate from your population, where would you stash them?" She held her hands out the same way I had, looking for any sense of motion. "Not in Ed's jail, I'm assuming. Correct?"

I shook my head. "We don't have a lot of interlopers in Alfheim," I said. "Just Brother, and the elves locked him in Vampland." Except that clearly hadn't worked. "But he's here."

She flicked her wrist as if to drop one of her magical tokens into her palm.

Nothing happened.

Wrenn peeled off her jacket. She pulled up her sleeves. "I'm not a powerful witch," she said. "I carry everything but my protection spells as tokens." She held out her hands.

I'd gotten a glimpse of the Celtic tattoos around her wrists when we talked on the deck. But they were a fae thing, so I hadn't asked, and we hadn't dwelled.

Tiny pearls of magical energy dotted each of the intricate inter-woven silver lines coiled around her wrists. Larger pearls clung to more tattoos twining up her inner forearms.

"Those are Heartway tokens," she said.

Most of them were a brilliant emerald green. Two were slightly bluish. "These look different," I said.

"Those two I purchased. The others are from Robin."

"Ah," I said. "I used to carry elven tracers." I showed her my inner arm. "If you look carefully, you might see shadows." The red magic of Portia Elizabeth's dress had pooled in one of those shadows.

"You're not now?" She pulled down her sleeve. "Because they'd be useful." She held out her arm again. "Beyond the glowing, all of my tokens are completely inert and non-responsive. Either the kami did something—I don't see any kami magic on my arms or in our cell, though—or we're somewhere fae magic cannot operate."

I peered at her arm. "Not even a hint of pink and silver."

She peered at my Yggdrasil tattoo. "Only elven blues and violets."

We were in a small windowless holding cell with a metal bunk, a crate, and a swinging light bulb. "This is a very strange pocket realm."

"There should be..." Wrenn trailed off. She frowned again and waved at the walls. "A way to get in and out."

Not windows, I thought. "We are *definitely* inside a spell," I said. "What are we looking for?" I asked.

"A way out." She pulled up her sleeves again and held her forearms in front of her like divining rods. "An..."

Exit, I thought, but the word wouldn't form on my lips. *A door. A gateway.*

Wrenn closed her eyes. "Usually, I use my phone to find..." One of her tattoos lifted up off her wrists—no, a braid inside the braid around her wrists lifted up as if disengaging itself from the other tattoos. Green and red magics flickered upward, some of it reaching for her Heartway tokens, and some pointing toward the wall directly across from the bunk.

She looked at me, her face as surprised as mine. "I..." She inhaled. "One of the Royals gave me that magic."

Wrenn said "one of the Royals" and not "Oberon." And I knew, from Ed's interactions in Texas, that a certain Queen of the Fae had paid Wrenn a visit.

I pointed at her arms. "We need to talk about that," I said. Because I was pretty damned sure my default mother-in-law had given my sister extra magic that was powerful enough to operate inside a kami jail. Maybe to help. Maybe not. Maybe to mess with her husband. Maybe to start a war with the kami.

Or maybe simply because she liked me and wanted to make sure I made it home to her daughter.

I figured for the moment, we should go with "Titania wants us to survive this" and use every extra ounce of help we could get.

I slammed my fists against the wall where Titania's magic pointed. Something shifted. A crack appeared.

Wrenn pulled her jacket back on and zipped it up. I nodded and zipped up mine.

I hit the wall again. The crack widened and expanded up and around a ninety-degree angle.

The edge of a door.

I gripped the edge high up, and Wrenn gripped low down. We pulled. The door snapped open.

And ocean water hit us full in the face.

CHAPTER 11

Our prison was submerged, and not in any of the many lakes around Mount Fuji. We were in cold, dark, ocean brine, which meant we were either too deep under for sunlight, or too deep into the night for daylight.

Please be nighttime, I thought as I stumbled back from the onslaught of cold, salty, organic-smelling water.

"How long can you hold your breath?" Wrenn asked.

"A long time," I said. "You?"

She backed into the crate. "Doesn't matter." She looked at me. "I can't swim. Never learned. Not after Victor told me..." She pinched her lips together. "It's not your fault I can't swim," she said as much to herself as to me.

Victor told her I'd tried to drown her to force him to make me a mate. Which was yet another of his flat-out, bald-faced lies. "I hate that man," I said.

Wrenn snorted. "Can *you* swim?" The water rushing in was already up to our thighs.

I wasn't big on water, either. "I managed to not drown myself when I walked the Arctic into Minnesota." I'd had lots of opportunities. A few mishaps, too. I'd always managed to paddle my way to shore. "I think some part of me has swimming muscle memory."

She looked back at the hole. "Well, I sincerely hope that part of you can hold onto me."

"Yeah," I said. I wasn't about to lose my just-found sister.

Wrenn's hip knocked against the crate. She looked down the wood and the salt-smelling water sloshing around it. Her eyes widened. "Look."

The side opposite us—the side that had been out of view against the wall—carried a yellow square tipped on its side like a diamond. Inside, what looked like a faceless flaming emoji head.

I stared at it for a split second. The tipped over yellow square was the international sign for danger. And the flaming O was—

"There are tanks of oxygen in the crate!" I said. The signs said nothing about what kind of tanks, though.

Wrenn slammed her fist against the top. The wood snapped and the crate tipped against the inflowing water, but she managed to open a good-sized hole.

She yanked out a scuba tank, complete with rebreather. She reached in again. "There's only one."

The water crested over the top of the crate and slushed inside. We didn't have a lot of time. "Put it on," I said.

She held it out. "I'm carrying protection spells I can use to help hold onto you." She pushed it at me. "You're bigger and stronger, and will get us to the surface faster."

The water hit my chest. "All right, all right." I loosened the straps on the harness as far as possible—it would likely still be too tight—and tried to snap the tanks to my back. "I have no idea how to do this safely." I didn't, and there was no way one of my constituent parts brought scuba muscle memory to my body. I was over two hundred years old.

I couldn't get the strap to snap. I was too big to wear the tanks. "You'll have to wear it."

Wrenn refused to take the tank. "We don't have time." She held her hands up out of the water and slapped at the active magic on her wrists. "Please override whatever's holding my tokens in check and let me access my protection and safety spells."

Nothing happened.

The water was up to her chin. We were going to drown if we didn't figure out how to get Titania's magic to work.

Work to protect me.

I laid my hand over the magic on her wrists. "I want to go home to Ellie," I said.

The magic reached out for my mate magic as if to make sure it was actually, for sure, dealing with me.

Then it flared up Wrenn's arms.

Fae magic burst around her in wave after wave of green and red. It coiled around me, cinched itself down like a rope, and anchored the tank to my back.

Wrenn inhaled and opened the valve. "Here's hoping this works."

Air hissed out of the mouthpiece just as the water crested over Wrenn's nose. She inhaled one last time and pulled herself close as the fae bubble contracted around us.

I took three breaths on the mouthpiece, then handed it to her. She took three breaths, gave me a thumbs up, and handed it back.

Titania's magic was holding the tank onto me, and Wrenn to my side. Even if she let go, I could feel the spring of the spell, and I'd be able to pull her back.

"Hold on," I said, and kicked toward the door.

We swam out into the ocean as we switched who inhaled the oxygen. Dots of light streamed down colors from above, so we weren't too deep. Or that far away from civilization. At least I hoped so. When magicals were involved, the lights could be decoy magic and we might surface in Point Nemo in the Pacific thousands of miles from any land.

Wrenn handed me back the mouthpiece. I took three more deep breaths and continued to kick toward what I hoped was the surface.

Wrenn tapped my shoulder and pointed behind us.

I twisted my head for a quick look.

From the outside, our prison was nothing more than a large

bubble wavering in the water. No signs of the crate, or the walls, or the light.

Just a pocket surrounded by a writhing coil of barely-visible sliver, pink, and sea-blue magic—a coil with a wide dragon head and a long dragon tail.

We were in the ocean with a Japanese *water dragon*.

It stuck its head into the prison-bubble, then pulled it out.

A wave of sound moved through the water—and through us. My inner ears rattled. My gut wiggled. My bones shook.

The dragon looked up just as a wave of brightness ran from its head to its tail, revealing shimmering scales along its long, sinewy body.

Wrenn pointed upward. She didn't want us near a dragon magical. I nodded and kicked harder. Wrenn also kicked, and after a moment, we fell into a rhythm of kick, kick, pass the mouthpiece, kick, kick, pass.

We rose. The lights grew brighter, but not at the rate they should have. We kicked ten feet, but those round lights only came a foot closer.

But the water became less dense. Still cold. Still dark and salty. But we were moving upward. We had to be.

I looked back again.

The dragon followed us upward. It had lost its dragon shape away from the bubble, and looked more like a shimmering reflection in the water, but I knew what it was. So did Wrenn. She took her three breaths and kicked harder.

What had felt like twenty feet of water above our head suddenly wasn't there anymore. We broke, gasping, into air.

We were in a bay. Tokyo Bay, I suspected, from the shape of the buildings and the huge suspension bridge in front of us. The bridge spanned the entire bay and was lit up with a full rainbow of colors. Every inch of coastline had been transformed for shipping. Massive container ships docked under equally massive cranes. Cars buzzed along all the roads and over the bridge, even though the sun was only just beginning to spread pinks along the eastern horizon.

Wrenn tapped my shoulder again. "Do you see the dragon?" Her fae spells still held us and the tank together.

I looked around. "No." Hopefully it would stay under the water and leave us alone now that we were at the surface.

"There's a platform," Wren pointed over my shoulder.

Behind us, above where we'd been imprisoned, sat a buoy with a floating platform big enough to hold three, maybe four people without tipping. The buoy light flashed like all the other buoys marking shipping lanes.

Both the platform and the buoy shimmered softly with kami magic.

"We could try for the shore," I said. It looked to be about a mile. "Your spells seem to be holding."

"The Queen's spells, you mean," she said.

"Yeah," I said. I helped her keep her head above the waves. We were both muscular enough that floating wasn't easy for either of us. Plus our boots and clothes pulled on our legs, and I wasn't about to drop the oxygen tanks, just in case. "We need to keep moving, either way."

A wave came through and Wrenn bobbed under for a second until I pulled her back up to the surface.

She pointed at the platform.

I didn't think she wanted to touch the kami-charmed wood any more than I did, but we didn't have a choice. Wrenn was strong, but she couldn't swim, and even though we were both nearly indestructible, neither of us wanted to test our invulnerability in Tokyo Bay.

The platform sat on top of four rows of pontoon floats, each painted bright yellow, so they were visible during the day. Several planks of weathered wood held them together. A low rail skirted around the outside on three sides. Someone had nailed a rickety-looking ladder to the open side.

I kicked us toward the platform hoping that the rungs hadn't been in ocean water so long that they would no longer hold my weight.

Wrenn gingerly reached for the ladder. The silver magic sniffed at her hand, but nothing else, and allowed her to climb up to the platform. "Careful," she said. "There are gaps up here."

I climbed up after her, the tank hanging off my shoulders now that I was no longer inside the fae protection spell, and hauled myself onto the planks. I handed her the tank and laid down on the widest board available. "Now what do we do?"

She unzipped her jacket, slid it off, and carefully wrung water out of it. I would do the same in a moment. For now, the cold only annoyed me, and I stared up at the sky.

"Someone will show up soon enough," Wrenn said. "We broke out of their prison."

Then what? I sat up and leaned forward, shaking my head to get as much water out of my hair as possible. "Do you speak enough Japanese to explain to the dragon that we were tossed here by a World Spirit because our brother is a demon vampire with multiple personalities?" I sat up and unzipped my jacket to wring it out. "Or maybe ask about Chip and Lollipop?" We had not just one missing kitsune, but two, now.

There was also that white one who knocked us out.

"That dragon was likely a manifestation of a local ocean god's magic." She looked down into the murky ocean. "If it had wanted to hurt us, it would have done so while we were underwater." She slipped her damp jacket back on. "It was probably more of a projection than an aspect." She looked over the side again. "At least I hope it was a projection. That level of shapeshifting is a power I've never seen before with any magical, no matter the kind."

Elves didn't shapeshift. Fae, neither. They cast glamour spells. "It looked like magic, not a creature."

She nodded.

We sat for a long moment in the cold saying nothing, two of Victor Frankenstein's three assembled offspring, both staring at the lights of Tokyo like the children we were not. We wouldn't freeze to death, or suffer too much, but like drowning, I didn't want to test hypothermia, either.

Not that we had a lot of choice.

The set of Wrenn's shoulders changed. When she finally looked at me, I could see she'd made a decision. "You said her name is Ellie," she said.

She wanted to know about my mate magic.

No need to lie about it. "Yes."

"And she's connected to Queen Titania."

I nodded. "Yes."

Wrenn inhaled deeply and exhaled slowly as if calming herself. "Me knowing is a threat to her. And you. Isn't it?"

Yes, I thought. "Probably." Wrenn was likely to forget by tomorrow evening, but I didn't say anything. The less information her fae magic had, the better.

She looked at me again. "Before I took Ed into the Heartway to find his kids, we made a no-deal deal. All our actions were in parallel as representatives of our two distinct jurisdictions. No promises. All exchanges were law enforcement to law enforcement." She sighed in what sounded like frustration. "I can't do that with you. You're not with the Alfheim Sheriff's Department."

"No. No, I'm not," I said. I had no interest in being a cop. No way could I sit in my vehicle all day watching for speeders. Or spend my time filling out paperwork. Ed, at least, had an administrative side to his job that had him working with people at the county and the state.

Mostly, though, I'd spent two hundred years working on *not* being scary. I wasn't going to throw all that work away by taking on a job that required intimidation.

"So we need to find some other equal footing," she said.

We needed a parity of power, because only a parity of power could deter a problematic fae response. Too much power her way, and some fae somewhere would take advantage. Too much power my way, and some fae somewhere would get mad.

Such was the way of the fae.

"Yes," I said.

Wrenn watched my mate magic dance on my shoulders. "Worry not, little sparkles," she said, "I am Royal Guard, so guarding royals is what I do." She patted my knee. "Brother is our priority anyway. No need for your Ellie to come up again."

"Yes," I repeated.

She nodded again. "I kind of feel a little like Romeo and Juliet here, being caught between fae and elf magicks like this."

My mate magic flared up again at the mention of Romeo and Juliet. *Romeo and Juliet was not a romance*, I tried to remind my mate magic. Not that it noticed. Not that it cared Wrenn liked Benta better, anyway.

"I think we now know why Raven hijacked you," I said.

Wrenn chuckled. "My satchel is still sitting on the table next to the door at Raven's Gaze. I inadvertently left it with the Raven World Spirit." She looked toward the brightening eastern horizon. "Which, by the way, is a breach of protocol that's going to get me kicked out of the Royal Guard. If she messes with my satchel."

Which Raven would, for sure. "*If* she messes with it," I said instead.

"If I had my Guard star, I'd have a lot more spells." She looked at her wrists. "And a lot more authority here."

Neither of us had much authority in Japan beyond being experts in all things Frankenstein. "I think we're on our own."

The sun crested over the eastern horizon and spread lovely pinks and salmons over Tokyo—and the yacht no more than a hundred yards from the platform.

A boat neither of us had noticed until the sun hit it.

"*Whoa*," Wrenn said as she leaned away from the suddenly appearing boat. "We have company."

CHAPTER 12

The yacht wasn't large for a sea-worthy boat—maybe forty feet—but was a sleek bullet unlike any of the big boats I'd seen on the lakes of Minnesota. No flags marred its lines. No markings broke up the silver, mirror-like finish. Only shadows moved behind its blacked-out windows. Even without the enchantments woven around its pink and silver hull, it would have been hard to notice.

Wrenn gripped my arm. "That boat's kami-owned."

Were we in for a fight?

A woman appeared from the blacked-out cabin. She leaned over the boat's rail and waved her arm.

A woman I'd never met but sort of recognized.

"Frank Victorsson!" she yelled.

I *did* recognize her.

"Chihiro?" I called. She looked the same as the photo Ellie had shown me—taller than most Japanese women and maybe a bit thinner. She wore a nondescript white collared shirt and a pair of chinos; her bobbed hair was longer than in her pictures, and now had a pink stripe flowing from her crown alongside her face. Her features struck me overall as oval—oval eyes, oval mouth, and oval chin and cheeks, which gave her a sense of sweetness on top of her keen mind.

The little bit of Chihiro Hatanaka I knew was kind, but she was also thorough. And tough. She'd talked me through many evenings of confusion and anger when I couldn't remember Ellie.

Wrenn looked at me, then at Chihiro, then back at me. "You know someone involved with the kami?"

"Chihiro!" I yelled. I turned to Wrenn. "It's a long story."

"Ah," she said. She clearly understood that Chihiro was part of my life with Ellie and that she shouldn't pry. "Noted."

Chihiro jumped up and down and waved her hands again. "Frank!" she yelled again.

"This whole thing is surreal," Wrenn said. "And I live with fae."

Chihiro ducked her head into the cabin again.

"Is she trustworth—"

Lollipop appeared between us, wedged between my shoulder and Wrenn's like a little fox sausage. She wiggled and blinked, and grabbed our arms so we wouldn't destabilize the platform.

"Hey!" Wrenn, thankfully, did not jump.

"Did you bring Chihiro?" I asked the kitsune. It was possible. They'd interacted in the past.

Lollipop shook her head *no*. She pulled a lollipop shaped like Titania's crest out of her mouth, swirled it at my mate magic, then held her fingers to her ear and lips as if she were speaking into a phone. Then she pointed at the boat.

Ellie called her? "How did..." I couldn't say her name with Lollipop so close. "How did our mutual friend know to call Chihiro?"

Lollipop pointed at my shoulders again, did a little winking dance with her fingers, then pulled a bright red heart from her mouth.

"Through our mate magic?" I looked at the magic swirling just above the skin of my hands. It had calmed down and wasn't as annoyingly obvious. Or maybe it had been busy giving Ellie updates I had no idea it was giving her.

Wrenn's eyebrow arched. Thankfully she didn't say anything.

"How did you find us?" I held up my hand again. "The mate magic?"

Lollipop put the candy back into her mouth. She pointed at the boat, made the phone gesture again, then tapped her own chest.

"The person on the boat called you? Raven didn't send you to fetch us?" Wrenn asked. "Or the elves?"

Lollipop shook her head *no*.

Wrenn glanced at me, then scrunched down a little so she was on eye level with Lollipop. "Kitsune," she said. "A jorōgumo is involved with a kelpie syndicate to traffic low powered magicals to vampires."

She didn't say anything about our brother.

Lollipop nodded *yes*.

Wrenn kept her attention on Lollipop. "That's why you came to Frank for help, correct?"

Lollipop nodded again.

"Dracula is in Japan," Wrenn said. "He freed himself from an elven prison. He's extraordinarily powerful." She glanced at me. "That seven-tail means the locals are aware and are surveilling him."

Lollipop blinked.

Wrenn watched Lollipop for comprehension. "We have a message we would like you to take to the local kami, okay?"

Lollipop nodded *yes* again.

"Frank works for the North American enclave of elves who locked away Dracula. I work for the Fae Royal Guard. Imprisoning us will not stop the syndicate nor the vampire and may cause a diplomatic nightmare for everyone."

More nods from Lollipop.

"Okay. Good," Wrenn said. "Will you take this message for us?"

Lollipop looked down as if she was about to vanish again.

"Wait." I touched the kitsune's shoulder. Brother had enlisted the local yōkai and was probably feeding on every magical he came across, including kitsune. "Did Dracula take Chip?" I asked.

Lollipop's eyes grew huge. Her lip trembled. She vigorously shook her head *no*, then burst into tears and threw herself into my arms.

"Did the traffickers take her?" Wrenn asked with a gentleness that surprised me, even though it shouldn't.

Lollipop nodded *yes*.

Their going after Chip and Lollipop made my blood boil. I didn't know why. The syndicate had trafficked many low-powered magicals, which should have been enough to make me want to break a few heads just on principle. But this made it personal.

Chip and Lollipop were the ones who had given me Chihiro's number. Without them, I never would have found Ellie.

I did owe them. I owed them big time.

I hugged Lollipop to my chest. "We'll do everything we can to help," I said. "Because that's what we do. Right, Wrenn? We help."

My sister nodded, too.

"Do you know where Chip is?" I asked. Even if we couldn't take down Brother immediately, maybe we could rescue Chip.

Lollipop shook her head *no* again.

"Have you been looking?" I asked.

She nodded just as vigorously against my chest.

"Please be careful," Wrenn said. "Promise us that you're being careful."

Lollipop nodded again and pulled a big finger-crossed emoji from her mouth.

The boat edged close enough that we could swing off the platform and onto the stern.

Lollipop vanished and my arms dropped to my belly, sending a shock through me and down into the platform.

Wrenn threw her hands wide for balance. "I wish they wouldn't do that."

Lollipop reappeared on the boat, next to the door into the cabin, and crunched in on herself. She sniffed and rubbed at her eyes and pressed her back into the wall behind her.

Chihiro stepped out of the cabin again. She patted Lollipop's shoulder before moving to the back of the boat. "We need to hurry. I must return this boat before the owner realizes it's missing."

Wrenn hopped over to the yacht first. I jumped over next and moved away from the equally sleek engines on the back.

Wrenn touched my elbow. She nodded toward the platform just as the sun fully crested the horizon.

The dragon shimmied up the side of the platform more like waves undulating in the ocean's innate magic than like any actual creature. It shimmered in the dawn light, silver and pink and blue and green, and set its huge head next to the boat.

Lollipop pulled a dragon head out of her mouth and held it out for Chihiro to see. Chihiro nodded, squeezed Lollipop's shoulder again, and stepped toward where Wrenn and I stood on the end of the boat.

"Please move to the kitsune," Chihiro said as she stepped between us and the dragon made of magic.

She moved aside her hair and touched a spot shimmering with its own magic behind her ear. Magical goggles manifested over her eyes, and earphones over her ears. The spell shimmered and shimmied like —but not in time with—the dragon. The headpiece's oscillation sped up, then slowed, then sped up again, changed colors, then changed back, until it landed on the pattern that matched the magicks of the beast.

"*Ohh,*" Wrenn said. "That spell's trade-worthy."

A seeing spell shaped in such a way as to allow a mundane to see magic? Every member of Ed's family should have one of those.

Chihiro bowed to the spirit. "Ōwatatsumi no kami," she said.

The dragon shook its great head.

Chihiro continued to bow. Lollipop slapped my arm, then bowed. Wrenn and I followed.

The dragon reared up into the dawn light like a shimmering heat mirage, then coiled itself around the boat. Kami magic rubbed against the fae magic on Wrenn's wrists, setting off small sparks. Power undulated around us. For a long, electric second, we were completely subsumed in silver and pink.

Then it was back to its coil on the platform with its massive head once again down by Chihiro.

A wave of pressure—concern, perhaps—moved from the dragon to Chihiro, then by us to Lollipop. The dragon god found something about this moment worrisome.

Chihiro nodded.

Another wave moved by, this one feeling like a dismissal.

Chihiro nodded again.

And with that, Ōwatatsumi no kami vanished.

Chihiro straightened. She touched behind her ear again and the seeing spell contracted back to a tiny mole-like spot. She stood at the end of the strange, shiny yacht haloed in the pinks of dawn as if she was the sun goddess herself.

But she wasn't. She was a woman, a mundane who, like Ed, had gotten pulled into the world of magicals. And we'd just watched her communicate with a magical kami unlike any I'd ever seen before.

"Frank." She smiled and bowed slightly. "It's good to finally meet in person."

Lollipop blinked a few times before returning her dragon head to her mouth.

"We must go." Chihiro pushed toward the cabin. She waved to us. "Come." Then to Lollipop: "You are safest with them." She nodded toward Wrenn and me.

I wasn't so sure about that.

Chihiro started up the engine again. "Hatanaka Chihiro," she said, saying her surname first as she nodded to Wrenn. "You are Frank's sister." She did not ask. "You are Fae Royal Guard." She looked Wrenn up and down. "You are not wearing a star."

Wrenn bowed to Chihiro and did not extend her hand. "Wrenn Goodfellow." She patted at her belt. "I left my star at home."

Chihiro looked me up and down, as well. "You are as big as I expected." Her grin said there was more to her comment than I knew.

My face must have betrayed me because she laughed. "I know these matters must stay private." She nodded toward Wrenn.

My sister shrugged.

"We have not yet found parity of power," I said.

Chihiro nodded. "Understood." She steered the boat away from the platform. She looked back once as if to make sure the ocean dragon had not returned, then accelerated the boat toward the shore.

"We were tossed into a middle of a Night Parade," I said.

"There was a kelpie," Wrenn said. "It was a meat market for the blood syndicate that took Chip."

I moved to the center of the boat. "Brother showed up. He ate the kelpie. Then a white seven-tailed kitsune headbutted me and we ended up under the sea." I pointed at the water.

"Which Ōwatatsumi no kami found interesting," Chihiro said. "It did not authorize the use of its territory for your prison."

"Was that why it gave off that wave of concern?" Wrenn asked.

Chihiro turned the boat toward a marina. "Oh, no." She pulled back on the accelerator and slowed the boat. "It questioned my unauthorized taking of this boat."

Wrenn leaned down and peered at the steering wheel edge-on. She ran a finger over the teak of the wheel. "The boat is kami owned, isn't it?" She looked up. "The magic is right at the surface, but it's there, and strong."

Chihiro blinked rapidly for a second, as if a terrifying memory surfaced.

But then it was gone. "Many of the kami do not believe that the syndicate or the gaijin vampire are... problems."

Lollipop nodded vigorously.

Chihiro looked down at the steering wheel. "Even though his godhood has cost many lives."

Godhood?

"What?" Wrenn stood up straight. "How?"

But it made sense. How else could a European demon—and you weren't going to get any more European than Dracula in a body built by Victor Frankenstein—come into Japan and quickly gain so much control over the local yōkai?

Becoming a god was the only way—and explained the change in personality.

"I will explain everything I know as soon as we get you two to safety," She eased the boat toward a dock inside an equally sleek boathouse.

I've felt in-over-my-head several times in my life. I was reborn into the world in-over-my-head. Every social interaction up until the elves found me had me drowning in what-ifs and why-nots. Plus I lived with magicals who doled out information on a need-to-know basis. So I should have the skills to parse what to do when I didn't know what to do.

But we were in Japan, inside a language and culture I did not know, surrounded by extraordinarily powerful and interconnected magicals of whom I had only a cursory knowledge.

I was beginning to feel overwhelmed.

Wrenn hopped off the yacht and helped tie the boat to the dock.

Lollipop snuggled up against my side and looked up at me like a little lost fox kit. I looked down at her. "We'll get Chip back," I said.

We wouldn't. I knew it. I suspect Wrenn knew it, too.

Not with the local kami refusing to understand that they had "problems."

I wasn't going to tell the sad little kitsune that. I wouldn't take away her hope.

Because hope was all we had.

CHAPTER 13

Gods weren't *here*, with us mundanes. Gods were the sparks of magic made when humanity rubbed against the natural world, not the products of those sparks. Not the elves, fae, kami, spirits, loa, or any of the other magicals walking the world with humanity. Gods were more... abstract.

No, not abstract. Invisible.

So what did that mean for Brother? Demon, as Wrenn called him. Dracula. Or perhaps the name given him by Chihiro: *Kyūketsuki no kami*, Vampire God.

What had my father unleashed onto the world?

I sat back against the buttery leather of the rented SUV's passenger seat. The first thing Chihiro did after Ellie called her was to rent the biggest vehicle she could find, to accommodate my height. It turned out to be a black, fully-appointed, right-hand-drive-converted, late-model Cadillac Escalade with black tinted windows, gold interior trim, and the softest black leather seats I'd ever touched.

The strangest part was sitting in the left side of the vehicle and not having a steering wheel. Several times I had to stop myself from stomping my foot on a non-existent brake pedal.

Not stomping did nothing to calm my barely contained panic. I had to stop my foot from moving, and my leg, and stop my fingers from tapping, and my mouth from running off question after question: How did Brother convince the yōkai of Tokyo that he was a god? How did he get here in the first place? How was Chihiro involved in all this? What day was it, anyway?

I wanted to break something.

But mostly, I *had* to talk to Ellie. "Chihiro," I asked, "could I use your phone?"

Chihiro squinted against the morning sun as she drove us toward the Tokyo suburbs. She was taking us to the local kami in much the same way I would have taken Wrenn to Arne and Dag if she'd shown up in the middle of something nefarious in Alfheim. Whether or not we'd meet the main Inari aspect—there were at least fifteen living in the Greater Tokyo Area—I did not know. Chihiro and Wrenn both doubted we would. But the best place to start was a restaurant tucked away in the streets outside of Tokyo proper.

So Chihiro drove. Traffic wasn't anywhere near what I'd expect for one of Earth's most populous cities, and we traveled at a good clip inside the concrete river that was one of Tokyo's major expressways. Congestion, it seemed, happened on the trains, not the roads.

Chihiro grabbed her phone out of a cupholder in the center console. She fiddled with it one-handed, then held it against the steering wheel so she could swipe her finger to unlock the screen. Then she handed it to me.

"Yours and hers are the only names in English," she said.

The screen in my hand looked remarkably like my own, with several of the same apps, plus several more I could sort of figure out from their logos. I opened her contacts and scrolled until I found Ellie's number.

She answered on the first ring. "Did you find him?" she said. No hello or anything. Just the frantic tone in my beloved's voice.

I have to go home, I thought. I *had* to. I couldn't stay here, this far from Ellie. Every muscle, every nerve, every scar and path of skin on my body was hyper-aware of her absence as if I'd been scalded all over by boiling water.

I was a frog inside a pot of hot mate magic and the only way I was going to get out was to *go home*.

"Yeah, she found us, love," I said.

"Frank!" I heard thumps. She must have been jumping up and down. "Are you okay? There were… bad things? Bad happening. Then you were unconscious for…" She sucked in her breath. "The elves don't know you've disappeared, but I felt it. I knew you'd moved to someplace familiar. Someplace the cottage recognized, so I called Chihiro because my gut said Tokyo. I didn't know if she'd be able to find you. At least not so quickly. Are you okay?" she asked again. "Is your sister with you?"

"I'm okay," I said. "We're both okay." I glanced over my shoulder at Wrenn in her place behind Chihiro. We both still smelled like the cold saltiness of Tokyo Bay but at least we'd carried enough blankets off the yacht to protect the Escalade's seats from our squishy clothes. "Lost our phones. No worse for wear, though," I said.

Wrenn raised an eyebrow.

"One of my little friends from Las Vegas showed up outside of Raven's Gaze," I said. Ellie knew about the kitsune and how they got me Chihiro's phone number. "Then Raven tossed us into that famous forest under Mount Fuji."

"Aokigahara?" Ellie asked.

"Yes," I said.

"That place is haunted, Frank. It's full of yūrei," Ellie said.

Yūrei and yōkai, I thought. Ghosts and demons.

Ghosts and demons that better stay away from my mate, I thought.

This was going to be impossible if I didn't get the mate magic to behave.

I closed my eyes and pinched the bridge of my nose. "I'm having a difficult time with…" What to say on an open line? "homesickness."

Ellie sucked in her breath again. She breathed out slowly, but inhaled sharply once more.

She was holding back sobs.

"Honey," I whispered. "I'll be home as soon as this is done." *Now, I* thought. I needed to go *now*. But I couldn't. I shouldn't. Not with Brother on the loose. "There's a reason Raven sent us here."

Wrenn shook her head as if to remind me that we shouldn't be too open about magic on unsecured lines.

"My family or yours?" Ellie asked.

"Mine and Wrenn's," I said.

Wrenn closed her eyes and pinched her lips together as if she, too, would rather this not be a Family Frankenstein problem.

"*Oh*," Ellie said. She understood.

"Yes," I answered. "He's gained an impressive following of like-minded... individuals... here."

"Oh, no," she breathed. "I'll get word to your local friends."

She'd have to go through Sophia. *Target*, I thought. But any other way and her concealment enchantments would disrupt information transfer. And the last thing we needed right now was a game of magical telephone diminishing the severity of the problem.

"Thank you." I turned toward and leaned against the passenger window to get the best version of privacy I could in a moving Escalade. "Please be careful."

"I will." She sighed. "I don't have a lot of time."

It was morning here, which meant evening there. The cottage was about to yank her inside and I wouldn't be able to talk to her again for about ten hours. "Text Chihiro every single number on your phone," I said. "I'll make more calls."

"Okay," she said. "I love you."

I swear my chest swelled like my heart was about to burst, which was the stupidest, most cliché thing the mate magic could have done to me. "I love you, too," I said.

Ellie ended the call.

I stared at the phone in my hand. When I looked up, Chihiro kept glancing at me as she sped us down the expressway, and behind us, my sister sat with one of the yacht blankets around her shoulders, seat-belted in, watching me clutch a cellphone like it was more valuable than the tank of oxygen that got us out of the kami holding cell.

"Do you see magic, as well, Ms. Goodfellow?" Chihiro asked.

"Call me Wrenn. Please." She sat forward and leaned between the seats. "It's blindingly bright in here, if that's what you're asking," she said.

Chihiro smiled the sweetest, happiest smile. "That is most excellent news."

Wrenn laughed. Chihiro laughed, too. I couldn't help but chuckle.

"No one made the effort when she lived here," Chihiro said. "Magical or mundane." She took us off onto a long exit ramp.

"You did," Wrenn said.

Chihiro nodded. "Yes, I did." She glanced in the rearview mirror at Wrenn. "I will tell you more once you and Frank have reached a parity of power." She glanced at the rearview mirror again. "It is good to help a friend without fear of reprisals or invasions, is it not?"

Wrenn pushed the blanket off her shoulders. "Fae Royal Guard do not operate on the same rules as most fae," she said. "Also, I'm not fae, even if I do work for them, but yes, we must be careful. Best to operate under the rules of fae engagement."

"We need to be cautious with fae magic," I said.

Wrenn pulled the blanket out from behind her back and carefully folded it. "I'm a witch. Or partially a witch." She leaned toward me. "Some part of me was a witch," she said. "It's the only explanation."

There was another explanation—Robin Goodfellow had wanted her to think she was a witch, so he gifted her with spells that imitated innate witch ability. But that possibility was a whole new can of worms. One I preferred to keep unopened at the moment.

Chihiro took us off the expressway onto a wide boulevard lined with an unending sea of buildings. Some were businesses, some were tall apartment complexes. Some were taller apartment buildings. Some were wide apartments with more businesses. They were all the same desert beige as every single suburb in the American Southwest.

Beige brick. Beige slat siding. Beige stucco. Beige metal. The only variation in color was if the beige was more blue-beige than gray-beige. A few here and there were dusty rose beige.

Not a single building looked to be older than about fifty years. All were packed close together with only small concrete-lined spaces in between. Several alleys snaked away from the road.

I'd expected more... personality? I'd at least expected something other than so much beige. And a lot fewer exposed electrical and utility lines. But then again, I'd only seen pictures of the "fun" parts of Japan—Mount Fuji and all its natural beauty and glory, the brilliant neon of parts of downtown Tokyo, the vermillion of the many Shinto temples that not only shaped this land, but also its magic.

Turned out cities were cities no matter where on Earth you were. Tokyo just happened to be more closer-built than most of the US cities I'd visited.

We drove for what felt like a long time, but I knew wasn't. The buildings changed some, growing squatter and shorter, but still painted in the same palette of many beiges. More trees appeared, then disappeared, then appeared again.

We turned off onto a narrow side road and the beige apartments gave way to shorter, tightly-packed beige homes interspersed with small tucked-away businesses. Not one of the homes had a yard, and every business had a low-slung door. A lone tree grew against a building on one corner. The next building had a set of potted plants.

The street became impossibly narrow, as if the entire community was built within a rabbit warren of alleyways. The Escalade was far too big to be rolling around the back streets of the Tokyo suburbs.

"I am taking you to a restaurant frequented by the local magicals," Chihiro said. "It is neutral territory."

The words "neutral territory" carried... something. The way Chihiro said the phrase, articulated the English, I couldn't tell. But I had a feeling the place we were going might be neutral in terms of magicals but was not magically neutral.

I glanced back at Wrenn. The expression on her face suggested that she, too, had picked the same variance in Chihiro's voice.

Wrenn leaned forward. "Chihiro," she said. "What's this restaurant called?"

"*Kōsaten*," Chihiro said. "Crossroads."

"The Tokyo Crossroads?" I blurted out. "The same Crossroads as the Las Vegas Crossroads? *That* Crossroads?" I'd made a bad deal in a Crossroads. Or part of a deal. I still wasn't quite sure which Vegas deal Raven traded, and for what. Or why.

"Crossroads?" Wrenn leaned forward. "Like burying a box in the middle of an intersection to call up a demon kind of crossroads?" She raised her hands. "Absolutely *not.*"

"You don't know about the restaurants?" I asked. She was Fae Royal Guard. And here I thought she knew everything.

"The restaurants where world edges meet," Chihiro said.

Wrenn blinked. Shock danced across her face. "Those aren't for *us,*" she breathed.

They're for gods, I thought.

We came to a corner. A second street split off to the east, and the main road curled around a high garden wall and a big tree that blocked all visuals. In the sky, low-flying small planes dropped in and out of a nearby airport.

Chihiro stopped. "It is not... nefarious," she said. "All the kami use it."

I looked back at Wrenn again. No matter how she tried to hide it, the shock had not dissipated.

What were we driving into?

Chihiro started up the Escalade again and rounded the curve.

A small red Honda Fit sat askew in the middle of the street, blocking passage in both directions. The windows looked tinted, but with red instead of black. Underneath, the interior also gleamed bright red in the morning sun.

The red shimmied with thick, viscous auras.

"The car." I pointed. "It's coated in a thick red magic."

Chihiro stared at it for a long moment. Her finger moved to touch the spell behind her ear, but she stopped and set her hand on the steering wheel again instead. "Red?" she asked.

Wrenn leaned forward. "Bright, vermillion red."

Chihiro continued to stare. "This path to *Kōsaten* is blocked, then." She put the Escalade into reverse and looked over her shoulder.

I turned in my seat to look out the back window at the same time Chihiro did.

The white kitsune from the forest appeared in the cargo area of the Escalade. He, she—I couldn't tell so I went with *they*—was bald with a thin, ageless, oval-shaped head and face. Brilliant golden eyes shimmered with kitsune magic. Bright white loose-fitting strapped-down fighting clothes covered a lithe, strong-looking androgynous body, and a tight white scarf wrapped around their long neck from their shoulders all the way up to under their chin and ears. The kitsune wore no gloves, and their nails were the same gleaming shimmering gold as their eyes.

Seven white fox tails burst into the space behind their body.

Chihiro yelled something in Japanese. The kitsune responded in kind as they lunged for Wrenn. Kitsune arms wrapped around my sister's head. But my sister was fast, like me. Her arm snapped upward and she latched her hand onto the back of the kitsune's head.

She yanked forward. The kitsune yip-snarled.

They both vanished.

CHAPTER 14

Chihiro slapped the steering wheel. "They are not here to cause harm!" she yelled out the window at the Honda sitting in the middle of the road.

Something inside the Honda moved.

I couldn't see for sure if it was the kitsune, or Wrenn, or just the magic, but I needed to make sure the kami weren't harming my sister. We had yet to actually talk to one, or introduce ourselves, or to explain how we'd landed here in Japan.

The only interaction we'd had was that seven-tailed kitsune tele-porting us away without warning. Twice.

I was out and running toward the Honda before Chihiro yelled again. If I literally reached through the red Honda's magic and ripped a door off the hinges I might get someone's attention.

"Frank!" she yelled. "Don't anger the Guardian!"

I skidded to a stop next to the car and reached for the door handle.

The white kitsune appeared in a crouch on the Honda's roof and for one brief second, we were eye-to-eye.

Every bit of the cunning and intelligence of a fox stared back at me —even more so than with Chip and Lollipop, and those two made a fun game of keeping me on my toes.

But they'd been playing. This kitsune was not.

The red magic of the Honda wiggled. The fox looked down briefly and gently spread their hands on the car's roof as if to tell the magic all was well. They had this.

Then the fox jumped up and planted a pristine white heel on my forehead.

I tensed my neck and slid my foot back to counter the kick, and at the same time grabbed the kitsune's ankle. "Hey!" I yelled. "Stop!"

A magical funnel appeared in front of the kitsune's head, one that looked as if I was about to get an enhanced sonic blast directly to my face. I instinctively let go of the kitsune and stepped back as quickly as I could.

It didn't help. The funnel followed my movements and an eruption of car-alarm-like gekkering fox screams hit my face at eardrum-splitting volume.

I yelped and covered my ears. "Stop!" I yelled.

The kitsune inhaled to start another blast. I looked up.

I don't know where the kitsune had dropped Wrenn. I hadn't seen her when I exited the Escalade. But the drop hadn't been far enough away for the kitsune's safety.

Wrenn leaped onto the hood. The Honda groaned, then shrieked as its metal distributed the force. Wrenn swept forward toward the roof and twisted as she snagged the kitsune's shin.

Tentacles of red and green magic rocketed out from under the cuffs of Wrenn's jacket and wrapped around the kitsune's legs. The fox looked down, then at Wrenn. Their face shifted from the flat businesslike determination of someone doing a job to what I could only call bemusement.

The kitsune thought my sister's Royal Guard magic was cute.

Fox tails manifested behind the kitsune and fanned out like seven white, silver, and pink-tipped spokes on a wheel, blazing in the morning sun.

Then the kitsune wrapped their hand around the red and green tentacles encircling their leg.

We were dealing with power levels much higher than Chip and

Lollipop. Higher also, I suspected, than many of the elves in Alfheim. Probably higher and better controlled than the vast majority of the fae with whom Wrenn dealt on a daily basis.

Which meant that the seven-tailed kitsune crouching on the roof of the compact Honda was a major threat to both Wrenn and me.

"Hey!" I bellowed as I planted my foot.

The kitsune looked at me just as I reached down and gripped the Honda's frame between the two wheels.

The car crackled and squeaked like a metal animal. My back strained. My biceps argued, but I was significantly bigger and stronger than the kitsune, at least physically.

My sister dropped her feet off the car's hood and landed next to me, her green and red magic still flaring outward from her arms and still around the kitsune's shin—and holding the fox to the roof. She reached down to help.

We flipped the Honda on its side.

The back window popped out. The windshield snapped and crackled as a spiderweb of cracks opened across its surface. The body groaned and popped, but the car flipped up easier than I thought it would.

Its underside was as bright red as its finish.

The kitsune fell off the roof and landed on the other side. We had a Honda scab between us, which likely would do nothing to stop the kitsune's magic. But at least it offered some—

The kitsune appeared on my back. Legs pinned my arms to my sides. Arms wrapped around my head. Fingers dug into my face.

Another sonic blast of fox gekkering cut into my ear—and my Yggdrasil tattoo.

Magic welled up from deep down in me—deeper than me—and hit the fox spirit so hard it knocked the kitsune off my body.

The kitsune slammed into the now-vertical underside of the Honda, dropped, and landed in another crouch.

"I am Fae Royal Guard!" Wrenn said. "This man works for the North American elves!"

The kitsune shrugged.

I spread my arms trying to get the kitsune to calm down. "Chip is missing!" Not that Chip was Chip's real name, but I could hope this kitsune understood who I meant. "Chip and Lollipop helped me. I owe them. I promised to help!" I said.

A ball of magic formed on the kitsune's hand.

Someone behind us yelled in Japanese.

Chihiro, magic-viewing enchantment wrapped around her eyes, ran toward us.

The kitsune closed their hand and the magic vanished. They yelled anger-filled words at Chihiro.

She stopped about ten feet away. "Speak English so they understand you, Ito Yuki!"

The kitsune's name must be Yuki, surname Ito. I offered my hand. "I'm Frank Victorsson," I said. "The member of the Fae Royal Guard is Wrenn Goodfellow."

"Goodfellow?" Yuki the kitsune's lip twitched. They ignored my hand and slowly stood. "Go home before we drop you back into the ocean."

Wrenn sighed. She crossed her arms. "Kami are just as stubborn as your elves, Frank," she said.

"Do we show up in your lands and 'help' you with your problems?" Yuki tugged on the wrappings around their forearm.

Chihiro moved closer. "You know that if the Elf Emperor requested help from any kami you would be in Iceland right now instead of harassing the two people on Earth who might be able to stop the gaijin vampire."

Yuki rolled their eyes. "It would take an extinction level event for the elves to ask for help."

"That is not the point, Yuki!" Chihiro yelled.

"We aren't elves," Wrenn said.

Yuki's eyes narrowed and their face took on an even more fox-like shape. "*You* are a fae cop." They looked at me. "And you..." They inhaled. "You are just another big loud American tainted by magic you do not understand."

I understood pretty damned well the magic that touched my life. "I see your tails." I waved my hand to outline the aura of silver and hints of pink shimmering just off the kitsune's skin. "You control the pink aspects of your kami magic quite well. Is that how you generate all the white around you?" I nodded at the Honda. "The car, too? Are you controlling the white and turning it red?"

Yuki laughed. "Are all Americans this ignorant?"

"Let us pass, Ito Yuki!" Chihiro said.

The kitsune pointed at the flipped Honda. "*I* did not set a Guardian here." They nodded toward me. "And this one inflicted damage."

"*You* attacked *me*," I said.

Wrenn held up her hands. "Could you call someone? Perhaps your boss." She motioned to the kitsune's white clothing.

Yuki Ito snarled. "Europeans are why we have had vampires in the first place. Now we have a European vampire who eats kitsune. Go away. Your help is not needed."

The kitsune waved us off. Their face danced with all sorts of emotions—distrust, annoyance, a hint of overwhelmed frenzy—but mostly anger. Yuki Ito was quite the angry fox.

"Clearly, it is," I said. *Let us help so we can find Chip*, I thought.

The kitsune looked up at my face. A flash of surprise danced across their ageless features, and then locked down. All the emotional expressions ceased. The businesslike mask returned.

Should I admit that the gaijin vampire was our brother? Probably not. "We can help with the vampire," I said again.

Yuki Ito examined the car. "No, you cannot."

"Yes, they can, Yuki," Chihiro said. "The two messengers sent to spy on the power hiding in Las Vegas? In the United States? They knew the moment they met Mr. Victorsson that he's special." She pointed at me.

Power hiding in Las Vegas?

There weren't any powerful magicals hiding in… The Crossroads Restaurant.

"The World Raven sent us here," I blurted out before I realized that bringing Raven into this was probably not a good idea. "She doesn't want Dracula in Japan anymore than you do."

Shock returned to Yuki's face. This time it stayed. "You think the *Kyūketsuki no kami* is *Dracula*?"

Yuki grabbed my arm and twisted to force me to roll my inner forearm upward.

I used to carry tracer enchantments on my skin. They once marched up each of my forearms like a little elven-powered battalion. They were one of the ways I felt useful to the elves—by basically being their hunting dog. I'd never thought of it that way, and I'd relied on them and the protection spells they'd tattooed on my scalp. But mostly I think I saw them as visible marks of my acceptance into the world of my magical adoptive family.

Then the tracers hurt Ellie. Not badly, but she couldn't touch them without receiving a bad shock. They kept me from my love.

And the Dracula aspect of Brother had figured out how to form them into a pike and to stab them through my heart, which seemed... a bit too on the nose.

Did I miss the tracers? Sometimes I was reminded that I no longer had an elven speed dial on my skin. But Ellie's comfort was more important. So was my freedom.

There are hints still there, though. Impressions, like little craters in my magical topography.

Yuki the seven-tailed white kitsune slapped their hand down on top of one of those depressions. "Like the vampire, this one is corrupted," Yuki hissed.

I looked down at my forearms. Why was I... Dracula had touched those depressions when he stole my tracer enchantments.

And now the kami thought I was a threat.

CHAPTER 15

I stood in the middle of a Tokyo alley-street next to a flipped Honda, with an ass-kicking kitsune telling me Brother wasn't the real issue here, but rather the "hiding power" magic that supposedly corrupted my ex-elven tracer tattoos. Even though they were one and the same.

I knew it in my gut. Or maybe I knew it in the magical depressions lining my forearms. But under a bright autumn sun, in Tokyo air remarkably similar to what I breathed in Alfheim, in the center of these wall-to-wall suburban homes, I understood the true threat: the body that carried Dracula and the combo-soul that had manifested a version of Brother who hugged yōkai, along with goodness knew what other vampiric horror.

The kitsune was *wrong*. I wasn't the problem here.

Wrenn snapped into a tight-yet-not-rigid stance that said *I dare you to throw a punch.* "You are clearly trained," she said. "You're carrying spellwork not typical to kitsunes." She pointed at her lips. "That trick concentrating your screechy fox gekkering? And the ease at which you teleport others? Neither is an off-the-shelf kitsune ability, even for seven-tails like you."

Yuki's eyes narrowed to slits.

I was correct; Yuki Ito had just as much difficulty keeping emotions under wraps as I did.

"You're Imperial Guard, aren't you?" Wrenn asked. "And yet you refuse to acknowledge that I am Royal Guard, which is a breach of protocol."

Yuki shrugged.

"Do you know what else is a breach of protocol?" Wrenn's upper lip twitched ever so slightly. "Taking our phones and our identification. Dropping us into an underwater prison. Do you know what these discourtesies are likely to trigger, kitsune?"

She stared at Yuki but the kitsune did not answer.

"A visit. Maybe from my mentor. The fae named Goodfellow." She nodded toward me. "Or perhaps the *Royal* who has taken a liking to my brother." She enunciated every single letter in "Royal" as if each was a separate syllables.

I crossed my arms. "I like the Queen. She's nice." I wasn't going to say anything at all about how Titania was nice. I still got the effect I wanted.

Yuki blinked.

"Give us back our phones." Wrenn held out her hand. "And if you don't want our help, stay out of our way."

Another angry-fox car-alarm gekkering screech erupted from Yuki.

I squinted and twisted my head, and somehow managed to keep myself from covering my ears. "Why do you do that?" I asked.

Chihiro held her arms at her sides, but her hands worked and her fingers danced. "Ito Yuki! You are a fool!"

Another car turned the corner, this one a black Acura roadster with equally black windows. It stopped at the corner next to the now-parked Escalade, and waited.

A depths-of-space black Acura had appeared out of nowhere. An Acura that carried magic with intent.

Yuki's expression changed from anger at us to the same business-only fighting face they'd had when they snatched Wrenn. They tapped the red Honda and said something in Japanese. Then they stepped forward, between Wrenn and me, and dropped into a fight stance. "You three leave. *Now.*" They pointed toward a gap between two of the houses.

Chihiro turned around and looked at the new vehicle. Then she looked back at me.

I knew something was wrong. Very, very *wrong.* We were being stalked like prey.

She was ten feet away, and over thirty from the Acura, but I wasn't sure she could make it to us in time.

Not that making it to us would matter. Not with the thick black magic—magic that shimmered and shimmied as if it was the shadow of the red magic on the Fit—oozing out of the Acura's seams.

"Get Chihiro!" I yelled at Yuki just as the driver of the black Acura accelerated.

The kitsune vanished.

I dove to the right. Three steps and a jump and Wrenn was on top of the garden wall to our left.

Chihiro dodged left also, toward the concrete garden wall, but the Acura leaped forward—not rolled or skidded or anything a car should do, but jumped—like a frog or a cat or... a giant black scarab-turtle.

A giant evil skittering thing snapped forward along the narrow alley-street directly for Chihiro.

She ran straight into the arms of the appearing Yuki Ito. The kitsune embraced Chihiro.

They both vanished.

The Acura skidded through where they'd been and slammed into the underside of the red Honda. Both cars groaned and shrieked. Sparks flew off the pavement as the cars skidded into the garden wall directly underneath Wrenn.

Magic exploded off the red Honda. It coiled upward from the vehicle, a shimmering snake only Wrenn and I could see, except it wasn't a snake.

What had Chihiro said when I jumped out of the Escalade? *Don't anger the Guardian.* Yuki Ito must have told it that now was the time to be angry.

"Dragon!" Wrenn yelled as she dropped off the wall into the garden behind.

Oranges and vermillion reds danced along the surface of the coils. Orange and black fringe "fur" appeared around a manifesting head. Arms appeared along the coils, each with three fingers.

It reared up, then sniffed at the black magic leaking from the Acura's seams.

Dragons, I thought. Kami magic wasn't just the power god-aspects carried. At least some of it was alive.

Like Sal. And probably Wrenn's sword, Redemption.

The red dragon had been between us and the Tokyo Crossroads—guarding it from interlopers who should not pass. So what was the black dragon?

The Acura's shadow magic snapped out at the red dragon, which reared back from the inky, ugly black as if the stuff stank worse than a bloated corpse.

The Honda's dragon shoved the Acura. Its tires smoked. It didn't want to move. But the dragon made from living magic pushed a midsized Acura away from the underside of its Honda as if it were a toy.

The engine, the sound system, the transmission, I don't know how, but the Acura howled like an angry, venomous robo-beast.

The red dragon snapped down onto the Acura and ripped off all four doors. They flew toward the houses on either side, four whipping automotive frisbees that embedded themselves into beige slat siding.

The black dragon fully erupted off the Acura. Where the first had oranges and vermillions, the corrupted dragon roiled with vomit-inducing greens and yellows.

"Wrenn!" I yelled again.

She appeared around the corner of the garden wall and jogged around the wrecks toward me.

The two dragons, both towering over their automobiles, crashed together. Real-world visible sparks filled the air. A concussive boom followed.

Buzzing, hair-raising power arched across the overhead electrical wires.

The red dragon coiled up and into the arching electricity. The black dragon dropped low and spread itself out along the pavement as if searching for something—or someone—to use as a weapon: A yōkai. Fleas and flies. Rats. Wrenn or me.

Wrenn grabbed my arm. "Run!"

A white-hot bolt of electricity jumped from the lines to the ground. The black dragon screamed. Static slapped Wrenn and I across our faces and a high-pitched ear-splitting buzz rattled our teeth.

We both turned to run.

I looked down at the ground. Not in a conscious way. More to give my body awareness of what was on the other side of me so that it could run away from the crashing, living magic behind us.

I saw the puddle. I saw the oily slick on its surface. Most of my brain thought nothing of it. We were in the middle of a fight involving damaged automobiles. It was just oil.

Just oil.

If I were Brother, I'd expect my siblings to attempt to go to the local magical authority. I'd be watching, probably leaving a yōkai—or low-demons—at every entry point protected by one of the dragon guardians.

Hell, he probably did that anyway, just to keep tabs on the kami.

So a part of me knew better. A part of me understood exactly into what I set my foot.

Unfortunately, that part didn't yell loudly enough for me to pay attention.

CHAPTER 16

Brother's oily low-demon magic coiled around my foot and…
I stood in an alley between slat-sided Japanese homes on lots
that to my American eyes were nothing more than postage stamps,
inside the sprawl of a city that dwarfed everything I knew in so, so
many ways. Between two Honda-built automobiles I recognized but
were still much, much different from the Fits and Acuras I knew at
home.

Seven-foot, three-hundred pound me was nothing but a semi-
living insect in the land of dragons and gods.

Wrenn looked between the dragons and me. "Frank?"

But this land should be a land of its own gods. "Vampires do not
belong in Japan," I muttered. Brother was like that one-tenth of one
percent of metastasized cancer cells that got by chemo.

Ivan's ghost had cleaned Brother's magic off my soul, but must not
have gotten it all, because that touch from the oily magic in the puddle
was enough for that one-tenth of one percent of remaining corrup-
tion to activate.

And I felt him, his presence. His draw. His violent twisted love and
his omnipresent touch.

"Brother," I breathed, as if I yearned for him and not Ellie.

Wrenn touched my arm. "Something's happening, isn't it?"

He was family. Our family. My family. Brother understood us. He was us. And we were him. We shouldn't hide from family, no matter our sins.

No one else was *us*. Not these Japanese magicals. Not these Japanese mundanes. They could only aspire to be us, but only we stood against all tides with the steadfast strength built into us by Victor Frankenstein.

These thoughts fell over my mind like a comforting blanket. They pressed down all the moment-to-moment framing I do: Is that person afraid of me? What are the norms here? Will this moment cause distress? Can I help?

Am I worthy of being here?

None of it mattered anymore, because I had the certainty of Brother's love. No one else mattered. Not Wrenn. Not Ellie. Not the elves or the kami or the fae. No magic but his gave me solace. Thinking of other magicks would only damage my relationship with the god-love that was my Victor-stitched family. Doing anything that did not feed that god-love would only cause me to be rejected. Again.

There were others who felt his love. Yōkai, whose gnawing cavernous needs sent them screaming through the night, now had Brother to apply salve to their pain.

Wrenn looked at my shoulders. "Something's wrong with your mate magic."

"I feel the best I have in centuries," I said. All my anger had purpose now. No more bending to the will of those lesser than me. The world was here for my taking and I now understood why.

I wasn't ugly. Mundanes only feared me because I was exactly what Victor built me to be—their master.

Wrenn reached out as if to touch my mate magic. "It looks *slimy*."

I grabbed her wrist. How dare this woman touch me?

Yet father had built her as proof of my ascendance.

She punched me in nose with her other fist and kneed me in the crotch so quickly I didn't realize what she was doing until sharp rupturing pain burst from my septum and my testicles.

I kept hold of her hand as I buckled over. She moved with me, twisting her grabbed arm down and landing her free hand on the back of my head.

Her leg came up and she slammed my forehead into her knee.

"Snap out of it!" she yelled in my ear. "You are not him," she growled. "You are *better than Victor.*"

I still gripped her hand. Crushed, actually, as I squeezed the life out of her fingers.

Yet she did not wince. She did not scream. She fought for her life.

"I'm fighting for *your* life," she said through gritted teeth, as if she'd read my mind.

My life is my own, I thought. The puddle on the ground—the one I'd stepped into because puddles did not matter—reflected back to me the fire in my own eyes.

"Damn it, Frank," Wrenn said. "You *cannot* fall under his control this easily."

His control? I would be free of every hold on my soul and body, including the silver of the elven tattoos along the side of my head.

"You're better than a kelpie," she said.

Of course I was better than a kelpie. I was better than *her*.

Her lips were right next to my ear. "You will never see Ellie again if you don't fight this, big brother."

Yet my mate magic still clung to my shoulders. "You don't know that," I said. I would have my family. All of them. Just as Brother had his yōkai.

"Yes, I do," she said with a softness I did not expect. With a tenderness that said she knew exactly how this would play out and how the fae would respond, and, probably, the elves. How the kami would likely kill both of us.

How I would lose my newly-found sister, and my newly-found love, and long-held elven family. All so a blanket of rage could smother the uncertain effort of actually thinking things through.

A shimmer reflected in the puddle. Something magical moved toward us at high speed.

I let go of her hand.

The two dragons twisted in the air as if they couldn't decide if they should pay attention to us or each other—or the new threat.

The red dragon reared up and its massive head moved side-to-side. It touched the overhead lines again.

I'd been out in electrical storms. Victor had used electricity to jumpstart my body. Yet this jiggled and tingled and hurt every bone and tissue all at the same time.

An arc of electricity hit the top of the Escalade as if Bjorn Thorsson had called down lightning. Brilliant light burst between the houses and everything turned white. Oven-like heat hit us from both directions. We both gasped and instinctively stepped backward—and directly into each other's backs.

The smell of ozone filled the air. The house to the left groaned. The one on the right rocked toward the alley-street, snapping and popping as metal and timber violently disengaged from each other, and burst into flames.

Down the alley-street, the Escalade snapped in two where the bolt had hit it, its roof blackened and smoldering and its tires on fire. On the other side, a crater smoldered where the bolt had hit the pavement.

The black shadow dragon pulled itself completely off the Acura. Then it leaned over and sniffed at Wrenn. It pulled back and shook its head. Then it sniffed me.

It reared up. Shadow magic coiled around it like a paper-thin tornado.

And it vanished.

The red dragon coiled up along the overhead lines, also lifting itself completely off its Honda—and taking all the extra redness off the vehicle. The undercarriage returned to its normal black and gray metal. The windows returned to their normal clearness.

Then the red dragon lifted its head into the air as if listening for the black dragon—and vanished as if chasing prey.

We were alone in the middle of a raging fire with our god brother.

CHAPTER 17

Fire licked at us from one side and filled the sky with choking smoke. Ozone added an almost bloodlike metallic tang to the air. Shadows fell over the little valley between the burning suburban Tokyo homes but the ash scared me the most.

Heat roared off the burning house. I ignored it. There would be no flashbacks to the fires of my formative years in Germany.

I twirled my finger in the air. "Brother makes ash bend to his will," I said. He'd stolen the ashen remains of Rose's life to form the dapper suit he'd worn when he first attacked me back in Alfheim. The Dracula aspect of his personality had taken that suit and refashioned it into Dracul armor—and a pike he'd stuck through my chest.

The pike that had almost killed me.

He was here, somewhere, reminding me I was better than that weak version of myself. I'd always been better. I rolled my neck and grinned at Wrenn.

"I need to get you out of here." Wrenn lifted her hands. "Make sure Frank gets home safely!" she said to the magic circling her wrists.

It burst outward as a bubble of red and green energy, and pushed back the heat and smoke—and whatever demon Brother had settled over my consciousness.

I sucked in my breath and leaned against Wrenn. "Damn..." I muttered.

Brother still yanked on my soul—no, my fatigue. He offered a simple way of processing life. No need for me to navigate the world anymore. I was safe and secure within his love.

It was so easy. So seductive.

I had to name it, this demon, even if it wasn't a literal demon. If I didn't, I would never get it under control and it might just grow into something with its own mind.

There was security in there, inside that blanket, and a sense of relief. Life was difficult and grand and full of other people's opinions. The oily magic covered over all of it like dirt over a grave. But it didn't bury and smother the world, it only buried and smothered how I interacted with it.

Or didn't. For a split second, my roiling ever-present pit of self-whatever—doubt, fatigue, excitement, all my second-guessing of my own reactions—become something different. Similar, yes, but emptier. Hollow, like a void. Like I felt when I walked the American South before carrying Rose into Alfheim.

A warrior's vibrating emptiness. The hole that becomes a thing that lodges itself at the end of your breastbone, under your ribs, just below your heart.

And then it slid away, the touch of a need that felt all too familiar yet was not me. Or Brother.

What had I just experienced? "I swear his oily magic is liquid cult. He's been serving it to creatures whose souls were already tainted." The yōkai, mostly. That rock of void had been nothing more than an ice cube floating in Brother's influence.

"Liquid cult, huh? Cherry or orange flavored?" Wrenn moved against my back again. "You okay now?"

I had to be. "We need to get out of here," I said. "He couldn't get into my head like this in Alfheim."

Wrenn looked down at her hands. "We're going to pay big time for this magic," she said.

Nothing useful from the fae came without a cost. "We'll deal with that when the bill comes due."

Wrenn moved so we were side by side. "We go that way, around the Escalade. Less smoke and I think I remember how to get us back to the main road."

"Okay." We both took a step toward the vehicle.

Our bubble moved with us, sliding over the pavement—and the ash on the ground.

I should have known better.

He manifested between us, inside the bubble, and so close I smelled the decay on his skin. Wrenn tried to twist away, but it did no good. We formed a triangle of Frankenstein's children, shoulder to shoulder to shoulder and surrounded by fae magic.

Without Dracula's armor, he wasn't quite a full foot taller than I. His eyes shimmered more red than they had before—more like the Dracul-blood color the armor had been than the deep fire-touched maroon of my and Wrenn's eyes. And he was still much more handsome than I was, with his strong, straight features and the charming lightning bolt scar on the side of his face and neck.

He still wore a dapper, exquisitely tailored dark gray suit, though this one had fine pinstripes to it.

The split-second look he slid over me said he did not care one bit about my soul, or my comfort, or my security. No acknowledgement showed in his eyes. No understanding that there were three of us in the bubble.

All the surprise and fear his sudden appearance generated melted with that look, as did any lingering need for his love.

His interest landed fully on Wrenn. "You," he said in perfect, Scottish-accented English. "You traded Victor for the Fae Royal Guard? How droll."

Wrenn froze, right there next to my elbow, as if her brain could not process what had manifested so close to her body. Nothing was supposed to get this close. Not to her. Not to me. Yet here he was.

He grabbed Wrenn and kissed her fully on the mouth.

The bubble popped. All the magic given to her by the Queen of the

Fae exploded off us in a blast so strong it threw both Brother and me down the street.

I crashed into the Escalade's broken windshield. My back hit hard, but nothing cracked, and I rolled off the SUV to the heating pavement.

Brother bounced off the concrete garden wall on the corner. He twisted his huge body in the air, only a foot or two off the ground, and landed in a crouch.

We couldn't see Wrenn through the thickening smoke. The air had turned hot and gray, much like it had been in Vampland.

"I do believe she remembers me," Brother said. He held out his fingers and sucked in ash as if it was water. Then he used his ash-hand to straighten and fill out his tie. He nodded in the direction Wrenn must have been. "The fae do excellent work. Scars like hers are difficult to repair."

She didn't have scars. Not physical ones. I was the one with the visible remnants of our father's torture.

Brother ran his finger over the pavement and looked at the tip as if assessing the quality of the fire's ash. "She was built to be a trophy," he said. He flicked the finger as if tossing away all the dirt and used the same hand to straighten his tie. "Why are *you* here?" He waved the hand at the acrid and smoke-filled air. "In Japan." He stood from his squat. "The Bride, I understand. There are kelpies about. She's Fae Royal Guard."

His lip curled and his eyes widened with pure, unadulterated hate.

The expression was gone as fast as it appeared.

He had experience with the Royal Guard. Experience that angered this personality enough that he still carried the resulting blinding rage.

"The kelpies are trafficking kitsune and yōkai," I said. "But you know that already." Maybe by agreeing I could get him talking. He did like to narrate his doings.

He sighed. "That jorōgumo? Madame Kobayashi. She runs the operation for the Emperor." He fiddled with his tie again. "I'm doing the kami a favor by disrupting their syndicate. Someone has to."

He shook his head as if he alone could save the taken yōkai.

He was attempting to gain power by defeating a rival for dominance amongst the darker Japanese magicals. Doing the kami a favor gave him cover.

"What are you going to do when you've defeated this Emperor?" The Emperor must be the same spirit Wrenn had told me about when we were in kami jail, which meant he was not only powerful, but nearly impossible to defeat.

So maybe Brother really was doing the kami a favor. But at what cost? Letting Brother gather yōkai as if they were lost children was like using malaria to beat back cancer.

His eyes narrowed. He smoothed the front of his impeccable suit jacket. "Shouldn't you be in that North American backwater shoveling snow and complaining about the weather? You could come with me. Choose to be with your family."

He wasn't going to launch into a monologue and tell me all his plans. This version of Brother seemed to be more in control of his megalomania. "You are not my family."

A split-second micro-expression of something I couldn't quite figure flashed across his face. Confusion, perhaps. Anger, for sure. He had plenty of that.

I had to find Wrenn. The heat and the smoke were beginning to thicken and we needed to get out of here before the local authorities showed up.

"Why are *you* here?" I asked. Time to be direct before cops and flames drove me to run.

His entire body did the same belligerent tightening I'd seen with the kelpie. The same *How dare you* full physical sneer.

He waved his hand at the burning Acura. "Providence."

Luck, then. "How did you get out of Vampland?" I yanked a hubcap off the Escalade as I stood up. It wasn't much of a weapon, but it would have to do for now.

He waved his hand in front of his face to clear away some of the smoke. "I am a *god*," he said.

A cult leader, yes. A monster, absolutely. But a god? He wasn't a god any more than his siblings were.

Wrenn appeared on top of the garden wall and directly above Brother. Her jacket smoked. Soot covered her face. She must have run through the burning house to get to us.

In each of her hands she carried a flaming knife.

Kitchen knives from one of the houses, big ones the length of her forearms, coated in what I suspected was lighter fluid. She leaned forward, a burning knife on either side of Brother's neck, and sliced in a way that should have taken off his head.

Nothing happened. He neither burned nor bled.

She stabbed at his shoulder. Again, nothing happened. Not even the ash-made cloth of his suit wrinkled.

He turned around to face her. He pointed at me. "You are so much more creative than our big oaf of a sibling."

She slashed at his face. Again, nothing happened.

He leaned toward her. "I have made a deal with Death, my love. Those toothpicks mean nothing to me."

"*Vampire*," she growled.

He grinned. "*My* Bride."

Wrenn landed a straight jab punch right into Brother's nose.

He didn't move, nor did he flinch. The grin widened, though. He grabbed her arm and leaned in to sniff—or bite—her wrist.

I whipped the hubcap at his shoulder blades.

My aim was a little off. I hit him on the temple, right at the side of his eye.

He let go of Wrenn and whipped around. "I'm going to stick my arm down your throat and pull out your innards one organ at a time!" he roared.

The ash lifted off him just enough that it looked like he went from a perfectly tailored suit to one that was off the rack and two sizes too big. It puffed a little bit as well, taking on a roundness that had not been there before.

There were low-demons under there, like there had been under his Dracul armor. Low-demons that were about to pour off his body and return to infecting, destroying, controlling—all those horrors I'd seen in Alfheim. All the greenish-black oily rage. All the possessing of small animals. Werewolves.

Yōkai.

The first one landed on my back in much the same way as Yuki Ito had when they teleported in. The second and third attacked my legs.

The fourth went for my throat.

CHAPTER 18

Somewhere in the distance, sirens wailed. Acrid smoke filled the air. The houses on either side popped and crackled. Brother's hand shot out. He caught Wrenn's neck.

The yōkai climbing my sides, sitting on my head, attempting to chew on my flesh, attacking from all sides—they breathed in the smoke. They chattered their sharp pointy teeth. They whistled and hooted.

I felt their piercing teeth and claws. I heard their grunts and groans. I heard several speaking distinct and seductively articulate Japanese. I felt caresses with the burning touches and the icy scratches.

But I could not see them. To my eyes, they were all a blur as if inside a distortion enchantment. Was this magic theirs? Brother's? Something new they shared as a group? His low-demon pets?

I grabbed whatever little monster was trying to dig its teeth into my neck and threw it against the Escalade. I tossed the one on my back toward the garden wall. I kicked at the two around my legs, but their blur was harder to see with the smoke in the air.

"Wrenn!" I yelled.

She slashed at Brother's face again, and again, but her knives made no difference.

Screaming, nipping shadows piled up against my legs. I tried to move, tried to shuffle my way toward Wrenn and Brother, but the blurs locked me in place.

The sirens grew louder. The local authorities were on their way, and I instinctively glanced up the alley-street toward the sound. I couldn't help if I was arrested and tossed into the notoriously strident Japanese legal system.

Where were the kami? That Guardian dragon? Yuki Ito? The locals were allowing a monster and his pack of followers to run rampant in their city.

"I could use some help here!" I yelled at no one in particular and at Tokyo in general. At the abundant kami who I had yet to meet. At the kitsune. At the universe itself.

It wasn't the kitsune who manifested next to me.

Waves of silver and gold washed over the blurs attacking me. A high-pitched scream followed.

Brother grabbed one of Wrenn's wrists. She still slashed at him with her free hand even though he could easily snap her bones. He looked down at the determination in her face. "You are so much like her," he said. Then he roared at the smoke.

"Let us go!" I yelled.

Something long and sharp slashed through the air in front of me and skewered a blur to the pavement. More slashes and the blurs flew away faster than they could climb and cling.

"You pick *now* to come out of your hideout?" Brother yelled. "You serve only yourself! I *will* win this war!"

A man manifested in the air between me and where Brother held Wrenn. He floated off the ground with his back to me. Gray peppered his long black hair, which floated out around his head like a static-electricity-caused crown.

He wore what looked to me to be modified samurai battle garb— silver, magic-infused plate and mail armor wrapped with red, black, and white silk for improved movement and speed. Shin and knee guards protected his legs. Gloves and guards protected his arms. Plating protected his shoulders. He lacked only the helmet.

He floated there, in the smoke, eye-to-eye with the monster, toes pointed down and his arms held in a way that said he was about to blast Brother's body back to its component vampire parts with a bolt of magic worthy of every living elf.

Brother yanked Wrenn toward his body.

The man whipped his arms.

I swear the ground jolted as if the entire southern island of Japan moved two feet to the east. I flung out my arms as I jolted with the world and managed, somehow, to stay on my feet.

Brother and Wrenn vanished just as he tossed his jolting magic. The blast hit the garden wall, exploding it with a massive boom. Concrete chunks blasted outward, as did a concussive wave that pushed back the smoke.

A block of the wall flew straight for my head.

Whatever—*whoever*—was helping clear the blurs from me shifted. Two long slices of energy appeared in front of my head. Energy slices that looked much too much like spider legs.

The legs snagged a ten-pound block of concrete out of the air inches from my face.

The man looked over his shoulder.

His eyes glowed red in an ageless face which pulled and tugged with rage and wrath.

I gasped. Who had come to my rescue?

The mask of wrath was gone so fast I questioned whether I had in fact seen it.

The man dropped slowly to the ground. He looked engaged and disengaged at the same time, as if he was watching me for clues and running scenarios about how I was going to react, and how best to manipulate me into doing what he wanted. Would I attack? Would I run? Did I know who he was? How much information did I already have?

The spider legs around me clattered toward him, shrinking as they moved, and coalescing into a tall, beautiful woman in a tight skirt and blood red pumps.

"Like I said," she said to the man, "the Kyūketsuki no kami attends to this one." She pointed at me.

I raised my hands. "Who are you?" From how every hair on my body was standing up, I was pretty sure I was in the presence of a powerful spirit manifestation.

This was the being responsible for selling Japanese magicals to the kelpies.

I was pretty sure I knew the name of the jorōgumo: Madam Kobayashi of Central Kobayashi Shipping and Transportation. I'd seen her in the forest.

Which meant the man was "The Emperor."

His eyebrow arched. He did not speak, though from how the jorōgumo responded, he was able to communicate his intentions to her. He pointed down the street, in the direction of the now-close sirens.

The jorōgumo turned toward me. "You will come with us," she said.

I slid my foot back. What was the rule? Do whatever you need to do to not get in the car with a kidnapper.

She rolled her eyes. "We hold your contract. You will do as we say."

Contract?

The silent man flicked his arms and his samurai garb switched to an expensive-looking black suit, white shirt, and blue tie.

He bared his teeth and held up two fingers in front of his mouth to indicate fangs, then he made a throat-cutting gesture. He finished by pointing at me.

He wanted me to kill Brother. Which I would have done, anyway.

"Where's Chip?" I yelled. Brother had Wrenn and these two had Chip and I was done playing games.

The woman looked at her nails. "You wish payment?" she intoned as if I was a customer.

"I don't work with traffickers," I said. Not now. Not ever. I'd take down Brother on my own.

145

The jorōgumo laughed. *"With?"* She shook her head. "My dear, that grand mangey thing with the dire wolves at its feet like Ignorance and Want was more than happy to take our payment for your contract of promised help."

My mouth opened as if it, by itself, had framed some reasoned argument for why these two could go drop themselves into the deepest parts of Mount Fuji, but nothing came out.

She winked. "Now you know why the kami dropped you into their little jail, big guy."

The man grinned.

"You will bring us the Vampire God's body," she said. "Once it is in our custody, we will mark your contract fulfilled."

The man crossed his arms.

I'd never consented to a "contract." I wasn't going to hand Brother over to a jorōgumo, either. And these two were the kelpies' contacts in Japan. If anything, I should hand *them* over to the local kami.

Lights flashed up the street. Sirens blared through the smoke.

The authorities had arrived.

I looked back at the two magicals. The jorōgumo nodded toward the yelling coming from behind the burning Escalade. "It's us or three months in a booking cell."

There had to be another option. I ran for the space between a smoking house and one that had not yet started to burn, but more lights flashed on the other side. We were surrounded by cops and fire-fighters.

I jumped up onto the garden wall the same way Wrenn had and grabbed the pine growing in the yard of the house that hadn't yet caught fire. Slippery bark bit into my skin while making my fingers slide across its surface, but I managed to swing up to the roof of the house.

The smoke was thinner up here, and for a second, I got a look at the neighborhood.

And beyond.

A few blocks away, another house went up in flames. Electrical lines sparked. In the other direction, toward Tokyo Bay, smoke rose from what had to be the shoreline.

The smoke wasn't just these houses. Swaths of the Tokyo suburbs burned.

It hadn't been a jolt of magic the Emperor tossed earlier. He'd triggered an earthquake.

Then the jorōgumo was right there, right in front of me, looking more disappointed than angry. She wrapped her super-strong magical legs around my body. And she *moved* me.

Except... she didn't. Because at the same moment she enfolded me in her golden silky magic, a fox arrived.

Yuki Ito had me, their arms around my head and their legs around my chest in a caress gentler than any of their other touches.

Fox kicked at spider. Spider slashed at fox.

And, thankfully, fox magic won.

CHAPTER 19

I woke up alone and flat on my back in the center of a cloud-like futon. I was low to the floor, on a pallet rather than a bed, and covered with several also-cloud-like throws made in lovely soft jewel-like blues and greens. I was still dressed, thankfully.

Late afternoon sun danced through rustling branches outside a high, medium-sized window lined by potted plants. Big plants, small plants, plants with huge dark green leaves, and other plants with tiny, tightly-bunched pale leaves. Other plants in terra cotta pots covered the dresser at the foot of the futon. More plants in huge glazed pots surrounded the door. The room smelled of life and loam.

A fish *plinked* in a small tank on the dresser, and all I could think of was how similar this place was to the new sunroom in Ellie's cottage.

Chatter floated in from a room on the other side of a wooden sliding door. People argued in English about something I could not make out.

"When the kyūketsuki vanished a month ago, I thought that perhaps we were free of European demons," said a lovely resonant voice I did not recognize.

"Nothing is forever, Sakuya-hime," said a voice I did recognize.

Yuki Ito was out there with a real kami beyond the malevolent spirit and the kitsune I'd already met—and a kami who handed us a silver lining to all this. Dracula's call had been fully international, which meant that Japan's vampires were locked away in Vampland.

"And now he escalates," the kami said. The anger in her voice moved like electricity through the walls.

"Yes," responded the kitsune.

Silver and pink magic leaked in around the door and gently touched my shoulder. "The big American Yuki rescued from Madame Kobayashi is awake," the voice said.

"His name is Frank Victorsson," Chihiro answered. "He works for the North American enclave of elves. He also has ties to Queen Titania."

The silver and pink magic leaking in around the door stiffened and pulled back. There must have been a nonverbal response I could not see.

"Not all Americans are tourists," Chihiro said.

"Yuki and I walked the ruins of Hiroshima and Nagasaki, Chihiro. We lived through the firebombing of our great city. We understand Americans well enough."

I was in the same house as a full-fledged kami, one who was probably of great power, and who had lived with the trauma that ended World War II. No wonder Yuki did not want me around.

"He had nothing to do with that, Sakuya-hime," Chihiro said. "He will help. That's why I called you."

I pushed aside the blankets and slowly stood up. My head swam a bit, but my body righted itself quickly, as was its norm.

"I hope this... excursion... is worth my time," said the voice named Sakuya-hime. "We are needed, Chihiro. You know that."

She must be referring to the earthquake.

"Yes, Sakuya-hime."

The door between the bedroom and the main living area slid open. "Frank," Chihiro said. "You're awake."

She'd changed into short sleeves. Magic I hadn't noticed before, looking much like her viewing spell, coiled around one of her elbows like a brace. I pointed.

"Later," she said.

I nodded and looked out over her head. The bedroom emptied into a combo living and dining room area. Bookshelves lined every wall, including in front of at least two windows, and were filled with as many plants as books. A small but comfortable couch sat in the corner to the left of the door. To the right, a bathroom. Straight ahead, a four-person dining room table with a small kitchen area behind it. Yuki Ito sat at the table at the end closest to me. The kami who must be Sakuya-hime sat across from the kitsune.

She leaned back in her chair and crossed her legs at the same time she turned her torso toward me. She wore an exquisitely tailored cherry-blossom-pink suit jacket and white blouse. Her matching pink skirt was shorter than I expected, and showed off thighs as smooth and lovely as any I'd seen on an elf. Her crisp black patent leather boots were soled with a red that somehow did not clash with the pink of her outfit.

Her movement was awash in the smooth grace only magicals and dancers had, and somehow did not wrinkle her impeccable clothes.

Like Chihiro, she had a pink streak in her severely cut hair, though hers looked natural, or as natural as pink hair could look. Also like Chihiro, she was tall for a Japanese woman, probably around five-seven or so out of the boots.

The haircut added age to delicate features which, if she dressed for it, would allow her to pass as a teenager.

But young, this kami was not. Her posture, expression, and keen eyes—and her extraordinary control of her natural magic—said I was dealing with an elder-elf-level magical.

The kami propped her elegant arm up on the back of her chair and watched me take in what I suspected was Chihiro's home.

"How long was I out?" I asked. Every one of my muscles hurt, worse than they did after an extra-cold-inducing long sleep.

She peered up at my face. "Two hours." She pointed at the window.

Two hours shouldn't be enough to cool me down with any significance, much less cause the frostbite-like stinging running through my upper back. "I don't usually pass out like that."

She patted my arm. "Yuki grabbed you at the same time as Madame Kobayashi." She nodded toward the kitsune. "The effect is equivalent to pulling you through a half-open veil gate."

I didn't have a lot of experience with popping through veils, beyond chasing a kelpie around inside a veil, which wasn't the same thing as moving through one, half-opened or not.

Kelpies.

"Did Yuki find Wrenn?" I asked even though Brother had already taken her when the kitsune arrived.

Chihiro touched my arm again. "No."

Did any of them know why she was missing? I looked over Chihiro's head. "The vampire took my sister," I said to the magicals at the table.

The kami held up her hand. "We know. We are looking."

"Look harder," I snapped. "The kelpies and their syndicate have caught the attention of the Fae King and Queen. Now one of the Royal Guard has gone missing in your city. Do you really think that's going to sit well with, say, the fae named Robin Goodfellow?" I rubbed at my aching forehead.

Yuki and the kami looked at each other.

"Frank."

I looked down at Chihiro. Her eyes were huge. I'd made a major faux pas snapping at a kami like that.

Chihiro touched my arm again. "Your cell phone is on the table," she said. "With Wrenn's." She inhaled and straightened up to her full height. "The Princess won't give them back quite yet."

Her face said if I didn't calm down, I'd never get them back.

I stretched my shoulders. "Princess?"

Chihiro moved closer. "She is an aspect of Konohanasakuya-hime, the kami of Mount Fuji." She tucked her hands into her pockets. "She will not tell you her full name, only her god aspect, so do not ask."

I nodded.

Chihiro motioned for me to move toward the table. "I called her, Frank. She is experienced with European magicals." She stepped closer again and stretched up so she could speak close to my ear. "She asked me what I know about Victor Frankenstein," she whispered.

I inhaled.

"So assume she knows a lot more than she's saying." Chihiro moved back.

I nodded.

She stepped to the side.

I bowed to the kami. "I apologize for my behavior," I said. "Waking up this way has left me surly."

The Princess nodded graciously.

"Please forgive me for not attempting to pronounce your name. I fear my Minnesota accent would cause an international incident." Hopefully, I hadn't made her mad enough to cause a war.

Sakuya-hime smiled a small, annoyed smile. She dropped her foot back to the floor and returned to her original position facing the table.

I walked over. Chihiro moved around the table to the kitchen to pick up a tray of cookies and fresh water. A flat metal teapot already sat in the center on a tray with two unused cups—and my wallet and our cell phones. Other earthenware cups sat in front of the kami and the kitsune.

Carefully, I pulled out the remaining chair. It, like nearly everything in my life, was too small, but at least it did not have arms. I sat as gently as I could, also minding the small table, and nodded to Sakuya-hime. "The elves of Alfheim locked the vampire claiming to be a god—he was Dracula then, as I'm sure you know already—inside a pocket realm with all the other vampires who disappeared a month ago. They'd be happy to do so again," I said.

"We know." Sakuya-hime leaned forward and the folds of her blouse subtly revealed her neck and a hint of cleavage. "And yet he is here, is he not?" She sat back and placed her hands on the table. "He calls himself Kyūketsuki no kami now." She slowly steepled her fingers as if expecting me to argue.

I rubbed at my shoulder, more to remind the Princess that surliness was not off the table than to work out any ache.

Sakuya-hime gave a small nod. "Vampires did not set foot in Japan until after the Anglo-Japanese Alliance of 1902," she said. "We eradicated the demons as they were discovered." She unsteepled her hands and set them flat on the table. "The last three disappeared a month ago. At first, we suspected the Emperor."

I glanced up at Chihiro.

"Emperor Sutoku," she said. "He is an onryō, a vengeful spirit. He caused a magical civil war here in Japan during World War I."

"There was no civil war," the Princess said. "The big war disguised a few magical skirmishes. That was all." She wrapped her elegant hands around her tea cup as if Chihiro had just told me something all kindergarteners knew.

"He is not like the vampires, Frank, nor is he like an aspect. He's a spirit. As long as there are mundanes who believe in him, he will continue to wreak havoc on Japan."

As long as there were mundanes who knew of the gods, there would be god aspects, be they elf, fae, kami, or any of the other magicals on Earth.

The Emperor must function the same way, but more continuously, because he was a spirit. "I've met him," I said. "He seemed vengeful."

Yuki Ito nodded as if impressed I'd survived.

"He caused the earthquake, didn't he?" I asked.

Sakuya-hime ignored my question and snapped her fingers at Chihiro. "My tea is cold."

Yuki Ito frowned. In the kitchen, Chihiro's shoulders slumped. She pushed away from the countertop and walked toward the table.

I wanted to snap my own fingers and roar *Apologize!* at the kami. Or to offer Chihiro a job with the elves. But I had no power to do either of those things. Nor did I know the true nature of the relationship Chihiro had with the kami, and in particular, Sakuya-hime.

Chihiro lifted the little teapot and began pouring new tea, first for the kami, then the kitsune, who touched her hand.

She set a cup in front of me.

"I will serve you when you come to visit," I said.

She grinned. Then with a small nod, she poured me tea and walked back toward the kitchen area with the pot in her hand.

I sipped. The tea was exceptional, brewed perfectly with just the right amount of high, sweet jasmine notes.

Chihiro, now watching from the kitchen area again, must have read my enjoyment of the tea on my face, because she smiled.

Sakuya-hime ignored Chihiro and sipped her tea. "How long do you think the kelpies have been trafficking low-powered magicals to the vampires? One century? Two? They established connections to Dracula's *original* court." Sakuya-hime straightened her blouse. "The fae King and Queen have allowed these activities since vampires first appeared."

"That doesn't mean the rest of us should allow it," I said.

Sakuya-hime shook her head. "Your Elf King kept two vampires in his town for seventy years, one of whom was Dracula's younger brother, and the other a fae witch who had lived," she twirled her finger at me, "surreptitiously, mind you, with the Normandy enclave of elves for several decades before they ran him off to live in a cave."

Ivan *had* been a witch who had lived with elves. Elves who betrayed him.

"And here you, and the woman you say is your sister, storm into one of our most sacred forests with your European faces and your European arrogance and upset the apple cart, as you enjoy saying."

"How is wanting to stop kelpies from trafficking your magicals upsetting the apple cart?" I asked. This was not a Tony the Evil Librarian level problem. This was much worse.

"Emperor Sutoku," Yuki said, "has been... keeping the vampire in check. They have been, up until today's skirmish, leaving mundanes alone." Yuki's expression said they were not happy with the arrangement.

"Until you two appeared, that is," Sakuya-hime said.

They'd been allowing a vengeful spirit to fight with a vampire who thought he was a god because by doing so, it kept them both occupied and away from the townspeople?

"That worked?" I asked. Evil magicals were not toddlers.

Or maybe they were. Just extraordinarily violent and destructive toddlers that the kami, for all their power, had to care for, because that's what the magic of Japan demanded.

Sakuya-hime sat back in her chair again. "We... guided them. Quietly. Like your King controlled his vampires."

Except here, the kami had no choice. Still, they allowed the Emperor to traffic less powerful magicals.

"*This* vampire is not Radu the Handsome," I said. "*This* vampire controls magicks capable of bending elven enchantments to his will." How much information should I share with the kami? "And ward off Fae Royal Guard spells. He can—and *is*—manipulating kami magic. He's taken control of one of your Guardian dragons."

Sakuya-hime lifted her arm and held her hand in as if it were the head of a beast and kissed the side of her hand as if it was a puppy. "One should chip one's pets," she said, "so one knows the homes they visit."

The kami had allowed Brother to infect a dragon just so they could keep tabs on him? "How inhumane," I said.

Yuki Ito shot me a surprised look, but it vanished immediately, before Sakuya-hime noticed.

"The vampire is *dangerous*." I pointed at my phone in the middle of the table. "That phone carries the personal numbers of a dozen elves, including King Odinsson and Queen Tyrsdottir. Pick it up. Call any of them. They will tell you magical to magical just how dangerous Brother is."

Oh, no, I thought. I'd called him Brother.

The satisfaction woven into the grin Sakuya-hime threw me was worse than anything I'd expect from a Loki elf.

This kami was not a trickster. She was, if I remembered correctly, an aspect of life, a goddess of spring and blossoms and all the gentle, delicate things of the Earth.

But she was also an aspect of the goddess of volcanoes, and one's only hope was to run from a volcano. Run as fast as you can and pray the pyroclastic flow churns in a different direction.

Yuki Ito crossed their arms. "Your name makes it obvious who you consider your father, Mr. Victorsson." They laced their hands behind their head. "Not that we'd expect subtlety from a man who lives with elves."

My mouth wanted so much to let out my inner Akeyla and just flat out ask them why they were like this. Why the dominance games and the refusal to help. Why they weren't cooperating in tracking a member of the Fae Royal Guard, either.

But I knew. The kami were not going to allow foreign magic on their land. They never had, and they weren't going to start now, even though they had a foreign vampire god in Tokyo. So they were doing what they'd always done with outsiders—use what they could until the cons outweighed the pros, then decisively "deal" with the issue.

They were quite good at dealing with magical and mundane threats. *Were* good at it, until World War II.

I pinched the bridge of my nose. I was *way* out of my depth here. "Perhaps," I said, "Sakuya-hime would feel more comfortable—diplomatically speaking—interacting with King Odinsson? Queen Tyrsdottir? Magnus Freyrsson?" I pointed at my phone.

"Why doesn't your Queen admit to her god aspect?" Yuki Ito asked. "We all are quite clear about the power we wield."

Sakuya-hime touched Yuki's arm. She held up a finger, but did not look at her companion. "He dug himself out of the pocket realm." She made a little digging motion. "He had—has, still, though we have not seen it—the end of what appeared to be a pike. He used it to literally excavate a hole back into The Land of the Living."

I blinked. I didn't know what to say, or how to respond. He'd literally dug himself out of Purgatory.

"Rumor amongst our demons and spirits is that another vampire exited with him." She sat back. "We suspect that he consumed the vampire because we have not found any trace of a companion."

Yuki Ito leaned forward. "He ate a kitsune when he exited." They glanced at me as if they understood I'd promised Chip and Lollipop help.

Sakuya-hime touched their arm again. "He did us a great courtesy eating an aspect of Tamamo-no-Mae. You know that."

Yuki yanked back their arm. "*Kitsune*," they snapped.

Sakuya-hime shook her head. "You will have your revenge."

Yuki's lip twitched.

I decided to test my suspicion. I stared directly at the fox. "Chip and Lollipop," I said.

I could not read the muscle twitches of their face. Was Yuki Ito surprised? Frightened? Unsure? All three?

Yuki slapped the table. "I will avenge!"

I mimicked the slap. Mine made the entire table shake. "How? Can *you* stop him?"

"Can you?" Sakuya-hime asked. "Emperor Sutoku thinks you can."

She knew about the Vegas Wolf deal. "I do not work for him."

Chihiro gasped and covered her mouth.

"Our sources say otherwise," Sakuya-hime said.

"Your sources are wrong," I countered.

"What weapons do you wield, Mr. Victorsson? How is it that you, a man who is neither mundane nor magical, has the power to bring Kyūketsuki no kami to heel? Does your sister wield the same power? What, exactly, did your father unleash onto the world?"

I had no answers. I hadn't before Raven tossed us into Japan, and I didn't now. "Vampires don't like my blood?" I offered. Except for the whole draining me dry to build a pocket borderland adjacent to The Land of the Dead.

Sakuya-hime laughed. "That *must* be the key." She stood up. "We are needed." She looked at Chihiro. "Do not call again unless you or your American can truly help."

Chihiro stepped out of the kitchen. "Sakuya-hime!" she said. "This is a mistake!"

The kami smoothed her lapels. "I will rescind your viewer, Hatanaka, if you do not cooperate."

Chihiro took a step backward.

157

The kami held up her hand. "Do not bring gaijins to Kōsaten, do you understand? Any more of these... indiscretions... and I will ask Inari Ōkami to ban you from the temples."

Chihiro backed against the kitchen countertop. She bowed her head. "Yes, Konohanasakuya-hime," she said.

And with that, an aspect of the goddess of Mount Fuji walked out into the Tokyo afternoon with her super-kitsune in tow.

CHAPTER 20

I f I'd learned anything in my life, it was that blind arrogance was the true universal of Earth's magicals. At least the elves of Alfheim seemed to be aware of their overconfidence.

Chihiro continued to stand with her back against her kitchen sink, her eyes huge and her skin pale. Out front, a car engine purred to life, and after a moment, vanished into the background noise of the Tokyo suburbs.

"But you have been inside a Crossroads," Chihiro muttered. "You told Ellie that you were inside the Crossroads in Las Vegas and she asked me about them because she had a vague memory of there being one here." She blinked fast a few times. "Or Berlin. Or Alice Springs."

I looked up at the ceiling. "Why are magicals so arrogant? That kami could make Magnus Freyrsson quake in his boots." I rubbed my forehead. "Why do they call themselves kami, anyway? Kami means 'god'. They're aspects."

Chihiro straightened. "Japan has not had the linguistic drift away from the god-ness inherent in the word 'kami' the same way as the words 'elf' and 'fae' have lost most of their potency." She walked toward the table. "I suspect it has to do with cultural continuity. We were not broken by the Romans."

"*Heh.*" I looked up at Chihiro as I pocketed my wallet and swiped my phone off the table. "She shouldn't talk to you like that even if she's more of a god than any of the other magicals," I said. "The elves don't treat anyone in town like that." Except maybe Ed.

I sighed and looked up at the ceiling again. I was intimately familiar with the rage that erupted when a person was mistreated. I was going to have a talk with Arne when this was done, and he was going to listen to me. No more assuming Ed would always be there to do their bidding. And if I could manage it, I'd do the same for Chihiro.

I pressed my phone's on button. Nothing happened.

I picked up Wrenn's and also tried to turn it on. Again, no power.

"Do you have a USB charger?" I held up the phone.

Chihiro pointed at her own phone on the counter, not far from where she stood.

I could call from her phone. I'd charge Wrenn's first. Unlike mine, hers could find portals. I probably couldn't get a compatible signal.

That was, if her phone agreed to cooperate.

I plugged in Wrenn's phone, then picked up Chihiro's phone. "May I?" I needed to check if Ellie had, in fact, texted Chihiro the numbers on her phone. At the very least, I could call Arne and Dag's home landline. I remembered that number. And the main Sheriff's Department number.

I glanced at the kitchen window. It was the middle of the night in Alfheim. I wouldn't be able to reach Ellie, though I could leave a message. One of the elves should answer, though. Or worst case, Ed.

I dialed Ellie's number. It, as I predicted, did not connect, and went to voicemail. "I'm with Chihiro. Check the news. He's escalated." I inhaled. "He took Wrenn." I inhaled again. "I love you and I promise to be careful." I had to hang up. I couldn't leave too much information. I just needed to hear her voice.

I needed to see her. Touch her.

Chihiro touched my arm.

I looked down at my love's friend. "Call Chihiro as soon as you get this," I said, and hung up.

Chihiro nodded once and patted my elbow. "I have a second charger somewhere." She walked away and into the bedroom.

My flock of bright blue puppy sparks swirled around my head and chest. "If you make it difficult for me to think, I might make a stupid mistake. And then what? You and I will never get home."

My mate magic fluttered, but it pulled in again, and settled down on my shoulders.

Was it listening to me? "Thank you," I said.

I scrolled through the many new English-language entries in Chihiro's phone. Ellie had definitely pulled through for us. Chihiro now had half of Alfheim in her phone, including all of the Gerouxs, Arne, Dag, Maura, Magnus, Ed's personal number, and two I didn't expect: Akeyla and Sophia.

"Arne first," I said, and dialed his number.

The connection clicked. Arne answered on the first ring. "Arne Odinsson," he said.

Chihiro set a second charger down next to my phone, then walked toward her television.

"It's Frank," I said.

"What's going on over there?" he asked. "Our not-an-oracle told Maura that you'd been flung into Tokyo. News reports say there was an earthquake."

Ellie really had come through and had gotten a message to Arne, like I'd asked.

Chihiro turned on her television.

"Yeah," I said. "He's here, Arne. He's escalating. He took Wrenn."

I swear Arne rubbed his face on the other side of the connection. "Dag's down at the restaurant. She's trying to get the new owner to talk to her."

"Good idea," I said.

"It'll take two days to get any of us there if she doesn't cooperate. That's the fastest, with available flights." He sighed.

They did not have a Heimdall elf, which meant they could not manipulate space as well as the fae. Or the kami.

Or a superpowered kitsune able to teleport other people. I looked over my shoulder. "Chihiro!" I called.

"How is it you know a woman in Tokyo, Frank?" Arne asked. Some of that irritation caused by Ellie's concealment enchantments edged into his voice.

"Those two kitsune in Las Vegas," I sort-of lied. It would, at least, give his mind a reason, and should calm down the irritation.

"Ah," he said. "How are they involved in all this?"

"Victims," I said.

New and more devastating images played across Chihiro's screen. Buildings burned, though their neighbors stood unscathed. My guess was that the death toll would have been significantly higher if Tokyo wasn't populated by so many magicals.

He exhaled. "Damn it."

"Yep," I responded.

"Any contact with the locals?" he asked. "I'll bring everyone I can get onto the flight."

Chihiro walked over.

"It'll take the elves two days to get here," I said to her.

She nodded.

"Unless you think Yuki will help." Yuki had the magicks to move me. Yuki could move the elves from Alfheim to Tokyo. Maybe.

Her eyes widened. "Alfheim is on the other side of the planet, Frank. That's a long way for someone like Yuki."

Maybe not.

"Lollipop found me," I said.

"Lollipop did not *move* you," she said. No, she just zeroed in on me.

"If you're suggesting what I think you are suggesting," Arne said, "you are asking a great deal from a... fox... I assume?"

"Yes," I answered.

Arne paused for a breath. "I'd rather not light beacons, son," he said. "For the safety of the town."

"Beacons?"

"More like runway lights, so the fox doesn't come in or launch out blind." He inhaled again. "But I will. That monster escaped from our jail and is now menacing their town. We must offer all the assistance we can."

Wrenn's phone beeped to life. A notification box popped up but disappeared again before I caught anything about her messages.

"Hold on, Arne." I picked up Wrenn's phone and swiped at it to see if I could get to the notifications again.

The box reappeared indicating three voice messages and seven texts, with a partial readout of the latest, which had come in only a ten minutes ago: "... NA Nordic friends have it?" it said.

"Oh, no," I said. "Arne, you may be dealing with Wrenn's employer. I think he might show up there looking for Red."

Chihiro plugged in my phone and set it down on the counter. Then she looked around my arm at the notifications on Wrenn's screen. She pointed. "Is that from..."

"I think so," I said.

She reached over my arm and pressed on the notification window. "Do you know how to unlock her phone?" she asked.

I shook my head *no*.

Arne swore in Old Norse. "Tell your friend that we will send who we can but I cannot deplete the town's protections, if *he's* coming around."

That *he* would be Robin Goodfellow. But what if it turned out to be King Oberon? "I understand."

"Text with any other news. I must go to my wife."

"I will," I said. "Stay safe, Arne," I added.

"You, too, son. You, too." Arne hung up.

Chihiro took Wrenn's phone from me. She ran her finger over the screen. "Do you think this thing could take us to Wrenn?"

I had no idea. "I know she finds gates with it." Then there was the issue of privacy. What if we somehow unlocked Wrenn's phone and the kami read all her fae secrets the way Robin Good-fellow was probably reading all of Ed's secrets off the clone Wrenn made?

Yet we had a great and terrible vampire to kill and a kelpie-run trafficking syndicate to destroy. Plus probably—most likely—multiple magical royal courts to appease, since all the vampire-destroying was going to make someone powerful angry.

Powerful magicals who allowed vampires to be "a little naughty" in order to keep their "bigger naughtiness" under control were about to have their apple carts upset. Except the whole naughty trade-off wasn't true. It had never been true and it never would be. Allowing those little naughties allowed the powerful "good" magicals to dance with their own dark sides.

Because every magical was both good and bad, just like mundane people. The question was on which side of that balance you fell.

And Arne, the All Father of a town called Alfheim, had kept Tony and Ivan around because he was too arrogant to understand that not even an Odin elf—two Odin elves, with Dagrun—can control something as uncontrollable as Dracula's "bad boyfriend" little brother, Radu the Handsome.

But there was something else there, with Arne's choices. Who filled his town? Dagrun, Benta, Magnus, Bjorn, Lennart, Maura, the many other powerful elves who had, over the last four centuries, congregated in Alfheim as if called to Valhalla by their chieftain god? The Alfheim Pack with its three Alphas and its prosperous, well-trained members? Me?

Now Ellie's cottage and the World Tree. And the World Raven. Not to mention the involvement of the fae.

All of which made me wonder about the collector side of Odin—the god of death who gifted men the tools they needed to die gloriously in battle just so they'd be available to help him during Ragnarok.

But the kami? The kami did not believe in the cyclic destruction of the gods and the world. The kami were just arrogant enough to think they had all their problems under control, including Brother, no matter how he ran rampant through their city.

Brother was evil. Brother was chaos. Both evil and chaos get their thrills from sowing confusion and disarray. And nothing covers wholesale victim-eating like a nice suit and the lie that you're here to help.

Not that I understood how the kami and their yōkai, yūrei, and other creatures interacted, or how the modern mundanes of Japan felt about their magicals, both good and bad. Honestly, I had no idea what the dynamics were here, and I suspected that learning those dynamics would be a year-long task.

We did not have a year. Not when a power-hungry vampire was involved. Not with Emperor Sutoku claiming he held my promise of help. Not with Fenrir sniffing around Alfheim.

I looked up at the ceiling yet again. Fenrir would come for the kami, too. The Midgard Serpent encircled the entire world, after all.

I looked down at Wrenn's phone again. Gates, at least, would get an elf or two here faster.

"Chihiro," I said. "I think we need to break into a Royal Guard phone."

CHAPTER 21

Over in the living room area of Chihiro's small home, the news switched to yet another fire in yet another part of Tokyo. Chihiro had turned off the sound so all I heard was the *plinking* of the fish tank in the bedroom and the faint, low vibrations of urban life as they rumbled through the walls and floor.

My brain made fire noises anyway.

Those three houses behind the reporter roared. The high rise behind the other reporter crackled and hissed. Water blasted from hoses.

People screamed.

"Japanese folklore," Chihiro's shoulders did the universal twitch that meant she used the word folklore ironically, "blames Emperor Sutoku for all disasters, human or natural." She looked up at my face. "We mundanes often understand better than we think we do."

I ran my finger over the screen again as if part of me hoped the phone was a tiny bit like Sal and would want to help. No such luck.

"What's his deal?" I asked.

Chihiro leaned against the counter next to the charging phones. "He's a spirit manifestation of a real Emperor who ruled Japan a millennia ago. There were sacred vows and court backstabbing. He

166

abdicated and was exiled. Then came blood and the severing of tongues." She moved to the table and pulled out a chair. "He was snubbed and his spirit now haunts the court and the nation. Bad crops? Sutoku did it. Samurai take over? Sutoku did that, too. Lose a war? Sutoku. Earthquake?" She waved her hand at the outer world. "Vampires eating magicals? Look to Sutoku." She sat down. "Sometimes it's true."

I left Wrenn's phone on the counter and sat down next to her. "Did he cause the earthquake?" *Because he was mad at me?* I thought.

She shrugged. "Maybe. Probably not. He's not a nature spirit. I mean, think about what would be involved in causing an earthquake. That amount and type of magic takes more than standing in the middle of the street waving one's hands."

So he'd been showboating. "I suspect he knew it was coming."

She sat back. "I think that's his real power." She picked up the remote and changed the channel. "He's prescient for events he can claim he did, to keep up his glamour of shock and awe." She flicked through channel after channel of disaster images. "Except the corrupt business dealings. Those are very real."

And vulnerable, unless you were terrified of the spirit who tossed out earthquakes. "I take it destroying him doesn't work." That was the thing with spirits. They weren't born. They just were. If the kami destroyed the Emperor, he'd still go home, get a good night's sleep, and come back the next day ready for a new fight.

She shook her head.

So the kami had been using Sutoku to hold Brother in check, and Brother to occupy the Emperor, and as long as the fight stayed away from mundanes, they let both of them prey on whatever non-kami magicals they could catch.

The kami were awfully cavalier with other magicals' lives. From what I'd seen so far, so were the fae. Which meant the elves were, too. They all were.

Thus was the way of magicals. They were bound by their magic. I leaned forward and pressed my palms against my forehead. "I have a headache," I muttered.

Chihiro laughed. She patted my back like the good default-sister-in-law she was. "What's the plan?" she asked.

I stood up again. "We unlock Wrenn's phone and ask it nicely to take me to her without alerting the King of the Fae or his Second in Command that I, a mere elf-adjacent mundane, had accessed fae high tech."

She nodded. "Then what?"

"I go get Wrenn."

She leaned back in the chair. "How? A taxi?"

"If I have to," I said. "By myself," I added. "I can take hits, Chihiro."

She frowned. "But can you speak Japanese? Read signs?"

I wasn't going to put her in any more danger.

Chihiro sighed. "There's a reason I've been able to help you, Frank." She tapped her ear. "A reason I have this." Then she tapped the magic around her elbow. "And this." She inhaled and resettled herself in her chair. "Ellie's concealment enchantments... change people."

"They haven't changed me," I said, before I gave it enough thought to form a good opinion. Because if I was honest with myself, if I did the introspection one should do after one interacts with fae and fae-built anything, I'd realize that yes, I had changed, and probably not all of it had been the falling-in-love kind of growth, either.

I mean, I was pretty sure I'd anchored Ellie's cottage to Alfheim by inviting the World Tree to take root.

Chihiro lifted an eyebrow. "You can call on magic now, can't you? Magicks not gifted to you?"

I nodded.

She patted her elbow. "The cottage injured me when it moved." She inhaled. "I lost my elbow. My bones shattered. Luckily, that was the only damage I took."

I had no idea. "Ellie thought you'd died."

She looked away. "We've talked about it."

Good, I thought. "The magic," I asked. "The kami helped?"

"The kami *noticed*." She patted her ear again. "The viewer was a gift. I can manipulate it in ways that only a magical should be able to."

She dropped her hand to the table. "The brace controls the pain. It's to keep me out of the mundane medical system."

"Ah," I said.

"Us," she waved her fingers between us. "Those who are so specifically touched, we are new, Frank. At least according to the kami. We should not exist. That's why they drew me into their world. I am an anomaly they wish to protect. Or control." She shrugged. "They do not know about Ellie, by the way. The concealments still keep me from talking about her."

The cottage left Chihiro with parting gifts, one nice. One not. How very fae.

"So I will help you find your sister," she said. "And if we can get Chip back, I will help you do that, too."

"Okay," I said. Arguing with her would not help any of us. She was correct about me needing help, anyway.

I reached for Wrenn's phone. I waved to activate the lock screen. "It's fully charged."

"That was fast," Chihiro leaned over to look.

Mine was still at twenty percent. I got up and rearranged the phones, plugging in Chihiro's and unplugging Wrenn's, then returned to the table.

"How do we do this?" I asked. I suspected the phone was completely unhackable via mundane methods, none of which I knew anyway.

Chihiro tapped the spot behind her ear. The goggles manifested. She picked up Wrenn's phone.

The goggles did the same roll through vibrational energies as it had when she'd called it up to talk to the dragon in Tokyo Bay; changing colors, shape, and density, and finally settling onto something that looked similar to, but not quite the same as, the red-and-green tooth-and-claw of fae magic.

"I think it's a smart chip," Chihiro said. "I think it will open for fae magic." She tipped her head to the side. "Guard magic." She looked up at me. "Law magic, Frank."

"I'm not a cop," I said. I wasn't affiliated with Alfheim's law enforcement.

She set down the phone. "But you *are* Paladin to King Odinsson of the Alfheim Elves."

I blinked.

"The Princess," she said.

"Is there anything the kami do not know?"

She shrugged. "Other than about Ellie? No."

I suddenly felt violated. Small. Naked. I wanted to yell that if they thought Brother was bad, wait until they saw me in a full rage. But I hadn't been that man in two centuries. I never would be again. I had vowed as much to myself, to the elves, and now to Ellie.

Because I was a paladin.

"Look at it this way. You and Wrenn now have parity of power."

We did. "At least there's a silver lining, huh?" I placed my hand on screen of Wrenn's phone. "I am Paladin to King and Queen Odinsson of the Alfheim Elves and I request law enforcement help to locate Wrenn Goodfellow of the Fae Royal Guard," I said to the device.

Nothing happened.

"I don't think it believes me," I said.

Chihiro leaned over the phone. "Your Queen has blessed this paladin," she said.

Red and green magic shot up out of the phone as the magical chip inside unfolded. It snapped toward Chihiro like a snake. She raised her hands, but it snapped again and pushed her away. Then it turned toward me.

It wasn't a cloud, or a snake, or a dragon. It was all technology with hexagonal cell-like structures, lines, and geometry. It snapped from state to state instead of dancing but was still the same thick red and green as all other fae magic.

If this magic was alive, it was alive in a whole different way than Sal or the dragons.

"It doesn't feel conscious," I said.

Chihiro watched it from her place against the table. "It's an algo-rithm—algorithms. It's running programs." She pointed at its interior.

170

"Several, but still not the millions a living creature runs microsecond to microsecond."

Gears. Lines. Shifting patterns. "Someone figured out how to *program* the geometry of the universe?" I'd seen the gearwork inside the fae magic somewhere, or at least something similar...

In Rose's ghost cottage. When I accidently opened the gate that brought Brother into Alfheim. Wrenn's phone carried the same basic underpinnings as the magic that pierced the veil between The Lands of the Living and the Dead.

"This is... terrifying," Chihiro said.

Those gears whirled inside the magic. Patterns rotated and pulsed.

It snapped at me again.

"I'm Wrenn's brother!" I held up my hands. "We need to find her! The Demon took her and I need to find them before he hurts her!" The magic held still for a moment, as if considering what I said. "The kelpie blood syndicate is here in Japan and she has a lead!" I tried.

The magic grabbed both of my arms and rolled them as if looking for Heartway tokens.

"I live with elves," I said.

Chihiro dropped into a chair. "Frank?"

The magic slammed down into the shadow of energy on my arm where Portia Elizabeth's red dress magic had pooled.

I managed to grab the phone just as it yanked me into the fae Heartway.

CHAPTER 22

Crossing veils is not thrilling or exciting. It's painful. Your body moves from one reality to another, and that—to the individual nerves, bones, tendons, and cells that do not understand what is happening to them—is *not right*.

A body becomes terrified. A body wonders if this move from one location in one realm to a new location in another means a state change. And the energy input needed to change states is how the delicate filigree of life is destroyed.

Fire to ice. Mundane to magical. Living to dead.

Or, in my case, Dead to living.

I did not remember a lot about my trip to the Las Vegas Crossroads. But then again, a lot of what happened there had been hidden from me behind walls of magic. Or, more precisely, behind veils. Crossroads were where worlds met, after all.

I remembered my disorientation. Not as much as when I woke up on Victor's table after what must have been time in The Land of the Dead. Or perhaps I was something completely new, a soul born at the transition.

Perhaps I share that newness with my sister. And my brother. Perhaps we are where worlds meet.

I didn't remember waking up on Victor's table. I remembered the lack of integration of my stitched-together body: The difference in grip strength between my left and right hands. The strange extra ruddiness captured by my left eye, but not my right. The unequal catching of pitches between my ears. How my right arm did not quite yet understand what my brain wanted it to do.

It wasn't until I realized I was alone that the world solidified. He'd run off, my "father." Run off and left me alone, and in freezer-burn-like physical anguish. Left me to navigate his dirty, now-abandoned laboratory. To learn how to talk, and walk, and to be a human.

The latter took a while. There are a lot of ways to be a man. Several of those ways help no one but a villain. Many did not help me.

Then came my obsessions with Victor, and my anger, and his promises. It ended on an ice floe. He called me "Demon."

Wrenn called our brother that word. Demon. But what was a demon? An angel? When something resists the entropy of The Land of the Dead, when it has enough will to spin itself into a thread of power, it can escape.

Like a virus.

I became aware that I was no longer in Chihiro's kitchen. I was no longer *anywhere*. No ground supported my feet, though this place had directionality. I knew up and down, side to side, front and back.

My eyes processed something, though calling it light would probably give it too much substantiality. Everything was flat, and even, and gray, as if I was inside entropy, or Death itself.

Except I was alive, and this place did not feel like The Land of the Dead. It felt new, and virgin, like the untapped spaces inside veils. Like what had been underneath the version of Magnus's farm inside the veil between Alfheim and the fae realm into which Titania had tried to pull Ellie. The place the elves had shaped with their magic to mirror the real world.

The place in which I stood now had yet to be shaped.

But how was I supposed to get out of here, or use this place, or find Wrenn?

My hand vibrated.

I looked down at my palm. I'd grabbed Wrenn's phone just as the techno-magic of its chip slammed me here.

"You tossed me into the Heartway, didn't you?" I asked it. I was in the fae transit system without any guide, or token, or markings indicating that I wasn't a threat. But I was also in a part without a gate, or a station, or even rails.

The phone's screen lit up. A completely blank map appeared. I looked down at Japan unmarred by any markings beyond one lone location dot.

"You're showing me my corresponding location in Japan, aren't you?"

No answer. If Chihiro was correct, the phone would not answer questions unless I asked it something its algorithms could process.

I peered at the screen. "I need to know where Wrenn is." Even if it just gave me a dot, I could figure out where to go in the real world. Maybe.

Nothing changed on the screen.

The elves had nothing like Wrenn's phone, or the transit system Oberon and the fae had built out of... what? Rail lines they placed because one of them had figured out how to program magic? Wrenn hadn't told me a lot about the Heartway, other than that it was her place of flashbacks.

Flashbacks that had occurred while she carried this phone.

I had no idea what information the system used to determine exit points, or even if there were possible exit points in Tokyo. But maybe I could glean some information about the hows and whys of the system by reviewing past transits.

"Wrenn," I said. "Please forgive me." I was about to do something I should not without permission. "Phone," I said. "I need to talk to Wrenn's Heartway memory of Brother. The Demon. The Vampire God." *Please don't drop me into one of her flashbacks*, I thought. *Just give me—*

Brother appeared directly in front of me. No pop, no change in air pressure like when one of the kitsune manifests, just a blink and he stood within arm's reach in this blank place, the eight-foot monster with his lightning bolt scar and his bits of Dracula.

He was dressed wrong. Old fashioned, like he'd walked out of a real daguerreotype photo. His suit was still dark gray, still with pinstripes, but he wore a well-tailored vest and the kind of shirt we all wore at the turn of the Twentieth Century.

He pulled a pocket watch from his vest, looked at it, then looked at me. "Interesting," he said.

"Where is she?" I asked.

He leaned closer and turned his head a little as if listening to a distant sound. Then he raised a finger and poked it at me.

Reality between us wobbled.

We were not in the same place. I doubted we were in the same realm. But something was allowing us to see each other.

I am going to pay dearly for accessing this magic, I thought.

"The fae did not lie. You did escape." He nodded approvingly. He leaned closer. "I sucked him dry then ripped off his head, brother. He will not menace any of us—"

He looked over his shoulder.

He was about to vanish again.

I had no idea what version of Brother I was looking at, or what flashback this was, but I couldn't let him disappear without trying to get some information.

I flung myself at the barrier between us and—

I was in a burning house, though I felt no heat. The house was a large Craftsman with high ceilings, ornate woodwork, and large front windows. Flames rolled up the walls and across the large rugs.

I felt *pain*. Blistering pain in all its forms—physical from the nerves in skin, emotional from a brain hijacking the same nerve system to tag a situation as bad, horrible, untenable, destructive. Pain that vibrated out into the veils between me and the hell of the house into which the phone's magic—Heartway magic—had just dropped me.

I groaned and stumbled, but I held onto the phone and I managed to keep on my feet. My mate magic, though, lifted off my shoulders and jiggled around my head as if the flames and the pain terrified it—

as if the blue sparkles dancing on my skin remembered Ellie's out-of-control witch fire.

"This isn't real," I whispered. "You're safe." The World Tree anchored the cottage. My mate was safe.

Brother's mate was not.

He stood between another male vampire and a woman—a fae—who lay dead on the floor. Another fae stood over her. A goat-legged, horned fae. His eyes glowed with the depths of eternity. He wore a uniform I assumed was Royal Guard.

The goat fae snickered, but his face and body were tight with anger. *"Else the Puck a liar call; So, good night unto you all,"* he said. "We're done here."

He vanished.

Puck? Wrenn said she'd been searching for Brother for two hundred years and here was her mentor all horned up like a god aspect killing Brother's mate?

The other vampire vomited. When he looked up, his eyes had crystalized to the color of ice. "You *turned* me, you bastard." And then he was gone through the open door.

What was I seeing?

Brother's face changed. His shoulders, also, and how he held his hands.

He was shifting into a completely different personality.

He was disassociating.

"This isn't helping!" I yelled at the Heartway magic. How would this moment of terror in Brother's life help me find Wrenn? How would it help anyone?

He shifted again—and looked directly at me. "Do you think the Queen would tolerate *you* paying the price for entering the Heartway this far from any gates?"

Shock hit me so hard I slid back my foot as if my body thought it should run.

The Heartway was squeezing the cost of my presence from Brother, or at least its own version of Brother. Could it do that? Could it literally eat itself to fuel its own magicks?

"*O quizás hice un trato con la Muerte,*" Brother said.

Spanish? He was disassociating. He had to be.

His suit changed color. Only for a flash, or a blink of my eyes. His eyes changed, too. Gone was the gray of his clothes and the fire in his eyes.

He was a corpse, for that moment. A hodgepodge of stitched together meat stood in the center of the burning house, drained of all life and living and any color other than the green pallor of nothingness.

Then this Heartway version of Brother grabbed onto the gearwork geometry underneath the Heartway, and all the veils, and the universe. The same gearwork the phone used to access the fae transit system.

He moved. Or Death moved him.

I knew exactly where he went. I knew through which veils he moved and I knew he landed in the one realm that would drain off the pain of this moment. He'd stay there a century until I called him home.

The burning house vanished as the Heartway ate up the residual pain lingering in the memory. Fae magic chewed it up and swallowed it whole to fuel the engines that allowed it to reach for me. I was a Paladin of Queen Titania. I had parity of power with Wrenn, a Paladin of King Oberon. It would provide me with the information I sought.

But I was dealing with a program, not an entity. Not Salvation, or Redemption, or one of the Guardian dragons. The magic on Wrenn's phone was in fact magic, but as Chihiro said, it was an algorithm.

And algorithms need input they understood, which it did not have in Japan.

Wrenn's phone could not *take* me to Wrenn. There were no Heartway gates there, and only the Tokyo Crossroads to act as the single switching station between fae and kami magicks.

The phone had no connected entrance and exit points. But it could *point.*

I looked down at the screen. A second point appeared close to mine in the vast blankness of the map of Japan. She was still in the city. "Hold that marker!" I said. "Keep it pinned so we can read it when we return to Tokyo."

I had a lead.

A lead that would probably have me face-to-face with Brother without magical backup. Or, more likely, with wrathful "backup" looking to take Brother into "custody." Plus I had no idea how incapacitated Wrenn was, or if she would be able to fight. Or if she'd already found a way to contact the Royal Guard.

I was going in blind. I needed a weapon.

The kami already refused to help and I shouldn't ask the fae magic in my hand. How was I supposed to handle this?

I looked up as if to ask the stars above.

I'd been focused on Brother's flashback and the information on Wrenn's phone. I hadn't looked *up* at what floated over my head.

At the *up* above this virgin place of nothingness.

There were megastructures to the universe, or so I'd read, or seen in a documentary. Threads of gravity on which galaxies hung like pearls. Surfaces of bubbles on which those galaxies sparkled like dewdrops. The veils, mostly, where creation built itself.

What floated above me in the deep blackness of nothingness wasn't a foam of bubbles expanding outward into incomprehensible spaces. I was looking at something much more familiar.

Those dewdrops rested on leaves held by mega-branches. Those branches spread outward from a single core trunk. And that trunk grew out of a space much like this one—infinite, undiscovered, and virgin.

And here, now, directly over my head, the roots of *everything* spread through the underbelly of existence.

Me, a simple man caught up in complex magic—a man trying to do the best for the people I loved—should never have been allowed to gaze upon the roots of the universe.

Roots feed all leaves, I thought. Or heard. Or both.

Something moved in those roots. Something shimmering with the darkest, blackest of magicks. Something powerful.

Hunger rolled off it as if its job was to remove the debris from the universe—to consume what should no longer exist.

I would not cower because if I was correct, if the coiling and uncoiling happening around the roots of the World Tree directly over my head was the creature I suspected it was, cowering would only get me consumed.

Because the magic in those roots ate the souls of murderers. Sinners.

Vampires. The wrathful and the evil.

All the souls who washed up on Hel's Corpse Shore.

"You are not a Japanese dragon," I whispered. Yet the creature was fully dragon.

No, this dragon was wholly Norse.

"Nidhogg," I whispered.

Then the jorōgumo yanked me back into The Land of the Living.

WRENN GOODFELLOW

CHAPTER 23

WRENN GOODFELLOW

Wrenn and Brother watched each other over a heavy ornate table built from a dark tropical hardwood. Two lit taper candles—one green and one red—sat in the middle of the table, each in a silver candleholder decorated with seven-pointed stars.

The candles were a nod to the magic Wrenn wore but could not wield with any real power.

Brother's chair was huge, like him, and made from a creamy dark brown leather. It clicked when it rolled over the bamboo floor, but otherwise glided with him when he moved as if it loved him as much as his yōkai minions.

Wrenn's chair was small and plastic with metal legs that did the flooring no favors.

The table sat at one end of the long room. A matching massive dark desk sat at the other. Windows—always shaded, to keep her from seeing outside—allowed in some filtered light.

The tall palm in the pot behind the desk did not seem to enjoy the abuse and lack of light, and she'd already dumped a pitcher of water on it hoping to save at least one living thing.

He'd refilled the pitcher and brought her take-out. "I am not the monster you think I am," he'd said.

They all said that, the monsters. They were all "we're one in the same, you and I. At least I have the guts to take action to make the world pay for my grievances." The villain's mantra.

She didn't touch the food, though it smelled savory and delectable. It still waited in its bag on the edge of the desk.

He hadn't taken her knives. They rested on the table in front of her, two ten-inch chef's blades stolen from one of the burning houses. The flames had been an ineffective spell which, like the knives themselves, had caused him no damage.

She hadn't taken his pike. It sat on the table in front of him, a three-foot-long broken bit of stolen magic. From what she'd learned from Frank, it was more of a death-straw than a pike.

She still smelled like the fires. He, on the other hand, smelled savory, like the food.

"So," he asked, "where do you want to spend our honeymoon?"

She was sure he'd stayed on this line of questioning specifically because it agitated her. She tried not to twitch.

Did he know about her flashbacks? The version of him in the Heartway? Were they somehow connected? She'd always assumed her Demon was all her and that the Heartway generated him to cause the pain it needed to fuel its transport spells.

But the world was not always what it seemed. She would not dwell. Dwelling would turn the twitches into shaking and the shaking into a blackout.

So she argued. Bantered. Anything to force her brain to separate this vampire from the ghost haunting her soul.

They'd already done the prerequisite back and forth: *I'm not your bride. Yes, you are. I know I'm not, but what are you? Sticks and stones, my sweet. Sticks and damned-to-Hell stones.*

Then he'd brought the food still sitting in the bag on the desk.

"Tell me about her," she said. There had to be a *her* somewhere in this story. He seemed fixated, and that fixation seemed more than simple juvenile male "Victor built a lady" posturing. He'd had a woman in his life at one time.

The thought of which also made her twitch. "She was fae, wasn't she?" There was an outside chance that he'd found a Loki elf, or one who was an aspect of Hel, the Norse goddess of the dead, but Wrenn doubted it. Hel elves were rarer than Loki elves and guarded by the enclaves. The fae made it their business to know where all the Loki and Hel elves lived, anyway.

Had he twitched when she'd asked about a woman? He'd twitched.

She grinned. "She was a baobhan sith, wasn't she? I've met baobhan sith who would be quite happy with eight feet of putrid death."

His lip curled.

Jackpot, Wrenn thought. She leaned forward. "I could find her for you," she said. "Easy Peasy Royal Guard Database Squeezy."

He chuckled.

She backed off. The last time he'd chuckled like that, he'd jumped the table and slapped her so hard she passed out.

She changed the subject. "The syndicate," she said.

He leaned back in his chair. "The kelpies are the linchpin, love," he said.

"Yes." Kelpies were often somewhat intelligent and easily bored, which was not a good combination in psychopathic fae.

Wrenn ran the tip of her finger along the handle of one of the knives, imitating how he'd caressed his pike.

He brought his hands together, touching only the tips of his pointer fingers and thumbs, in a gesture that looked like he was about to toss a spell in her direction. "Kami magic lingers, making magicals from this ecosystem valuable." He shrugged. "Their biggest supplier has always been Emperor Sutoku via Central Kobayashi Shipping and Transportation. There are others."

There were always others.

He leaned forward. "Do you have any idea how easy it was for me to turn yōkai and some of the oni against Sutoku? He does nothing for them."

As Frank figured, their vampire brother had been building an army of disaffected dark kami magicals, with the goal of taking out his dark magical competition—with Emperor Sutoku being the biggest and strongest target. Once he'd accumulated enough power, his plan had been to set up some sort of treaty with the kami, and then to turn his attention to the mundanes of Japan.

It was a good plan. He'd just started his attacks on the Emperor when the World Raven tossed her and Frank here.

Another week of accumulating power and the entirety of Japan would have been engulfed in a major magical war—which, she suspected, had already started. The earthquake right after he'd taken her could not have helped. The sounds of sirens, yelling, even the smash of a traffic accident outside meant something big was happening in the wider world.

All of which meant that he had not taken her someplace sheltered.

He sat back again. "I will be leaving soon. The gaze of the great elven eye has landed upon my dealings here now that you and our dear oaf of a brother have arrived. It is time to build anew in a different land without distractions." He grinned. "Come with me. I will teach you how to be a real witch." He flicked his hand and his low-demons coiled off his fingers into an elegant double-helix.

"And yet you say you wish to build anew without distractions."

He slowly turned his chair enough that he could put his feet up on the table. "So I kill you instead."

Yet she was still alive, still in his little suite, still being used as a sounding board.

"How much of you is Dracula?" she asked.

He sighed. "Lord Dracula whispers still. He wants information about the fate of Radu the Handsome."

Maybe every part of him was lonely. This personality certainly was. The banter, the food, the *I'm not a monster* all added up to *Please talk to me*. He'd want a hug next.

"You don't know?" she asked about Radu.

He shook his head. "I am free of the constraints of family."

"Ah," she said. "A wise choice." Except when you were lonely.

His eyes narrowed.

She sat back. "Why aren't you out there harassing the Emperor, or the kami? Or Frank. I mean, you put a lot of effort into harassing him when you entered Alfheim."

He grabbed the pike, but did not pick it up off the table. "That was not me."

Bingo, she thought. "Then who was it?"

He blinked a few times. "The one Frank calls Brother." He inhaled. "I am the Vampire God." He swung up the pike and pointed it at her. "I am *all* my parts."

She pushed back the chair just as he swung up the pike. It stopped only inches from her nose. "Let me go," she breathed.

He dropped the pike. It slammed into the table, bouncing up and then landing on her knives.

A cloud of low-demons puffed around its tip and the entire piece vanished.

He could vanish exactly the same way any time he wanted. "Why are you still here?" she whispered. "You could have left already." But she knew. He was lonely.

His army of yōkai was not enough. She suspected the reason he'd attacked Frank in Alfheim was the loneliness. This eight-foot-tall vampire had come out of The Land of the Dead solely because he'd latched onto someone with whom he could dance.

His brother. His sister.

He wasn't interested in her as his bride. That was obvious. He just wanted a companion and his yōkai weren't doing it for him. Neither were all the whispers inside his Vampire God head.

"Get up!" He vanished and appeared directly behind her. "Do you think I will sneak away? Do you think I will leave this land and allow them to believe that their tongueless ghost Emperor bested me?" He grabbed her by the neck. "I will rule Japan!"

Low-demons flowed off his arm and onto Wrenn.

She'd made a mistake. She should have read his reactions better and stopped arguing, or agreeing, or simply talking to him, before he escalated.

Because the vampires always escalated.

At least he didn't slap her into unconsciousness this time.

"Time to turn yōkai," he breathed into her ear as they vanished.

CHAPTER 24

FRANK VICTORSSON

The jorōgumo named Madame Kobayashi skittered toward me on massive magical spider legs. A demon born within the Japanese ecosystem, she was a creature who should not touch, or see, or learn about the true roots of Yggdrasil sprawled above us.

She did not look up. She had no need to do so. I was her target.

Nidhogg watched.

The Norse dragon did not have the fur mane of the Japanese dragons, or the circularity to its head, body, nostrils, or ears. Nidhogg, the eater of sinners, was more black than black itself, as if the color of its surface ate all other colors. As if the blue-black of a death bruise that danced along its edges was nothing more than a reflection.

It looked down at us with an arrow-shaped head and eyes of obsidian glass. It reared back like the kami dragons, though, and coiled the same way.

Would it take Madame Kobayashi?

"So big and handsome," she purred in my ear. "So warm and tasty for my babies."

Nidhogg dropped its head out of the roots and sniffed at the place on her back where her demon body transitioned from human to spider.

The dragon could take both of us. It could take only her, or me.

Jurisdiction? the dragon asked in my head, except "jurisdiction" wasn't quite the correct word for the thought it sent me. The dragon did not recognize a Japanese demon as food.

I was under the roots of the World Tree in a fae place between places being threatened by a jorōgumo and somehow I'd caught the attention of an extraordinarily dangerous Norse dragon. I should be terrified. I should be roaring and punching, but like when Wrenn and I first manifested in Japan, when we fully realized Brother walked this land, I had no idea what to do. The shock was too strong.

"I need your help," was all I got out. What else could I tell it? I held no glee in sending it after Madame Kobayashi. She might be a demon, but she was still a person. I wasn't kami. It was not my place to release magic of such finality onto her.

Yet I thought I could judge Brother.

"I will give you all the help you desire," Madame Kobayashi purred, obviously thinking I'd been speaking to her.

My attention snapped away from the dragon to the spider demon baring her fangs inches from my face. Her front legs coiled around my body. There was no slime, or putrid death smells, or the rancid corpses I expected with a demon. Only the terrifying gossamer ghost tickles of icy cobwebs.

She spun me once, twice...

Nidgogg vanished.

The third revolution flung me almost all the way back into Tokyo. Nothing around us moved. Not the haze hanging in the air, or the emergency vehicle rounding the corner. Not the jorōgumo.

She stood perfectly still, her hands poised as if she was about to coil me in another spell, just out of arm's reach on the concrete walk. Here, she appeared in her human glamour. This time she wore a tight-fitting black suit jacket, a tight tailored short skirt, and stiletto heels with bright gold soles.

She'd pulled me back into the real world with real dimensions—up and down, left and right, front and back. They were just not the same dimensions as where I'd been. Not the same up. Not the same down.

Not the weird comprehension of the incomprehensibly huge megastructures of the universe.

My brain was understandably confused.

And hot. We were standing close to a source of heat. I tried to blink but I was frozen along with the world.

I spun one more time.

We popped fully through the veil and manifested fully in a Tokyo intersection I recognized. Steel and concrete towers surrounded the wide streets. White bars painted onto the tarmac marked the pedestrian pathways. Massive billboards displaying national and international companies. A handful of well-groomed trees. Dancing displays. Neon. Fire engines. Now screaming and speeding emergency vehicles.

And fire. Smoke billowed out of broken windows at the top of one of the glass and steel towers. Flames crackled behind glass doors. A thick stinging haze filled the air, my eyes, and my lungs.

Shibuya Crossing burned.

"Madame Kobayashi," I said to the jorōgumo. "Yuki Ito grabbed me from your embrace when those houses burned." And stole me from the Emperor.

She winked.

I coughed and pointed at the buildings. "Why did you bring me here?" I yelled. "What did you do?"

She clicked right up to me, so close I could smell her sweet breath. "Me?" She tapped her chest. "*You* did this."

"How?" Creepy shivers ran up my back. The frozen sense of shock I'd had while in the Heartway space had dissipated when she spun me back to the real world and I wanted to pick her up and set her a good ten feet away.

A weird shadowed inner membrane flickered over her eyeballs when she rolled her eyes. "Why do you associate with kitsune?"

Something exploded a block away and I instinctively ducked. The area had been cleared of civilians, so the only other people around were official rescue.

Where were the kami? "What happened here?"

The jorōgumo stroked my chest. "The Emperor has a temper." She shrugged.

"He destroyed downtown Tokyo?" What the hell was I dealing with here? He was worse than any Loki elf.

She shrugged and held up six fingers. "Single digit casualties so far." She dropped her hands to her hips. "He may be angry, but he understands that if he annoys our Inari aspects too much they will destroy his —our—business dealings." She tapped my chin. "We *cannot* have that."

"But he destroys everyone else's business dealings with impunity, huh?" I asked.

"He *is* Emperor Sutoku." She shrugged again as she clicked away from me. "He is why the mundanes have insurance." She turned her back and held out her arms toward the evacuated buildings.

I had to get away from the jorōgumo and from the spirit Emperor with the temper who thought he owned a contract to which I'd inadvertently consented. I had to rid myself of this distraction.

I could rid Japan of him, too. He was exactly the kind of snack Nidhogg enjoyed.

Had the dragon followed us into the real world? I looked around. No sign of any magic other than Madame Kobayashi's golden threads.

Such decisions were not mine to make. I could, though, leverage a threat to which the Emperor might attend. If Nidhogg wanted to help, and if it could. It might not be able to manifest in the real world. Or in Japan. Or, as with Madame Kobayashi, it might not recognize the Emperor as food.

I needed info. And I needed to find Wrenn.

I looked down at my hand.

The map of Japan on Wrenn's screen had changed to a normal map outlining streets and buildings.

The red marker showing my sister's location had vanished.

I swore under my breath and tucked the phone into my pocket.

The jorōgumo looked over her shoulder. "What did you trade for my promise of help?" I asked as a distraction. "If it was anything more than a bottle of bourbon, you got screwed."

Madame Kobayashi swung her hips as she clicked her stilettos back toward me. She placed her hand on my chest again and tilted her head without answering my question.

It was obvious why the Emperor wanted Brother. Part of me wanted to let them fight and to not interfere, but not at the cost of deaths and burning buildings, no matter how much insurance the mundanes had. People's lives were being destroyed, and destroyed lives always led to more deaths down the road. Maybe in days, maybe years, but the destruction would kill a lot more people than the six to which she'd admitted.

"Where are the kami?" I asked. The elves would have descended on her the moment she pulled me back into the real world.

"Minimizing the casualty count." She waved her hand at the destruction around us. "Gathering up the lesser to keep them safe from us."

The look of disdain that flashed across her spider demon face said it all. This yōkai was more than happy to send her fellow magicals to their deaths.

I'd been fooling myself all the years I lived in Alfheim thinking that magicals weren't cutthroat or envious or full of gleeful murder. Part of me wondered if the elves were just biding time. Maybe the world was about to see an eruption of Minnesota Not-so-Nice that wasn't all that different from the one currently happening in Tokyo.

At least the kami had finally decided to do something about the trafficking of their less powerful. For the moment.

"Start yelling, Mr. Victorsson. Be the bait you were meant to be. Bring me the Vampire God." She spread her arms wide and turned in a circle.

So now I was bait. "Then what?" I needed magical backup to kill him. "You're going to take him into custody? What does that mean?" The kami did not seem all that interested in helping me put him down.

"It means, Mr. Victorsson, that you will never have to deal with him again." She sashayed toward me again—or skittered. Or both at the same time. A shiver moved up then down my spine. "Or I sell you instead."

They were going to *traffic* Brother? "Who's your buyer?" I asked. "The Gulf Coast Clans?" Or Clan, at this point, after Dracula's Call pulled in so many of them. The Gulf Coast vamps were the only ones I could think of who would put this much effort into getting the Vampire God back into America. "Is this some stupid ploy to send him after the elves again?" Blood and revenge, the two forces that fed vampires.

She tipped her head to the side and rolled her eyes as if I was the dumbest mundane on Earth.

So it wasn't the Gulf Coast Clans. I took a step toward her. "Who's your buyer, jorōgumo?"

The wrath and fury that manifested on her face mirrored the intensity of what I'd seen on the Emperor's back at the houses.

The next thing I knew, she had her fingers around my neck. "Show respect, tasty male."

The shock of her speed made me blink. "Tasty. *Heh*," I said.

A fire truck raced around the corner, sirens blaring and lights flashing. Not one of the firefighters noticed us or even looked in our direction. "You're hiding me from mundane eyes?"

She flicked the tip of my nose with her other hand.

Perhaps her wrath and rage were contagious. Perhaps they weren't hers to begin with and nothing more than the Emperor's way of controlling her. Maybe when she grabbed my neck, that control leaked onto me.

Or maybe I'd just had enough of the one-note spider demon and her predictable ways.

I grabbed *her* neck. And I shoved.

My arms were considerably longer than hers in her human form. Her fingers slid off my throat as I lifted her straight out and up into the air.

Her body let go, but her magic did not. Golden energy coiled tightly and pressed down on my windpipe.

She sneered. I slammed her into the walk under our feet.

The concrete shattered. Dust billowed up and mixed with the smoke and haze. A low boom echoed off the emptied buildings. And I held her down in the crater she'd made, my fingers spasming with fury and a roar trying to get out around the golden rope around my neck.

"Release me," I croaked.

Her magic tightened.

I sucked in what air I could and pressed her deeper into the broken concrete.

I could hold my breath longer than a regular mundane. I functioned better longer before I blacked out. But the tunnel vision started and the rage wanted me to snap vertebrae, or stomp on her gut, or pull off her spider legs one by one.

What was happening to me?

I let go of the jorōgumo and tried to stumble backward. I tried, but her golden magic still coiled around my neck and I could not breathe.

The tunnel closed down and I swear I heard the jorōgumo chitter.

A bolt of silver magic hit me full in the face. The golden coil around my neck snapped off. Someone yelled in Japanese.

I was on the ground looking up at a magical in a white hat and a blue uniform. He offered me his hand. "You are Victorsson?" he asked.

His natural magic shifted more toward silver than pink and red. He was muscular too, wide at the shoulders and narrow at the waist.

A kami had come to my rescue.

I looked around him. The fire truck had circled around the block and now waited on the other side of the wide crosswalk.

Madame Kobayashi had vanished into the fires.

"Some of us believe the Emperor needs containment," the kami said. "And the Vampire God."

"The kami who came to us believed the opposite," I said as I tried to catch my breath through the heat and the haze.

He moved his hands and a bubble of silver magic cleared the air around us. "There are significantly more of us in Tokyo than there are elves in your town, Mr. Victorsson."

As if numbers alone accounted for the lack of unity.

Thing was, they did. Alfheim's elves argued, and I'd already experienced an international Conclave.

"More here to damage," the kami said.

I breathed in deeply as I stood up. I towered over the first responder kami. He did not seem to notice.

"You will need to deal with whatever contract the Emperor holds on you yourself," he said.

I brushed off my shirt. "I suspected as much." Did I dare tell this kami I might have a weapon that could do the Emperor real damage?

He stepped closer. "We do *not* want fae involvement."

"No one does," I said. We were all probably going to get some, anyway.

He nodded at that. "So getting the Royal Guard woman away from the Vampire God also falls on you."

"Again, I suspected as much."

He glanced around me at the fire truck. "I must return to my duties." He looked up at the Yggdrasil tattoo on the side of my face. "*Hmmm,*" he said.

Then he whistled.

A Guardian dragon manifested behind the kami. This one was smaller than the one outside the Crossroads, and shimmered more toward bright purples and blues than the red of the other one.

"So it's true. You see magic," the kami said.

I nodded.

"Take him where he needs to be," the kami said. Then he bowed before jogging toward the fire truck.

"Wait!" I called. "What's your name?"

The kami only smiled.

The dragon reared up and watched him go.

"Do *you* have a name?" I asked the dragon-shaped magic coiling around me.

救出です, it said in my head the same way Nidhogg had spoken to me, or how Sal made her wishes known.

I had no idea how to translate what the living kami magic said, but at least I knew I could communicate somewhat with it.

I pulled out Wrenn's phone. "I need to find the owner of this device." I swiped my hand over the screen, hoping it hadn't relocked. "The phone had her location, but it lost it when Madame Kobayashi grabbed me."

The Guardian dragon reared up again. It lunged at the phone, coiling its tail around my arm and yanking the device toward its body.

"Hey!" I yelled.

It shook the phone as if trying to get it to activate, which it did. The dragon sniffed at the screen. It frowned. The magic frowned and dropped the phone onto the concrete.

It bounced and landed on my foot. I scooped it up hoping the dragon hadn't broken it.

"Be careful," I said. "This thing is the only way we're going to find Wrenn." I swiped at the screen again. At least the phone survived.

The dragon reared up and turned west like a puppy that had heard a noise outside.

"What?" I asked.

The dragon opened wide its mouth and swallowed me whole.

CHAPTER 25

WRENN GOODFELLOW

The Vampire God grabbed Wrenn's neck. His low-demons darted down his arm at the same time he yanked her forward. They moved.

The suite and the savory smell of noodle takeout vanished. There was nothing then, for a split second. No up. No down. No sense of travel or velocity or acceleration. No gravity, either, and no air. *Vacuum,* her brain started to comprehend, and then it was gone. They manifested again in the real world someplace they hadn't been before.

Plane, her mind registered. Then the Vampire God unceremoniously let go of her neck and she dropped toward the ground. She flailed forward, doing her damnedest to step out of being instantly moved from a chair to a wide-open space with nothing under her backside but concrete.

She'd expected as much, though, when he grabbed her back in the suite. She got a leg out, and even though he'd thrown her off balance, she managed to stand up without falling to the concrete floor.

He raised an eyebrow in clear appreciation of her reflexes—which was bad. The "nicer" she became in his eyes, the more likely that he'd continue with his Bride obsession.

"Where are we?" she spat out. Her mouth tasted like slime. Thankfully flavorless slime, but slick like she had snail snot on her tongue.

The low-demons, she thought. He'd coated her with his pets to bring her inside his teleportation bubble.

She spit onto the concrete. "Frank didn't warn me about the *slime*." She coughed and wiped her mouth.

They were in a hangar. A medium-sized one, from the height of the ceiling. Not big enough for a passenger airliner but big enough for a rich-person's multi-seater, or the small cargo jet under which they'd manifested. A bay door stood open on the side. If the vampire wasn't careful, he'd smack his head on the wing.

He grabbed her by the neck again and turned her around so she faced him. "They like you, my love," he purred in a surprisingly sexy voice. "They want to be close to you, like me."

You have all the predator moves, don't you? she thought. He could purr all he wanted but he was still a vampire. Still a demon. "Rumbly baritones never worked on me, sweetheart," she purred right back at him.

He grinned, which turned into a chuckle. He let go and straightened his tie.

The tie straightening thing was a tell. He seemed to do it when he wanted to be taken seriously.

"It's sundown," he said.

Definitely serious. Vivid evening pinks and oranges flowed in through the hangar's open door and spread across the horizon outside. Smoke from the Tokyo fires shaded much of the remaining light, but some did manage to reflect off the windows of a small airport tower.

Wrenn squinted and shaded her eyes. The sunset hadn't quite disappeared and still managed to throw a long shadow away from the hangar doors. Two shadows, actually, with the line of a second just visible on the tarmac, suggesting a second hangar next door.

A single runway separated the hangars from the terminal and the tower.

The vampire had taken her to what was likely a privately owned airfield outside of Tokyo proper. From what she could see through the doors, buildings surrounded the field, so they were still in a suburban area. The air smelled fresher and clearer than it had at the suite, without any haze. No sirens wailed. Not a lot of damage out here from the earthquake, though smoke drifted up from an area to the east as if a fire had recently been extinguished.

Nothing was marked and the entire airfield shimmered with magic.

"Where are we?" she asked again.

What had he said just before grabbing her? *Time to turn yōkai.* Which meant he'd taken her to where the yōkai were. She had a suspicion that if she could look closely at the plane, or the tables against the walls, she'd find the less obvious marks. "This is a Cen-Ko airfield, isn't it?"

He touched a finger to his nose and winked.

"If you turn them, you'll lose control," she said. A lot of the time master vamps lost thrall control once they fully turned prey, but not always. It depended on power level discrepancies, innate dominant and submissive tendencies, time of the year, a vampire's favorite color.... Mostly there was no way to tell how much control a master retained beyond a well-placed seeing spell or a well educated guess.

And her guess was that after only a month in Japan, he had no real understanding of what he was dealing with here magically—and not just in the many and varied yōkai he had in his thrall, but with the entire kami ecosystem.

If she was lucky, she might be able to exploit his lack of knowledge.

That was, if he didn't do the same to her first. She was a vampire hunter. Not a fae diplomat to the kami. She might know more than Frank, but she knew precious little.

"Yes, yes." He waved his hand as if he'd already thought of and figured out every angle.

Perhaps there was a maintenance cart nearby. Anything that might provide a weapon of some sort. She wouldn't make it to any of the tables against the hangar's far wall. He'd vanish and pop into her path before she made it two steps.

He sidestepped to stay in her field of vision. "That's the point, darling," he said.

He wanted her attention. Needed it, really. "You won't be a god if they don't need you anymore," she said.

"Yes, I will." He smoothed the tie again.

"The kami are going to strip you of your low-demons and stake you to an eastern-facing rock to watch the sunrise. You know that, don't you?" she said. "They may be tolerating you for some unfathomable reason—"

"I annoy Emperor Sutoku," he interrupted.

"—but that will not last," she finished. "You are European. You are vampire. You are the worst gaijin of all the gaijins and their use for you will come to an end."

He shrugged. "Then I salt and burn their earth."

Vampires were never this practical. Never working toward one goal but with an alternative plan in place in case they were foiled and wished to, as he said, salt and burn what they left behind. Destruction left in their wake was always a tantrum. A brief but intense fireball.

He winked. "What we are about to do is going to be the equivalent of a nuke turning the ground to glass."

He was going to magically nuke Tokyo. "You think that's funny?" she yelled. "Poetic? This is why your baobhan sith left you! That's some nose-picking boggart level bull—"

He slapped her across the face. Hard, too, like a punch.

She tasted blood. He'd split her lip. It would heal itself shortly but her head swam and nausea threatened to reinforce for her just how mundane she really was.

"Evangeline did not *leave*. One of your goat-boy Royal Guard captains found us." He inhaled sharply through flared nostrils. "One must not defile one's fae body with low-demons, my love," he rumbled in much the same sexy tone he'd used before. But this time, it had an edge. This time, its daring underpinnings said *death*.

Wrenn pressed her palm against her lips but otherwise did not move. No jerking. No twitching. Just standing stone still inside her shock as she forced herself to process the secrets he'd just said out loud.

The baobhan sith had called herself Evangeline. He'd clearly thought of her as his mate, or as much of a mate as dark creatures can have. And a goat-footed Royal Guard captain had come for her.

A goat-footed captain.

"How did he find you?" she whispered, still standing like a stone. Still with her hand on her lips.

"Her son was not careful."

A *witch*, she thought.

"I turned him."

When she and Frank had appeared in the Aokigahara Forest, when they'd first seen him, they'd both been so in shock they'd frozen. It hadn't lasted long.

A goat-footed captain with enough power to handle a baobhan sith, the Vampire God, their low-demons, and her witch son had killed his mate.

This, though… this made her want to drop to the concrete and curl into a ball.

His eyebrow arched. "Goodfellow, is it? The fae name you took?" He stepped so close their noses almost touched. "And here I thought our dear brother calling himself Victorsson in the grand Old Norse way was the most prostrating example of submissiveness any of us could possibly manifest."

She spit in his face.

He raised his hand to slap her again, but stopped, hand out and palm open.

He grabbed her neck instead.

Again, low-demons. And again, they moved.

CHAPTER 26

WRENN GOODFELLOW

W renn and the Vampire God reappeared inside another—no, *the other*—hangar.

Same concrete floor. Same open door, though at a slightly different angle to the small airport tower that was now fully lit up with exterior lights.

This hangar did not have a cargo plane. This one was full of cargo —large crates, all the same size, all looking as if they would fit two end-to-end inside one of those huge shipping containers they stack on ships at ports. All with metal side panels and wood joins.

Eight in total. Every single crate was wrapped in a tightly woven cocoon of golden magic. To mundane eyes, they would look like just more big boxes of stuff to be shipped off to other parts of the world.

Except they weren't boxes of stuff.

"This is the jorōgumo's work, isn't it?" she asked. How long had the syndicate been keeping yōkai in those crates?

A syndicate run by kelpies that preyed on yōkai. On fae. They'd take low-powered elves, too, if they thought they could get away with it. Maybe a troll or one of the other Nordic creatures, if they could find them.

And the fae royalty and their lying Seconds-in-Command did not care. All this time Robin knew about her vampiric sibling. Even if the goat-footed captain hadn't been Robin, he'd been Royal Guard, so Robin knew. He knew. The son of a bitch *knew*.

The vampire ran his hand over the closest golden shells. "Madame Kobayashi does fine work, does she not?"

He flicked out his arm, snapped his wrist, and the pike appeared in his hand. He thrust it into the cocoon of magic.

Strands of gold popped away from the pike's tip like disengaging magnetic lines.

And it was all *too much*.

She did not panic. Locked up, yes. Blacked out, though only during the worst, most painful flashbacks. Her job was not one where panic was an acceptable response to any circumstance.

Even betrayal.

The vampire might be lying, she thought. *He might be poking at me to trigger the panic.*

"Do you remember Victor's lab?" He pressed the pike tip deep into the jorōgumo's magic. "The electricity in the air? The chemical smell? The unbridled, raw magic?"

She slid her foot back. Would he notice if she ran? Where would she go? How would she get help? She didn't have her phone, and even if she did, who would she call?

"Reminds you of this place, does it not?" The pike broke through the magic cocoon. "Move again and I'll break your arm."

She stood still once again. There might be someone in there who needed her help, anyway.

The entire spell disengaged.

The crate underneath had been painted a bright blood red and a huge happy apple danced on the side. The label was in both Japanese and English, and said only "perishable."

"Do you know why the kami allow this?" he asked.

She had a guess. "To placate the Emperor," she answered. An Emperor for whom the fae had no analog. Mundanes did not ascend the same way in Europe as they did in Japan or any of the other Asian nations. Unless, of course, they turned vampire.

He knocked on the side of the crate. "The excuse is to limit the activity of yōkai harmful to mundanes, but yes, you are correct. They enjoy the 'a little naughtiness allows them to keep their bigger evils under control' excuse as much as those North American elves did with Radu the Handsome."

Though she doubted Radu—Tony Biterson, Frank called him—had eaten any of the locals. The elves would not have allowed it. *Ed* would not have allowed it.

The vampire put his ear against the crate. "*Hmmm...*" he said. Then he slammed the pike under one of the wood side pieces.

The side popped off and dropped to the concrete floor. The inside was as black as the night, and all shadow. Nothing stepped out.

"Look at that." He winked at Wrenn, turned, and slammed his pike into another crate. This one immediately unraveled as if the pike had learned from the first how to destroy the jorōgumo's magic.

This time, the crate was blue and decorated with a dancing pear. The side dropped off and hit the concrete floor. Again, nothing but the depths of shadows inside.

What was happening here? Were there more spells inside? Wrenn saw only the blackness.

The third crate was another red one with an apple. The fourth, orange with a fruit she couldn't identify. The fifth, yellow, with rice. The six and seventh, red again.

He popped the side of the last crate, the one farthest away near the back wall of the hangar. The panel hit the floor with the same resounding snap as the other crates.

This time, something screamed. This time, something flew out of the blackness. Something shadow-shrouded and bat-like.

It was gone, out the open hangar door, in the blink of an eye.

Behind Wrenn, something in the first crate made a slurping sound. She whipped around, arms up, ready to punch.

There were bodies in there. Big bodies, little bodies. Mundane-presenting bodies and bodies that were not, at all, humanoid. Fish bodies. Horse bodies. Body parts.

The fae had an unending array of fairies, goblins, pixies—both helpful and sinister things. But the creatures here? She had no idea.

The vampire twirled the pike, and with one smooth motion, flipped it over his shoulder and attached it to his back with some sort of scabbard spell. He walked toward her. Thankfully, he didn't vanish and reappear, but instead circled her in an ever-tightening spiral.

He stopped behind her, his chest pressed against her back. His hand moved to her shoulder and he gently, lovingly caressed the side of her neck. "Turning you will take extra magicks," he purred in her ear in his sexy voice.

Frank said vampires did not like their blood, including, it seemed, their brother.

He extended his hand out in front of them. "I ravish what I cannot have," he purred, and snapped his fingers.

They roiled out of the crates, an unending stream of creatures, crawling over each other, under each other, hopping, jumping, flying... moving as one large mass of magical beings out of their cells and into the real world.

They pressed her against the Vampire God. She should have pushed back enough to hold her ground. She should have been strong enough not to take what little shelter his massive body offered.

Yet she did. And he rejoiced.

He kissed her cheek and vanished.

"Damn it!" she yelled, and dropped to the concrete floor as the yōkai poured over her.

He stood in the middle of the open hangar door in his impeccable gray suit and his blood red tie, watching her watch him. Yōkai splashed around him as if he were the vortex in the center of their whirlpool—as if he were the jorōgumo on the rock checking this Night Parade for the most vulnerable.

His fangs descended. He yanked a creature out of the teeming coiling magical pool of bodies around him. It shrieked, but didn't much fight. She wondered if it had the strength, after being locked inside the crate.

He bit into its neck but pulled off immediately and gently set it back into the waves of others.

He wasn't feeding. He was doing as he promised. He was turning yōkai into vampires.

He stared directly at her, and clasped his hands behind his back.

All those teeming yōkai bodies shuddered. What had been the waves of silvers, pinks, magentas, reds in their magic became dark and slippery. They lifted up as one—like a yōkai blister on the tarmac—and stiffened magically and physically around their Vampire God.

"*Oh, no,*" Wrenn breathed. He'd turned one, maybe two. And those newly vamped yōkai were turning the others.

He picked up one of his newly-turned yōkai. He held it up, said something to it she could not parse, then pointed out beyond the fence surrounding the airfield.

He was about to release something much worse than a Night Parade onto the surrounding houses. The newly-turned had trouble controlling their urges—magicals and mundanes alike—and who knew what urges were already in that group before he added blood-lust to their menu.

If those vamped yōkai got loose, Tokyo would have a plague on its hands. From the way they roiled and crawled over each other, a plague that would look more like a zombie movie than anything vampiric.

She had no weapons, so she couldn't fight, nor did she have her phone, so she couldn't call for magical help. And she had to keep any mundanes as far from the airfield as possible.

The Vampire God vanished only to reappear farther away but still inside the teeming yōkai. Once again, he reached into the horde, pulled out a victim, and bit into its neck.

"I could use a little help here," she whispered to the universe. "Kami! It's time to get your magical asses down here, or *that,*" she nodded toward the mass of yōkai falling out onto the tarmac, "is going to eat your city!"

Nothing happened.

She shouldn't call on the fae. Not on Robin. Never again on Robin. Not on any of the royals. Not… she looked down at her wrists. Not on the Queen.

A price would be coming due soon enough for the Queen's magic. For her. For Frank. Maybe for the elves of Alfheim.

She looked back at the flood of turned and turning yōkai just as the Vampire God dropped yet another vampiric seed into the churning bodies. She looked down at her wrists one more time.

"I need a little—"

"*Stop!*"

Wrenn turned toward the open maw of the shadow-filled crate.

"No fae," the voice said. Three glowing fox tails manifested in the shadows. They wiggled, straightened, wiggled again, and the shadows inside the crate vanished.

"Lollipop?" Wrenn asked. This kitsune was the right size, with the same number of tails, and was also wearing silver lamé booty shorts.

The kitsune favored her left leg as she slowly walked out of the crate. Dirt marred her face and matted her hair. She wore a Hawaiian print shirt instead of a puffy yellow jacket. Her face was also rounder than Lollipop's and her eyes were larger.

The kitsune hopped on one foot and leaned against the edge of the crate.

This was not Lollipop. "Who are you?" Wrenn offered her hand.

The kitsune hopped down the open side but tripped as she stepped down to the concrete. "Who are *you?*"

Wrenn had her. "Wrenn Goodfellow. I'm Frank's sister."

She looked Wrenn up and down. "Nice to meet you, Frank's Royal Guard sister." Magic manifested around the kitsune's hands. "I will call." She nodded to mass of turning yōkai. "They will remember we're here the moment I do."

They would. "I need a weapon."

The kitsune hopped away from Wrenn. She held out her right hand, then her left. Then she inhaled and flicked her fingers.

Katanas appeared in each of her fists, both pointed downward.

Both with their tips resting on the concrete. Both with red leather crisscrossing their grips. "Fire would be better," she said.

Fire was one of the few things that permanently killed a vampire.

She held out the katana in her right hand. Wrenn took it.

"You're Chip, aren't you?" Wrenn asked.

The kitsune dropped her broken foot to the concrete. She winced but did not falter. Silver, red, and black fox magic coiled around her battered body. "Yes," she said. "Ready?"

"We promised Lollipop that we'd get you back." Wrenn dropped into a fighting stance. "If the Vampire God appears next to us, you vanish. Got it? Leave."

Chip squeezed Wrenn's arm, but did not answer. She raised her voice to the sky and released a gekkering scream worthy of anything Yuki Ito had dropped on Wrenn and Frank.

A wave moved through the horde. They stopped still as if shocked.

Hundreds of icy vampire eyes turned toward Wrenn and Chip.

Chip lifted her katana and dropped into a fighting stance. "They're coming."

He was twenty feet from them, just inside the hangar door, the monster at the center of this, in his impeccable ash suit and his godlike attitude.

"Well, well, well," he said.

Chip yelled at him in Japanese.

He shrugged.

"You call yourself Kyūketsuki no kami yet you haven't learned our language?" Chip yelled. She yelled again in Japanese, but this time around him at the horde behind him.

The yōkai wiggled. The Vampire God laughed.

And Chip grinned. "Three," she said.

The Vampire God frowned.

"Two."

Chip counting meant they had incoming. Wrenn raised her katana and mirrored Chip's fighting stance.

A Guardian dragon appeared directly over the Vampire God,

about ten feet over his head, all wiggly silver, red, blue, and purple magic. It coiled into a ball, then coughed.

"*One!*" Chip yelled with much more glee than someone with a broken foot should be able to muster, and limp-ran into the melee.

The dragon *coughed* like it had a hairball.

And spit Frank directly onto their vampire brother.

CHAPTER 27

FRANK VICTORSSON

I'd been inside magic many times. Usually it's a bubble and either you're inside, or you're outside. Inside might look different than the outside, but it was a space and you could move, unless it was a constraint spell. But most of those were more like being tied up than being inside a construct.

The dragon was all that. I was inside with no understanding of what was happening outside. And I could not move.

Oranges and reds danced around my head. Different shades of silvers ranging from bluish ghost colors to greenish verdigris to champagne squiggled into the warm red tones, then backed out for a count of seven before squiggling back in. The magic contracted with each of the color shifts, squeezing down on me to the point of claustrophobia, then expanding outward when the silver backed out.

I was pretty sure I was seeing and feeling the dragon breathe. I was inside *breathing magic*.

Until I wasn't.

I fell off a cliff once. Not a real cliff, more like the top of a very steep hill, somewhere north of the Arctic Circle. It's all rocks and wind up there when the ice retreats, and I'd only recently left my father behind. I'd tripped and dropped a good fifteen feet off the side of that very steep hill.

Then, I'd landed on gravel. Now, I didn't so much trip and drop. More like was spewed. The dragon hacked up hairball me and spat me onto my brother.

Same effect, though.

He looked up. I thought, *Well, this is it*, and as best I could in midair, hit his head with my shoulder.

I was honestly surprised he didn't just flick his low-demons and vanish. The shock of a dragon dropping me on him held him in place long enough for me to do damage—to him, and to me.

My shoulder hit his head and his neck snapped to the right at an angle that should have killed him. He buckled as my three hundred pounds landed fully on his chest. We both grunted. My shoulder dislocated. But unlike my brother, I had a vampire to cushion my drop to the concrete.

Two, maybe three of his bones snapped. My left knee took way too much torque but managed to not break. I landed on top of him, scrambling to get my good hand up and pressing his face into the concrete, or my good knee in his gut. Anything to hold him down long enough to figure out how to kill him.

Which I couldn't. I needed fire, or a weapon to destroy his heart, and with only one good arm, I didn't have the strength to take off his head.

"Frank! Roll!"

I saw the flash out of the corner of my eye and rolled off my vampire brother just as a katana slashed down toward his throat.

He raised his arm to protect his face and vanished. The katana hit concrete and the swinging kitsune landed in my lap.

"Chip?" I asked. "You're alive!"

She patted my cheek. "Missed you too, handsome," she said.

Wrenn ran up. "About time you showed up." She held her katana ready. "He'll be back."

He would. I popped my shoulder back into its socket. White hot pain seared up my neck. I groaned but I knew it was temporary. I'd have enough functionality to fight soon and full functionality by morning.

Chip pushed at something on the concrete with her foot. "Yuck."

She'd missed his throat but she'd gotten his hand. Low-demons crawled on it like worms. It twitched.

Chip kicked it away into... a horde. Shadows. Hissing slippery black things jittering and jabbing like a big pile of zombies.

I hadn't noticed. I'd been busy falling on my brother. But I noticed now. "What..." I pointed.

"He freed the captive yōkai so he could turn them," Wrenn said.

They were no more than twenty feet away, outside what looked to be an airplane hangar, on tarmac.

"Why aren't they attacking?" Chip rolled off me, carefully favoring her other foot.

I looked at Wrenn. She looked at me.

"Vamp-proof blood has its advantages," she said.

Lollipop suddenly appeared pretty much on top of me, where Chip had been moments before. She squeaked and threw herself at Chip.

They hugged. Chip kissed Lollipop's forehead. Then she pointed at the horde.

Lollipop vanished only to reappear on the edge of the horde, inside the roiling yōkai. She wrapped her arms around a small creature I did not recognize.

They both vanished.

Chip raised her katana. "We will remove the uninfected."

Then she, too, vanished.

Wrenn offered her hand. "Look," she nodded at the horde.

Several kitsune popped in and out of the group. Some were dressed in modern gear like Chip and Lollipop. Some looked to be in traditional Japanese grab. I counted three tails, and six, and one eight. They herded the infected, and they grabbed their fellow magicals who had not yet been infected, vanishing with them in their arms.

Two were in all white.

The kami might not want to step in, but the kitsune had this. Would they stop the Emperor from trafficking Japan's low powered magicals? Would I ever truly be free of whatever contract the Emperor thought he'd purchased? I had no idea.

Brother was my priority now. "We need to—"

At this point, I shouldn't have been surprised when a magical dropped out of nowhere onto my back. I should expect a chokehold, kicks, maybe even screaming in my ear.

What I didn't expect was the electricity, and *who* landed on my back this time.

He had no tongue with which to yell at me, but he could growl. Every cell in my body jolted. Wrenn's eyes rounded in shock.

Then there was yet another telltale puff of air as a teleportation displacement happened, this one not on my back, but between Wrenn and me.

Brother snorted when he realized the Emperor was about to bite off my ear. His neck still bulged where I'd broken it, and he only had one hand, but he was very much still the Vampire God. And he was incensed.

His one hand shot out and grabbed Wrenn by her katana-holding wrist. He couldn't grab me, so he did the one thing he could: He kissed me.

And we all moved.

CHAPTER 28

Our brother had control. Not the Emperor. Not Wrenn. Certainly not me. The Vampire God decided where we landed.

Should he be blamed for his evil? He was a vampire. At his core, he was all the demons cast off by the living. All those little needs to suck the joy, the love, the life from others. Because those needs were what Dracula found in his Land of the Dead pit. The raging human biological imperative to hold grudges.

Some were righteous, of course, and probably did not become demons. Maybe. I'd never met an angel, so I did not know. Most were ugly, small, petty, vicious, and utterly motivated by entitled anger at perceived slights—at the inability of primates to just let it go.

So that was our brother: The Vampire God, the King of Petty Slights, the Monarch of Whining, the Narcissist in Charge... the child who was so, so very much like our father.

They raged against the world, my brother and my father. They coiled themselves into something tight and horrific and they inflicted outward because the inside needed to be filled.

Vampires. How did you deal with them? The person had a right to exist—to grow and change—but the anger did not. The trick was figuring out if you were dealing with a person or a demon.

Or more demon than person.

We manifested on a rough-hewn wooden floor under an open skylight. A rod extended from the side of a massive wood-and-metal table, through the hole, and into the night beyond. Cloudy jars lined shelves, which lined the walls. A threshold at one end led into a shadowed room beyond, and other than the skylight, was the only exit.

We were in a lab. No, in *the* lab.

Brother tossed Wrenn toward the threshold. "You *ran!*" he roared.

He pushed me—and the Emperor, who was still on my back—toward the table.

The Emperor let go. Momentum carried him, though, and he smashed into one of the jar-filled shelves.

Brother pointed at him with his one still-connected hand. "Why are *you* here?" he roared. "You escaped The Land of the Dead but we are *not the same!*"

Manifestly, no, they were not the same. But fundamentally? They were both demons. The Emperor was a demon made of the spun-up slights of a single man and Brother was a walking graveyard of neediness.

The Emperor grabbed the metal leg of the massive table. Power crackled.

Lightning hit the rod.

The entire room turned bright white. I ducked. Wrenn dropped into a ball. Her katana clattered across the floor.

Brother faced the blinding light blasting off the rod. He pointed at the Emperor. "You think we are here because of a *storm?*" He tapped his shoulder with his sliced-off wrist. "We are here because of *gods!*"

Not his shoulder. The place where I'd stabbed him with the wood dagger. The one Akeyla set on fire and caused him to disassociate.

He whipped around and pointed at me. "You know my love. I tried to give you that love in the forest and in the city, but you are *afraid of me.* You bested Dracula. You were the one with the strength to stand at my side as I make this world mine. My brother. My family. We were to be Zeus and Hades." He pointed at Wrenn. "She was to be our Persephone!"

Wrenn inched toward her katana. Her skin had paled to sheet white, and the pupils of her eyes were all I could see, but she kept her wits. She moved toward the weapon.

I thrust my chin at Brother, more to keep his attention than in belligerence. "Wrong pantheon," I said.

He laughed and looked at the wrist of his missing hand. "Wasn't it Tyr who stuck his hand into the mouth of a wolf? Or in this case, a fox."

I glanced at Wrenn just as she wrapped her hand around the katana's handle.

Brother whipped around. "You chose *me* to haunt you all this time?" He inhaled deeply as if he smelled the freshest field of violets anywhere. "Oh, I know all about the Heartway. *She* was fae!"

She? The fae woman in the burning house. "Your mate?" I asked.

He turned back to me. "Mate?" he asked, as if the thought of a mate had never occurred to him. But it had. I saw it in his eyes. He thought about it all the time when he was this personality. And it hurt.

There was a thread here, between his hope that I was his equal, to having experienced such a life with the fae who had been his mate.

He'd wanted Wrenn for that role. That, too, was clear on his face. But she'd already rejected him. I had, as well. Three times, now. Yet he persisted. With her as well, I guess. Persisted because we represented something he remembered having, even if it hadn't been true.

Or maybe it had been. I'd only seen the end.

And here we were, the two living family members who could soothe his ragings. Who were supposed to do the soothing because he could not—*would* not—do it for himself.

Brother roared at the sky and with one grand wave of his remaining hand, snatched the Emperor off the floor. "Kami magic *lingers.*" His fangs descended. "I will transcend my godhood—"

Wrenn slammed the katana upward, through his spine, and into his heart.

He looked down at the kitsune metal poking out of his chest. He snorted and looked over his shoulder at Wrenn. "You're next," he said.

The silent onryō of Japanese entitled grudges grinned. And the vengeful ghost of Emperor Sutoku latched onto the protruding metal point of a magical katana.

Electricity flared around them like a pale halo. Brother's body stiffened. The Emperor chuckled. And something happened that should not have happened. But we were in the Heartway, and the Emperor was not the only vengeful spirit here.

Wrenn had told me about her flashbacks. About how she'd see the lab, and she'd see Brother rip Victor's head from his body.

That Brother manifested around the Brother we'd brought here. They overlaid each other like ghosts on an old-time television screen, except the ghost that belonged here had a script, where the interloper did not.

This time, instead of biting into Victor, the onryō of Brother bit into the onryō Emperor Sutoku. I counted one, two, three... The empty corpse of a spirit dropped to the floor.

"No, no, *no*..." Wrenn muttered. She stood perfectly still, shocked frozen. As was our Brother. The real one, not the ghost.

The moment he came out of his shock, he would kill her. Right here, right in front of me. I was about to lose my just-found sister to a scourge who haunted us both.

Except... I did have a weapon.

"Look up," I said.

Wrenn, frozen as she was, did not move. Brother did, though. He looked up, as I had asked him to do.

The magic in those roots ate the souls of the wrathful and the evil. All the souls who washed up on Hel's Corpse Shore.

"I told you. Wrong pantheon," I said.

Obsidian eyes glared down at both versions of Brother, and obsidian teeth snapped. *Jurisdiction?* it asked.

I was not kami, nor was I elf. But I was the man accepted by the World Tree. "He is my brother," I answered.

Understood, the dragon answered.

I didn't understand, even if I knew it was enough. There was no other way to free the world of him. And to free him from his pain.

Wrath tightened Brother's face. He knew what was coming. He was about to be consumed by the dragon who cleaned out the universe's debris. "I am the Vampire God—"

Nidhogg dropped down. And Nidhogg swallowed Brother whole.

They disappeared into the coiling roots of the universe. And then those roots, like Brother and the dragon, vanished.

"Thank you, Nidhogg," I whispered.

Wrenn gasped and reached out. "What..."

I offered my arm. "The World Tree likes me," I said.

She blinked. "Is he... they..."

"Gone to the Corpse Shore," I said. "Hel does not give up her dead. He will not be coming back." We'd vanquished Brother. "We need to get out of here."

She blinked a few more times, still clearly as stunned as I was. "Frank." She pointed at the floor.

He'd left behind the pike. The one Dracula had fashioned from my elven protection spells. Did I dare pick it up? Touch it in any way? That thing had almost killed me.

Wrenn looked at my face, then at the pike, then back at me. Her expression settled into the practical and determined cop face.

She picked it up off the floor. "I think this is yours," she said.

"Yeah," I said. I didn't move to take it. I stared at it instead. "I don't know what to do with it."

"Give it to the elves," she said.

Handing it over to Arne seemed the wisest choice. I didn't want it at the cottage. "Oh," I patted at my pockets. "I have your phone." I pulled it out. "Can you get us out of here?"

She dropped two tokens into her palms and handed one to me as she took the phone. "I think so." She unlocked the device. "There are no Heartway stops in Japan." She held it out. "Hold on. I think we're going to need to—"

CHAPTER 29

I became aware of the bar stool under my backside. A bar manifested in front of me, and a mirror behind it. Bottles of liquor with labels I could not read lined the mirror. A tap sat an arm's length to my right, and a bowl of peanuts to my left. Above, a wood overhang held goblets, horns, wine and shot glasses, mugs—just about anything anyone had used at any time to hold fermented or distilled beverages.

Sheets of vermillion, silver, and pink magic rippled between the mirror and the bar. They shimmered and coiled, and coalesced into a bartender.

He was nondescript with the kind of short haircut that made his black hair fluff up and flop over on the top of his head. His eyes, cheeks, and lips all had a sense of angles to them, as if he was more graphically designed than born a person, and the inverted triangle of his torso seemed exaggerated, though not so much that it seemed odd.

Wrenn, next to me on her own stool, set the pike on the bar. "—transition through a kami gate," she finished.

The bartender wiped down a glass with a bar towel before setting it down in front of me. "Glad I could help you two find each other." He did the same for Wrenn.

"You're the dragon?" I asked.

He tossed me an exasperated look and poured a finger of a beautiful silver liquid into my glass. The scents of honey and fresh spring cherry blossoms rose from the liquor. I inhaled, but did not pick up the glass.

Wrenn did pick up hers, and inhaled deeply. "I think my attempts to move in the Heartway were once again hijacked," she said. She set down the glass and swiped at her phone's screen.

The bartender nodded toward Wrenn's phone. "Orders came down to bring you two up to the restaurant." He set another wiped-down glass at the empty stool on my other side. "For a drink before you left our land."

I turned around, expecting to see the restaurant and what I hoped would be an army of kami behind me.

All I saw was shadows and fog.

This Crossroads wanted me to see less of its workings than the Vegas one had. I looked back at bartending dragon man.

I'd been at this bar before. Or one like it. The entire structure—the bar, the stools, the overhang, the set-in mirror in the back—the whole thing had been carved from one massive dark piece of wood.

One tree. One world. I splayed my fingers across the bar's glossy surface. *Leave her alone*, I thought. No one carved the World Tree. I would snap the neck of any man or god who threatened Creation herself.

The bartender nodded approvingly. He leaned over the bar. "All trees drop branches." He stepped back. "The kami would like a word."

A man manifested on the empty stool. Innate silver and pink magic danced along his skin. He looked strong, with wide shoulders and a muscular body. Like the bartender, he wore his hair shaved up on the sides, but shorter on the top. He also wore nondescript clothes —a white button-down shirt and khakis—and like Arne Odinsson, could have walked unnoticed anywhere in the world in this guise.

I doubted I'd get to see his full kami form.

"You're an Inari aspect, correct?" I asked. Or I hoped. "You're in charge around here?"

His face stayed flat for a beat as if he needed a second to figure out how to distort his answer to most benefit his side, then a crooked grin appeared on his face. "Yes," he said.

He was not in charge. I suspected he represented the Inari aspect who *was* in charge, but it wasn't this kami.

Hopefully, he was the local Magnus. "We dealt with the Vampire God and your Emperor Sutoku," I said.

The Inari aspect tapped the bar and motioned to the bartender, who filled the glass he'd set down before the kami appeared. The bartender poured a finger of the silver liquor, which the kami threw back in one gulp.

I leaned against the smooth wood of the bar and rubbed my face.

Wrenn looked around me. "We apologize if we messed up diplomatic protocols," she said. "We were tossed here by a World Spirit."

The kami tapped the bar and pointed at the glass, which the bartender immediately filled. He swirled the glass but did not drink. "You two have caused us a level of trouble we have worked for centuries to avoid." He downed his drink. "The Emperor never stays dead."

"I'm sorry to hear that," I said. "It is not a magical problem I would wish on anyone." It wasn't. "Did you clean up his mess?"

"The earthquake *you* incited? The loss of so many of our magicals to a vampire *you* angered?" This Inari aspect was as exasperating as a kitsune. "Yes." The kami sipped at the liquid. He continued to watch me as if he expected I'd figure out whatever it was I needed to figure. I half expected a test when we were done.

This time, I was the one who did not respond.

"Vampires always escalate, do they not?" he finally asked. Again with the patronizing questions and the high school social studies teacher demeanor.

They did. Every demon, vampire, evil spirit, smart-mouthed kelpie, or villain. If they didn't escalate, they wouldn't need to be put down. It wasn't trajectory, or even velocity. We all rode the same arrow of time. It was acceleration that snapped necks and caused harm.

"Which is why they must be dealt with," Wrenn said.

The kami sniffed. "*Channeled.*"

Why was this kami being so arrogant? And paternalistic. "The kelpie and a jorōgumo were using a Night Parade as a meat market," I said.

The bartender chuckled.

The Inari aspect grinned. "That was not a Night Parade."

Not the point, I thought. "Come to Minnesota and we'll see how well you differentiate between various elven happenings."

Wrenn touched my arm.

I was being short with a kami. I shouldn't be, for diplomacy, but something told me to hold my ground.

Holding one's ground was the best way to handle an elf, too.

The Inari aspect smiled. "I like you."

"Good to know." I just wanted to go home.

To Ellie. I looked down at my hands just as my little blue puppies decided it was safe to come out of hiding. They stretched and flicked around, but did not flare upward. Thankfully, they stayed next to my skin.

The kami laughed. "Isn't it *you betcha*, or some such phrasing?"

I turned my body square to his and drew myself up to my full height without answering. I had no desire to play this game. I just wanted to *go home*.

Behind the bar, the dragon-in-human-form leaned against the back wall, the mirror, and all the shelves of liquor. He seemed quite entertained by me holding my own with an Inari aspect, and I was beginning to wonder who was really the most powerful magical here.

The kami quickly sobered. His face shifted from jovial to stern with just the change in tension with which he held the muscles around his eyes. "Tell your king that we will no longer tolerate elves or any elf-adjacent magicals in Japan, Mr. Victorsson." He tapped his glass. "Or New Zealand."

I glanced at Wrenn. Like me, she seemed confused.

"And you, Ms. Goodfellow," the kami said. "Tell your Guard that we will no longer tolerate fae in Japan. *Any* fae. Am I clear?" He suddenly took a few peanuts from the bowl and tossed them into his mouth.

"Good to know," she said in a pitch-perfect imitation of my tone.

The bartender looked at the Inari aspect, then back at us, then at the Inari aspect again as if as surprised by kami's proclamation as we were.

I knew he did not agree. He and the kami firefighter had sent me to deal with Brother, which meant factions, or more likely, the kami equivalent of dueling enclaves.

None of which mattered to me anymore. I'd leave the diplomacy to the elves.

The kami placed his hands on his knees, elbows out to his side, and straightened his back as if he was about to launch into a wrestling hold. "Ask your elves how they handle their Loki elves."

There it was again, that little nip at the back of my mind about how I did not understand the true workings of magic. I had my model —I saw sheets of power and I lived in a town full of magicals—but my corner of the magical universe was just that. A corner.

Or, more precisely, I'd learned what I'd needed to learn to operate in a magical world—just enough to be able to calculate Newtonian trajectories and acceleration. I didn't understand relativity, special or general.

That was reserved for bigger political players than I.

And instead of helping—instead of explaining what I needed to know—they talked up Loki elves.

The Inari aspect tapped his glass and motioned to the bartender. The barkeep shook his head and reached into the shelves. He poured a new liquor, this one a mesmerizing, shimmering white, like snow, or rice, or the clothes of Yuki Ito.

The bartender shrugged. "I told you this was a mistake," he said to the kami.

"Mistake?" I asked.

The kami downed the white liquor, then flipped the glass and slammed it down onto the bar. "Perhaps you should consider your allegiances, paladin." He waved to the bartender. "This conversation is over."

He snapped his fingers and, hopefully for the final time, we moved.

CHAPTER 30

I sucked in restaurant air. Real restaurant air—dry, filtered yet fortified with the scent of cooking meat and garlic cheesy bread. A Prince song boomed out of overhead speakers. Bright midmorning sun streamed through the "Now open for takeout" painted backward across big dining room windows and made me squint.

Wrenn's satchel sat on the table next to her hip along with my cell phone. My phone, which I'd left at Chihiro's.

We were in Raven's Gaze. Home. In Alfheim.

Raven stood about ten feet away, in the shadows, watching us. She'd changed out of her usual white t-shirt and was wearing an "Alfheim Gossiping Squirrels" Sprout League t-shirt under her motorcycle jacket.

She looked down at the Ratatoskr-with-a-bat logo on her chest. "Like it? The baby Alpha gave it to me."

"You talked to Jax?" I asked. She hadn't been talking to anyone as far as I knew. Now she was talking to the kids?

Target, I thought, and not just Sophia.

"He tagged along when his mommy and daddy came by to have a chat." She smoothed the shirt. "The wolves here are brave and smart," she said offhandedly. "Nice of the kid to offer up this tuft of fur."

Wrenn tossed me a *What now?* look.

Raven grinned and extended her hand. "Welcome back," she said as she walked to Wrenn. "I'll take that."

She reached for the pike.

Wrenn did not give it up. "It belongs to Frank," she said.

Raven dropped her hand to her side. "Yes, it does." She turned toward me. "You have options. You can try to give it to one of your Odin elves. They won't take it. Remember how they reacted to that notebook and the dagger? Same principle."

I had no idea what "principle" she was referring to, though I suspected she was correct in her description of how the elves would react to an artifact made out of corrupted elven enchantments.

"You can take it to your sweetie," Raven said. "Ask her to put it with those bridles." She looked directly at Wrenn. "Not a good idea."

Wrenn dropped into full cop stance but did not take the bait.

Raven extended her hand again. "Or you can give it to me." She grinned. "It's not like you can keep it safely stowed in your garage."

With Rose's notebook, I thought. The notebook that had disappeared.

I swiped my phone off the table.

"The cute kitsune with the lollipop dropped that off," Raven said. "She had a new translator with her. A seven-tail dressed all in white." She fanned out her fingers, five on one hand and two on the other. "Oh!" She reached into the pocket of her jeans. "They left this for you, my dear."

She held out a flip phone to Wrenn. "Something about law enforcement to law enforcement, in case we all have a syndicate problem again."

Wrenn looked down at the phone. She nodded once and took it from Raven.

She still did not hand over the pike.

Raven sighed. "Your promises have been fully discharged," she said to me.

She meant the contract Emperor Sutoku purchased off of the Las Vegas Wolf. "I didn't deliver Brother," I said.

"Didn't you?" She shrugged. "The version of the Emperor who purchased the contract is also dead, so there's that."

Could it be so simple? "Is that why you sent us to Japan? To force an end to the promise-of-help contract stupidity I did not consent to in the first place?" Not to stop the syndicate, or even to "deliver" Brother permanently from the world. Because this had to come back to Raven somehow.

She gave me an adult version of Akeyla's "dumbest uncle" look. Then she extended her hand again. "Give me the pike."

The pike.

My recalcitrant gut said to say *No!* but I knew better than to anger a World Spirit. "You could have told us before you tossed us into Japan that you wanted Dracula's pike," I said instead.

She scoffed. "And chance that those imperialistic kami bastards would figure out exactly what that mountain of fangy nastiness used to dig into their backyard?" She held up her hands as if giving up at the same time she glanced at Wrenn.

Her meaning was clear: Anything capable of digging into reality needed to stay out of kami hands. And fae. And elven.

Wrenn looked down at the gray rod in her hand, then up at me.

What was I supposed to do? Force it onto the elves? Put Ellie at risk by asking her to put it with the bridles, as Raven suggested?

No risking Ellie. Not now. Not ever.

My mate magic flared around me as if I stood inside a blue flame. "I need to go home, Raven," I said.

Raven extended her hand again.

I nodded to Wrenn.

My sister sighed. She held out the pike to Raven. "Check it for low-demons," she said.

Nothing squirmed on its surface. I suspected that if it'd had a few low-demons left on it, the kami had cleaned them off before they hijacked us to their Crossroads. "It's inert," I said.

Raven gingerly took the pike. She spun it around like a baton and peered at its tip. "I will keep it safe."

She would. She'd also use it, of that I was sure.

Wrenn picked up her satchel. "I'd like to go home. Take a shower." She nodded toward me. "We can talk later. I need to check in with the Guard."

Going home was all I wanted, too. "Yeah," I said. We had a lot to discuss about the Queen's magic, what happened with Brother, and what it all meant, especially Nidhogg.

Ellie first.

Raven pointed out the window at the parking lot. "Your ride to Paul Bunyan is here."

I looked through the window just as Arne and Dag exited Arne's sedan. So Raven wasn't going to snap her fingers and send Wrenn back to Oberon's Castle.

"Great," Wrenn said.

Outside, Mark Ellis jogged up to Arne.

Raven pushed us toward the door. "The wolves have had the restaurant under twenty-four-hour surveillance since I sent you two on your excursion, on top of all the elven alarm spells." She rolled her eyes. "Go on."

We both looked out the window just as Mark pointed at the restaurant.

I waved. Behind me, a flutter and a small gust of wind.

I didn't have to look to know Raven had just vanished.

Wrenn shouldered her satchel. "I won't ask you to take me." She waved at my mate magic.

"Thank you." I was going to lose what little control I'd managed with Raven the moment we opened that door. "I'm going to move right on past them, you know," I said.

She chuckled and opened the door and...

My mate magic bolted outside like the puppies it was. It yipped and wagged its tail and ran in circles because it was home.

Arne said something to me. "Later," I answered.

Mark grinned like a werewolf sensing mate magic. Dag patted my arm as I walked by. Wrenn waved goodbye.

Bloodyhood was still parked where I'd left it, at the back of the parking lot, next to Mark's sedan. And I somehow managed to call

Ellie. Ten minutes later, I pulled in among the trees down the road from my place, as close to the cottage I as could get my truck.

Ellie burst out through the branches just as I opened Bloodyhood's door. "Frank!" she said as she jumped into my arms.

All I knew was the blissful wonder of happy mate magic. All I saw was Ellie.

"You're home!" she said.

Yes. Yes I was.

EPILOGUE ONE

Cen-Ko Airfield, Tokyo Prefecture, Japan...

A nthea the vampire sat at the peak of the hangar's roof, at the flat top of the curve directly over the center of the grand doors. She had no place to hide from the rising sun up here. No place at all, really, since this was a private airfield and not public, and no one was around to invite her into any of the buildings.

Still, she had a good twenty minutes. Her black, black dress would take her somewhere safe before the sun became an actual problem, anyway.

She'd followed her love to this place, though he'd ceased to be her love after they'd emerged from under the world. When he'd changed. Started to change. Then he'd changed again.

She did not like change.

"Valkyries must be able to handle change," she muttered. Her dress *was* change, but not an aspect of it like the elves and kami were aspects of gods. Her dress was more like that onryō Emperor who simply *was*. The dress was a taker of life, and love, and of things in its way. It caused hungers and voids when it deleted. Famines, really.

But it, like her, was trying to be good. Balance was the key, like how she sat now with her feet over the edge of a hangar roof. She might fall. She might not. The thrill came from threading the needle.

A lot had changed down below.

Her love—the monster who carried her love—had made victims of the already victimized when he turned those poor yōkai.

If he had been her love, he would not have done what he did. He would have found the balance.

Kitsune came. Not ones like the one the monster had eaten. These kitsune knew how to fight. By her estimate, they'd saved at least half of the other magicals who had been locked in those crates. But from the yelling and the magic being thrown around by the five full-fledged kami god aspects currently cleaning up the mess, their actions had only added to the chaos.

She hummed a little and watched a seven-tailed kitsune in white argue with an Inari aspect. "Someone's got a backbone," she said. She liked magicals with backbones. They were fun to play with. And kitsune were special. Not many magicals had international mundane buy-in. Like werewolves and vampires, they were one of the world's rising magical groups.

She could, if her dress were willing to do so, help the kitsune in white by taking care of the kami onryō problem for good. Such permanent magic, though, came with a great price, and she was unsure if these kami would be willing to pay it. She'd already wielded it once, to test and to learn, and the price had been great. Her love was gone now. She would never see him again, even if that sneaky jorōgumo had absconded with his hand.

Such was the price she paid for facilitating the meeting of the Norse aspect of her dress, the dragon *Níðhöggr*, and the Son of Wood and Rage.

"Perhaps we should go to Spain," she said to the dress. Walk the Rioja Valley where her love once lived. "To the lands of Castilla."

No, the dress whispered. If she were to become a valkyrie, she needed to gather her sisters. They were no longer harbingers, and even though they destroyed, they also built. Without them, without the circuits they facilitated, nothing in the universe would give enough of a damn to put up a fight against their fourth.

"We know where red sister is," she muttered.

Yes, the dress answered. The American desert. She would come when called. The Son of Wood and Rage would bring back their white sister.

The fourth, of course, had been eaten by the Norse dragon.

Her love. Her sister. Her brother. "I'm sorry," she said. They were supposed to be four, even if their fourth was the most ubiquitous.

The black obsidian gloss of her dress shimmered with all the colors of the universe, as if the magic had eaten reality. She was not to worry. Their fourth would find them again.

Death always did.

THE CASTILIAN

A SPECIAL SHORT STORY

CHAPTER 1

The Rioja Region of Castile, Spain, December, 1491…

The cold sand and silt loam working between Cristoval Armand
Martinez's toes was not his land, nor was the gnarled grapevine
under his equally naked fingers his crop. The heavy wool cloak over
his shoulders belonged to the battalions of the army he served. The
boots sitting empty next to his winter-chilled feet were, like the rest
of his well-worn fighting leathers, tokens held by men whose lives
were not their own.

He, like the land, belonged to the Crown of Castile.

He stared down at his naked feet as he wiggled his toes into the
cold dirt and salty dust under the vine. The air was the same as he
remembered it—thinner up the side of the mountain but not so thin it
made him hunger for each breath. The sky gleamed the brighter blue
that mountain skies always held, as if the dome of Heaven had chosen
to edge toward the brilliant violets of eternity, but the glowing
wonder of the sun thinned the color the way the elevation thinned
the air.

Grapes loved these hills, and he knew the vine next to his cold-pricked toes intimately. Fifteen years past, he had planted it, and the others like it, in a curved row along the side of this particular foothill above the Oja River. The vines had grown wide along their posts before the frigid wind rolling off the mountains sent them into dormancy. Below, the river rumbled by in gray winter sluggishness. Above, the Obarenes Mountains held tight to the dirty browns of winter.

Yet this place, and his memories of it, were not his. Like the rich vino pressed from the grapes of this field, he had been rendered out of this land and sold away. For all he knew, his daughter might still hold this field. He'd left before she'd been given a name.

She had been beautiful, his little bean of a child. He had meant the vines to someday be part of her dowry. Then he went to war.

First the War of Castilian Succession, and the famine of the soul that followed when his Queen, Isabella, took the whiny Aragonian into her bed. Then came Granada, and what the Crown demanded be the end of the *Reconquista*.

He had ridden into war. Spilled blood not his own, even from his own wounds. And splinters of his immortal soul pierced the veil to pin each corpse to its death place.

A Muslim near Cordoba. A Jew in Navarre. An entire battalion under the castled skies of Castile. His soul pinned the lands of the Crown, for the Crown. And he knew—not believed, not pretended, but *knew*—he should carry something for his works. Perhaps his lands again. But more importantly, something other than the hollowness.

Hollow was the puppet of the Crown. Hollow was its beast. Hollow was the place inside his being where his immortal soul should rest.

He was less than a man now. Only men came home to these hills and their rivers. To the warm summer sun and the vivid blue skies. To the fields and vineyards and the music of the cities and villages. He felt the truth in his chest every morning, the hollowness and the stiffness and the flat nothingness that would not be *him* if he had his soul.

The Church offered absolution for his sins. It had never been enough. His home could not have a monster such as him on its lands. Terror followed hollow men, and he had a daughter here, somewhere.

A new wind rolled between the posts and the vines, this one strong enough to cause a sharp pain to his naked toes. He sighed, wondering if such sensations meant that he wasn't the monster he knew himself to be. He should fight those sensations the way he fought for the Crown.

He was not his duty. The Queen's decree was.

He would do his duty and deliver the mercenary to the battles surrounding Granada. Then he would await his puppeteer's next pulls.

A gust rolled out of the mountains. It pressed him forward as it coiled around his body, wrapping strands of his black hair around his face and whistling by his ears. He let it push against his back, and leaned away from the vines and toward rocky banks of the Oja below. Then the gust was gone, the last of his heat with it, and a shiver raked from his core out to his uncovered fingers and toes.

The Scot—the mercenary to be delivered—stood two paces away breathing warmth onto his hands. "Bracin' breeze ye have here, Castilian," he said. He watched Cristoval for a reaction, and when he did not get one, he sniffed with one nostril in a way that lifted only one half of his face.

The gales and gusts coming down off the Obarenes were not breezes. They were *wrong*, even on the shortest day of the year. Even without a soul, Cristoval understood their wrongness. But a Scot would not understand. For him, such frozen howlings were normal.

The Scot called himself a *guardabosque* and had refused to give his true name—he said for everyone's safety—and had settled not on *neach-raoin*, the Gaelic version of his occupation, but on the English term "Ranger."

Cristoval did not understand the joke, nor did he care to. He only wanted access to the man's sword and the war stallions that came with him.

Ranger was shorter than Cristoval, though they carried the same width to their shoulders. The Scot's hair was as black as his own, with a distinctive wave, though the Scot's carried hints of greens and grays instead of the underlying warm golds and reds of Cristoval's. The Scot watched the world with sea green eyes, unlike Cristoval's own deep leather brown. But mostly it was the Scot's black clothing, and the black bridle and saddle worn by his stallions, that set him apart.

Today, with the cold, Ranger wore black britches tucked into his massive black war boots, though he preferred his kilt. His tunic and cloak were the same black as his hair. The only color on his person was the sea green metal-and-glass stallion brooch pinning his cloak to his shoulder.

"Get on wi' yer festival o' sobs, Castilian," Ranger said in a low, slow growl. His eyes narrowed also, and his neck tensed.

He was bored, and as Cristoval had seen already on English shores, a bored Ranger meant dark times for the local villagers.

The Scot's blackened soul would cast a useful terror onto the people of Granada. Cristoval was not going to release that onto the village down the river, or onto Calahorra, their goal for tonight's lodgings.

Calahorra—the town which had, along with many silver pieces, been part of the deal to get the Scot to leave the shores of his lake.

Cristoval had sailed north to recruit mercenaries for the final war of the *Reconquista*, to find the fabled killers who lived along the shores of Scotland's deepest, darkest lakes. Men described in ways that sent shivers down Cristoval's back even though he understood nothing of the words spoken.

Ranger had found *him* shortly after he had ventured into Scotland's lake country—the man had walked out of a dark misty night, dressed in his black kilt, with his three equally black war stallions behind him. Ranger had sniffed like a wolf at Cristoval's face, and cocked an eyebrow. "I smell Vascone on ye. An' Roman. *Hmmm....*" he'd said, speaking names and words for ancients a Scot should not know about. Names and words for ancients the Church refused to acknowledge but Cristoval's people remembered. "Ye'll take me t' Calahorra."

The city sat on the northwestern side of La Rioja. There had been blood spilled in Calahorra by the ancients of whom Ranger spoke. War had come, then diseases. Talk of cannibalism still swirled in the local tales even after all the centuries. And the Scot wanted to tour the location like a vacationing royal before he rode into an equally gruesome battle.

Cristoval had watched Ranger dispatch a group of English on the coast not far from their ship to Castilla. The Scot had inhaled the smell of burning and bleeding flesh as if it were the sweetest of perfumes. And not once had he shown mercy to the captive women.

Cristoval should have recoiled at Ranger's macabre fetishes and gleeful murders. Part of him that wasn't fully hollow had. But his body was not his own. He had his duties.

Men such as Ranger, as grotesque as they were, ended battles quickly. They were as wrong as the cold rolling down onto Cristoval's vines. As wrong as Cristoval's acceptance of Ranger's way. But Ranger was also the edge the Crown of Castile would use to slice Granada into edible morsels. So Cristoval had made his deal, and then immediately brought the Scot and his three massive black war stallions across to Castilla.

The stop in his home lands for this little moment of what? Pity? Mournfulness for what he had lost? Like his lack of recoil, Cristoval's hollowness swallowed all responses.

The largest of Ranger's stallions snorted. Breath curled from his muzzle. He tossed his big head and pawed at the ground as if he was the bored one, not his rider.

The three beasts stood in semicircle behind Ranger. They were all as black as their rider's adornments, except for the silver in their bridles and the strange, ghostly green of their eyes.

They had the same color eyes, the man and the beasts, even though Cristoval knew such things were not possible. "A trick o' the sun," Ranger had said on the ship as they crossed to Castilla, and had waved off the question.

Cristoval curled his toes into the loam one last time and looked up at the blue sky.

"Ye made a deal, Castilian," Ranger growled.

Cristoval shook the dirt from his toes. Slowly, he retrieved a stocking from the interior of his boot. The farther from his lake, the testier the Scot—and the stallions, none of which Cristoval rode —became.

This, he allowed his hollowness to swallow.

"I did," he said as he settled his foot into his boot. The cold had left him with pins and needles along his heel, but he'd dealt with worse. This, at least, said he lived.

Ranger sniffed at the air the same way he'd sniffed at Cristoval that night by the lake. Like a wolf, or a stallion, or something even more soulless than Cristoval.

Ranger fiddled with the black saddle on the back of his preferred stallion. The saddle vanished into the beast's coat and unless you knew it was there, was nearly impossible to see. "I told ye. First the chapel, then the battle, aye?"

Ranger's reason for touring Calahorra: *Capilla de las Almas Perdidas*, the Chapel of Lost Souls. Cristoval knew of the place in question. Everyone in La Rioja knew of the Chapel, though only a few knew its location.

It was not a place of dissolution, or isolation, even though it sat at the bottom of a hole inside a cave accessible only through a hidden vaulted entrance. Sun streamed down into that hole, bouncing off the golden rock and the clean white of marble, turning black shadows red. Angels sang there, with the whistles of mountain winds.

It was not a place for Ranger.

Cristoval pulled on his other boot. "Why the fascination with the Chapel?" he asked. He had asked at other times. He doubted he would get an answer this time, either.

Ranger patted the forehead of his stallion. "Nae much longer, brother," he said to the beast.

The Scot held his hand at eye level. "Church." He dropped his hand level with his shoulders. "My friend Quintus, may he continue his rebellions in those Underworld fields the Romans loved sae much."

He dropped his hand level with his belly. "Yer ancestral Vascones an' their lovely gods." Then he dropped it to his hips. "An' things *sae* much older."

Cristoval stood in front of his vines, boots on his feet, his cloak adjusted and gloves returned to his now burning-with-cold fingers.

He had been correct. The Scot wished a macabre tour before he started his new killing spree. Even a blackened soul was a soul capable of enjoyment. Cristoval would not begrudge the man his joys.

Ranger inhaled sharply. He stepped toward Cristoval. "I can smell a yearnin' from the far side o' my loch." He sniffed again. "Any yearnin'."

Cristoval adjusted his cloak. "I yearn only to serve the Crown of Castile." His voice sounded as hollow as his soul.

Ranger laughed and slapped his knee. "Nae, Castilian." He took another step closer. "Ye yearn for what ye dinnae have." He twirled a finger in the air. "Ye did when I found ye on the shores o' my brother's loch, an' ye do now. Though..." He made a show of inhaling deeply. "This place o' vines brings up a yearnin' for..." He inhaled again. "A daughter!"

The grin Ranger threw Cristoval would have made a lesser man step back. But he was Cristoval Armand Martinez, warrior of the Crown, death in the eyes of infidels, and a man who did not care. A black-haired Scot would not shake his steady if soulless constitution.

Cristoval set his hand on his knife's hilt anyway.

Ranger pointed and laughed again. "Ye're *adorable*, my friend!" He stepped back to his stallions. "We've bigger plans than Spanish lasses, eh, brothers?"

All three stallions snorted.

"See, my boys agree." Ranger strutted over to his massive beasts. "Be a good man, Castilian, an' answer for us. How old would she be, now?" He inhaled again. "Old enough, I wager."

"Do not threaten a Christian woman while standing on Castilian soil," Cristoval said. *Do not threaten my daughter*, he thought. His lovely bean. The reason for the vines in which they stood. That one little bit of yearning that said maybe, perhaps, he hadn't lost all the splinters of his soul.

Another peal of Ranger's big, vicious laugh burst from the Scot's chest. "We love how ye Catholics are sae blind t' the obvious around ye," Ranger said. "In the end, it'll make it easier for my King."

Had Cristoval been used by James IV, the Crown of Scotland? Had he brought in a mercenary who meant ill to his Queen and her idiot husband?

Ranger's eyes narrowed. "Ye're wonderin' if I care about your wee Spanish battles." He squared his shoulders. He returned to his saddled stallion, and in one swift motion, vaulted onto the beast's back.

The beast whipped his head as if annoyed at being mounted, and whinnied out his disdain.

Ranger leaned forward and whispered something Cristoval could not hear, then flicked the beast's ear. The stallion snorted a response, and pawed at the cold dirt. "Nae more than I care about the Stewarts an' the Tudors, Castilian."

Cristoval had made a deal with a demon. Or a spy. He'd crossed to Scotland and he'd gone through the motions and he'd done what his Queen required because he was hollow and he had no soul with which to view another warrior's heart. He'd seen a mighty sword and mightier stallions suitable for the Queen's generals.

The trip to the Chapel had been one day's extra riding and a chance for him to touch his land again.

To yearn.

"What are you?" Cristoval asked.

Ranger frowned. "My brothers an' I, we dinnae have much touch wi' men, unless ye're like-minded." He reined the stallion around so he could look down at Cristoval. "Ye're more like-minded than ye believe yerself t' be, Castilian."

Cristoval felt a push at his mind. A sensation. A *filling*. He'd felt a smaller version of the same filling in Scotland, on the shores of the loch, when Ranger said, "Ye'll take me t' Calahorra."

He had a duty to th' Crown. He had no soul and his duty at least kept th' hollow in his chest from consumin' his flesh.

The smallest of stallions nudged Cristoval's shoulder.

"Get on your mare an' take us where we need t' be," Ranger growled.

"*Capilla de las Almas Perdidas,*" Cristoval muttered. The Chapel of Lost Souls.

Maybe he'd find a splinter of his own inside.

CHAPTER 2

Cristoval's mare did not like Ranger's stallions. He should listen to his horse's small twitches and sidesteps as much as he should listen to his own still, small voices. But the Crown wanted Granada.

Cristoval rubbed his mare's head. "I'm surprised you care," he said. The horse had seen as many battles as he had, and not once had the beast bolted. Perhaps the consistent yet faint hint of brackish water the stallions produced after a good gallop made her skittish.

Or perhaps...

He blinked a few times. That whore Isabella had sent him out. He'd tripped across ocean waters to a cold hell full of devil men in black who called equally black stallions "brother." He'd left his home for her. He'd lost his land and his child.

He would deliver the mercenary. Then he would deal with the lass who called herself Queen. Perhaps he'd take care of the ex-wife, the other whore who took his child.

But first, he would do his brothers well, and escort them to a place of glory, so that they could all bathe in its beauty and godliness. All the lands of Iberia—and the lands of the Isles—were dotted with holy places claimed in the name of the one true God. As they should be.

One could not find Heaven unless the signposts were marked correctly.

They left the Oja behind and rode hard west along the base of the mountains toward Calahorra, and arrived at the peak with the hidden chapel just before midday. Trees became shrubs as they climbed. Rocks became boulders.

A stream had cut into a crag and opened a crack to the sky in the ceiling of what had once been a vaulted cave. Noon light bounced down through the crack and drew wide, overlapping, shadowed patterns on the vault's gravel floor.

Cristoval left his mare at the entrance so that she could drink from a small stream and graze on the low scrub.

Ranger pointed. "In there?" he asked.

The valley was not visible from the entrance. "We must follow the light," Cristoval answered. *Stay within the line of light cast through the crack and walk the ways to Heaven,* he thought.

They stepped into the vault. A line of light blazed on the gravel floor from the crack above. Dust swirled up into it like living fireflies. The air moved with the light, pushing against their backs, inward toward the open sink hole—and the chapel—in the center of the cave complex.

There were hidden paintings in these rocks. Lines drawn with charcoal and ocher of animals that did not exist in Spain. Some were recognizable, like the lions. Other were stout, one-horned beasts. A few were striped or spotted ponies. They were all tucked away deep in the side caves, and ignored by the Church.

Ranger walked to the side of the line of light, three steps to the side of Cristoval and in front of his stallions. He did not carry their reins; they followed of their own accord, also staying out of the blazing golden warm beauty marking their way. Cristoval stayed out of the light as well, more because it decreased his ability to see the walls and the path ahead than because it felt sacrilegious.

Old Latin words had been carved into the cave's walls. Most had been worn down, either by water or fingers, but Cristoval picked out *anima mea* and other words he knew came from scriptures.

The passage narrowed. The stallions shifted to clacking along the gravel in single file. Sunshine blazed down from above so brightly Cristoval felt it as a vibration, a continuous boom, filling his bones and his eyes and his ears.

He stepped around the corner and into a patch of winter-dead grass. Three steps in, a boulder so tall and wide it fully blocked his view stood between him and the interior of the Chapel's sinkhole.

He reached out, touching moss and slick lichens, and ran his finger over the rock's surface.

Ranger stepped up to his side. "It's inscribed." He scraped off some of the moss and exposed an alphabet Cristoval did not recognize. "*Leave these souls lost*, it says. *Heh*. Go awa', Castilian."

He shoved Cristoval backward.

Cristoval stumbled. Ranger was strong, but Cristoval had been in many fights, and his body understood how to stay on its feet. He twisted to the side, just missing hitting his head on the rocky wall, dropped to a crouch and—

Ranger's hold snapped off Cristoval's mind the way a weak spot in twine snapped when stretched too far. That twine had been yanked up from inside Cristoval and spun out of cold anger at his remarried wife, at his Queen for sending him into battles, at himself for looking away when Ranger murdered those women on the English coast. They were little angers, things that did not press through his hollowness, but brushed up against it.

And Ranger had coiled them around his mind.

Ranger chuckled. "Well, look at that," he said to the first stallion.

The beast chuckled, too, then snorted.

"Nay," Ranger answered the stallion. "Ye ken pushin' the like-minded is taxin'. We need our wits." Ranger patted the stallion's neck. "Take your brothers in."

The stallion brayed to the other two, then nodded and walked around the boulder.

Ranger crouched in front of Cristoval. "I'm goin' tae kill ye now." He glanced around the boulder. He rubbed at the side of his nose. "But first, those yearnin's o' yours. I ken the one fer the lost lass babe.

That's simple." His brow knitted together. "There's a flatness t' ye, which I ken all too well. I've come to believe it's what fighters like ye do t' yerselves t' make all the killin' fine." He leaned closer. "Makes it easy for ye t' do th' biddin' o' your Crown, aye? All th' tasks, big an' little."

Cristoval did not answer.

Ranger grinned. "Unless ye like th' killin'. Then ye dinnae need t' strip out that part o' yer soul."

Cristoval shifted his weight and moved his hand to the hilt of the knife he carried on his belt.

Ranger's grin turned into an expression of mock confusion. "But it's the *other* yearnin' I dinnae ken. The *real* one under all the rest."

Cristoval pulled the knife from its sheath.

Ranger grabbed his hand before the knife cleared Cristoval's cloak.

On the other side of the boulder, one of the stallions brayed. Clomps followed—clomps that changed to footfalls as they reverberated throughout the space.

"Ranger!" a man who should not be there in the Chapel behind the boulder called. A man who did not come in with them. "We found the entrance!"

"Aye, brother, I'm comin'," Ranger called. Then to Cristoval: "Your *Capilla de las Almas Perdidas* was built atop a shrine t' a god named Pluto, the King o' the Underworld." He nodded toward what waited on the other side of the boulder. "That shrine was built atop an older one t' a god named Berobreo, the King o' th' Otherworlds."

Castilla was dotted with chapels and churches built over pagan shrines. That was how believers learned the true path of the one true God.

Ranger slammed Cristoval's arm against the rock. Cristoval yelped and the knife fell from his hand. "We're here t' *Reconquista* it for the King o' the Fae."

Fae? The Church had driven away all such spirits.

The Scot leaned close to Cristoval. "I just cannae put my finger on what's in that heart o' yours." He shook his head. "Ye do like the murderin', ye ken. I smell it on yer blackened soul."

And that's where Ranger was wrong. "I don't have a soul," Cristoval said.

Ranger's eyebrow arched. "A Catholic who doesnae believe he has a soul!" Ranger laughed. "Well then, let's kill ye where the lost souls be." He dragged Cristoval toward the boulder. "Perhaps you'll find yours in the heap."

Cristoval kicked at the gravel and the dead grass. He pawed at Ranger's arms. He growled and hit but the Scot dragged him around the boulder and into the bright noon light.

The Chapel wasn't a chapel like any built by Spanish Christians, or any mosque built by the Muslims of the Emirates, and looked more like the old Roman ruins dotting the Castilla. White marble columns held up a marble roof. Steps led up to the doorless entrance. Strange statuary and carvings of gods, chariots, horses, and other animals covered the colonnade. The building wasn't wider than a normal house, but it extended all the way to the back wall of the sink hole, and into the rock itself.

The noon sun set the polished marble aglow. Cristoval squinted.

Another Scot walked out of the darkness inside the chapel. He was taller than Ranger but not as wide. His features were almost identical, with the same square jaw and black-as-night hair. He smoothed the front of his tunic. "Dinnae need a sacrifice, Ranger," he said. He wore a black kilt and black war boots identical to Rangers.

The stallions were gone. Ranger's "brothers" were about.

He knew Ranger was *wrong*. He knew the stallions were *wrong*, also. And Ranger had said they worked in service of the King of the Fae.

He knew the old tales. "You're not supposed to be able to leave your lakes," he muttered. He knew some of the old tales of other lands, too. Of selkies and Norse elves and these men.

Kelpies.

Ranger laughed. "Ye have nae idea how true magic works, do ye, wee Catholic Castilian?"

The kelpie standing on the steps frowned. "Will ye kill him, please?" He pointed at Cristoval. "We have work, Ranger."

Ranger hauled Cristoval to his feet and brushed off his cloak. "He doesnae have a soul, Seamus," he said. "He might be useful when we're sniffin' 'round down there."

The one Ranger called Seamus rolled his eyes. "He's *mundane*." He said "mundane" as if being one was the worst filth in the world.

Perhaps he was the worst filth. Perhaps that was why he lost his soul one shard at a time.

Ranger pushed him forward. "Who's in charge here, brother?" he snarled.

Seamus did not respond, nor did his expression change. He kept his face perfectly unchanged from the hate he threw at Cristoval.

Perhaps he had not heard Ranger. More likely he did not agree, and not agreeing meant that Cristoval had a wedge he could hack between these demons. The fewer of them who left this place, the better.

Ranger pushed him again and he tripped up the steps to the narrow colonnade. Two lit torches in stands framed a marble crypt in the center of the floor inside. The Chapel held nothing else. No pews. No altar. Nothing but the two torches and a crypt the kelpies had managed to open.

Ranger pushed him inside. The acrid wet smell of mildew and decay hit Cristoval full force and he covered his mouth. He stumbled forward, his face covered in the corner of his elbow, and looked down into the crypt.

The other two kelpies were down there, about a full floor below the crypt, both holding torches in a room that appeared to be about the size of one stable stall. Neither seemed upset about the smell.

There was nothing down there but the kelpies. No markings on the walls. Nothing dead to make that smell. No holes in the marble bricks lining the small room. No dust. Nothing but pristine white marble and two evil demon Scots.

The kelpie called Seamus jumped over the side of the crypt. He landed gracefully in the middle of the small room without a thud or even too much of an outward flicker of his kilt.

He looked up. "There's a gate here," he said. "I smell it."

A gate to Hell. It had to be. Nothing else would reek so.

"Up." Ranger lifted Cristoval up to the edge of the crypt.

"No, no," Cristoval kicked. He might not have a soul but he was still alive. He would not walk willingly into Hell.

Ranger pushed.

Cristoval dropped toward the floor, but he was a fighter, and his body understood what to do. He rolled out of his landing and directly into one of the other two kelpies.

A big black boot heel hit his hip. "What's the mundane for?" the kelpie said.

Cristoval rolled back into the middle of the small room. There was no way he'd get out now. Not without help from the kelpies. He'd die down here inside Death's air. He yanked his tunic up over his mouth and nose.

Ranger landed just as gracefully as Seamus. "An offerin', in case."

Seamus made a face as if Ranger was the stupidest kelpie he'd ever met. "What difference does it make?" Seamus kicked at Cristoval again.

He caught the kelpie's leg, one hand on his calf and the other on the inside of his knee.

Cristoval snapped the hand on the knee downward.

Seamus dropped onto his side. He huffed in the rancid air, and when he sat up, wisps of something bright and glowing trailed from the sides of his sea green eyes.

The rancid air charged as if lightning had just struck.

Cristoval should not have drawn the ire of a kelpie. He should not have tempted this fate, in here with a creature that could not be real, with no way out other than to journey into Hell.

Ranger chuckled. "Maybe some blood magic, boys?" He threw his arms wide and almost hit the fourth kelpie in the small space.

The strange aurora-like pale green light trailed through the shadows when Seamus jumped to a squat.

He grinned like a rabid wolf.

The kelpie's punch hit the side of Cristoval's head. He swung with it, doing his best to send the force into a spin instead of his bones, and slammed into the cold marble bricks of the crypt's wall.

They were smoother than they should have been, the bricks. So smooth he slid down them as if they were the slipperiest ice the winter had ever made.

Slippery like Hell itself. Not the brimstone Hell of his Catholic Queen. Real Hell, where nothing moved, and nothing mattered. Where torment was distilled to its unmeasurable essence and made so pure that it and only it spun into heat and flame.

For a split second, its gray filled his eyes, and its flat diffuse dust filled his nose and coated his throat. He'd been kicked into the gate to the Underworld, or the Otherworlds, as Ranger said. He was about to fall through, cold, forgotten, unfinished.

His hollowness welcomed vanishing into the nothingness. He had not truly felt or sensed or considered since he lost the first shard of his soul, in that first battle, when he slashed open a fellow Spaniard because Castile and Aragon could not find their ways. He'd lost the last splinter on sandy ground outside the gates of Granada.

So this evenness of death was nothing new.

But it was not his hidden yearning, to be dead.

He knew this because yearnings were the last to die. Yearnings spun for a moment or two in the timelessness of the Underworld while the rest of a man stopped caring.

He wanted to live, or to finish living. He had not yet lived, not truly. He had walked, yes. Walked away from this daughter and his wife and his vines because he was the property of the Crown.

But the yearning for life wasn't his hidden yearning. No.

He'd walked away because he was the property of the Crown.

He wanted to be free.

Cristoval dropped to the floor. He rolled over onto his back and looked up at the crypt entrance, at the blazing sunshine of life flowing into the rancid hole in the Earth where he lay dying. And there, at the corners of the hole, between the lip of the vault opening and the white marble stone of the walls, sat demons.

He didn't think the kelpies saw them. They argued amongst themselves, both gleeful that they'd killed a mundane and annoyed that the killin' was distractin' from their work. So they didn't look up.

The demons roiled up there, one black, one white, one red, and one a green-gray pallor. Four balls of something opposite of the flat nothingness of Hell, but not opposite its intent. They jiggled and flowed in and out of themselves as if they stole all the caring a soul held so that they could kick it into Hell. Four spheres, perhaps, or droplets, of what the Church taught no longer existed. Of magic and power and no man's Crown.

He knew the demons. He was a fighter and a Catholic man of war, no matter how he tried to ignore the Church's useless absolutions and teachings. He knew the ways, both new and old. He'd lived those demons: The First, the white, the *Reconquista* and the diseases that came with it. Then the Second, the red blood of War. The Third, the hungers, the yearnings, the Famine of souls and bodies. And the Fourth, the pallor of Death.

"You four had no idea what your King sent you to find, did you?" he choked out. A magical King had sacrificed the lesser of his kind, the warriors, the fodder who were owned and expendable, to procure demonic weapons. "Who's going to ride each of you as you go forth and destroy?"

Their King had sent them to gather the horrors inside a marble Pandora's Box.

Cristoval spat a laugh from his heavy chest. Four literal Horsemen had been sent from Scotland to find a gate to Hell and were about to become the Apocalypse.

The irony of the moment filled him with a joy he had not felt since the day he had held his bean of a baby daughter.

Yet the Horses of the Apocalypse needed riders.

All four of the kelpies looked up. Seamus yelled in Gaelic. Ranger reached up his hands as if truly, utterly surprised.

And then the white demon was upon Ranger, coiling in and around the black adornments that were his britches, and boots, and bridle. The red and black demons fell on the kelpies whose names

Cristoval did not know, coiling through their hair, filling their eyes and ears and nostrils.

The last dropped between Cristoval and Seamus. It wriggled like a droplet of water, like one of the kelpie's lochs, until it snapped a tentacle toward Cristoval.

You yearn for freedom, it said to him. *Yet you have no soul with which to yearn.*

"Yes," he whispered with what felt like his final breath.

Seamus bellowed. He moved to slam his fists into the ball but froze when Death touched him with yet another tentacle.

The kelpies' souls yearn only for war. Death wiggled. *We understand war.*

Yes, they did.

We wish to understand the world.

He would have chuckled if he'd had the wind to do so. "You *are* the world," he whispered.

Death wiggled with his words as if attempting to place them within its own context. *No. We are the wind in the world's branches, the frost on its leaves, the worm in its roots.*

"And you are its end," Cristoval said. His body, his world. *The world.*

Yes, Death said.

"Yes," he answered. It would send him on his way through the gate into The Land of the Dead because that was what Death did. It might send the kelpies through as well, and return to its resting place at the corners of the entrance into this place.

Do you understand what freedom is? Death asked.

"I understand you," he breathed. He would not lie to Death. He understood the hell of war but he did not understand his own yearnings. If he did, he would not be dying at the bottom of magical marble crypt.

Is freedom possible?

"Only you can answer that." Death had him, then, coiling under his tunic and britches. It filled the hollowness in his chest with itself. It flowed down his legs and into his boots, and wrapped its cold flat nothingness around his feet.

They tingled, his toes, as Death released his heat.

I release you from duty to the Crown, Death said. Then it snapped out to Seamus, taking him as Cristoval's mount.

He could do as he pleased, now. Could Death? Any of the Horsemen? They would have to test those winds, that frost, those worms.

And together, they rode out of their own accord.

EPILOGUE TWO

Cen-Ko Distribution Warehouse, Osaka, Japan...

I smay-Giselda St. Martin's stilettos clicked across the warehouse's floor. The place was horrifically dusty, to the point the air looked more like a fog bank than anything breathable. She sneezed once and rubbed her nose, and blinked back the debris in the air.

She slipped a little on the dust-slicked floor but righted herself before the jorōgumo noticed. "You do understand the gravity of this situation," she said.

The jorōgumo's disdain for "the simple mundane" Ismay was as thick as the stale air in this terrible little place. The warehouse itself wasn't much bigger than a store front, and easily missed by taxies and delivery trucks alike.

Those Siberian elves had come through for her with the hacked fae phone. It, plus her werewolf bodyguard, meant she met the jorōgumo on equal footing, even if she was simple.

Magicals. They were all fat arrogant bastards. And they would all pay.

The jorōgumo stopped in front of a scuffed-up blue and white plastic cooler. The thing looked as if it had gone through many work crews' lunch times. "It's in here."

Ismay scoffed. "I paid you for the whole body," she said, though she did not need the whole body. She only needed a very specific part of the body. She'd paid for the whole because the less information this jorōgumo had, the better.

The jorōgumo's eyes narrowed. "The whole body no longer exists." She flipped open the cooler.

Ismay looked down at the hand of the Vampire God.

"Do you want it or not?" the jorōgumo asked.

Ismay sighed more to put on a good show than out of glee. "Yes. But I'm not paying for the whole body."

The jorōgumo slammed the cooler closed. "Fine." She picked it up and handed it to Ismay. "Get out. Do *not* come back, do you understand? Japan is closed to outsider magic."

Ismay took the cooler. She did not break eye contact with the jorōgumo as she bowed her goodbye. "I understand," she said.

She turned on the spikey heel of her four-thousand-dollar shoe and click-clicked her way back to her waiting taxi.

The jorōgumo had no idea what she'd done. What she'd given up. The hand, if the wolf told her the truth, contained tendons from the only mundane part of the Vampire God. Except he hadn't been mundane. He'd been transformed into a Rider.

Ismay-Giselda St. Martin, the newly-minted CEO of Mednidyne Pharmaceuticals now that her idiotic brother had gotten himself killed by werewolves and elves over an equally-idiotic vendetta, took her prize and left Japan.

Because she could have anything she wanted now. Power. Immortality. Patent upon patent upon patent.

She no longer needed Fenrir's blessing. Why would she?

The Apocalypse was hers.

MAGIC SCORNED

What's worse than Ragnarok?
The Apocalypse.

A violent revolt rocks the fae realms. The talking axe and sword stir up an old beef between King Odinsson and King Oberon. Ancient jotunn magic rears its head. And Robin Goodfellow unleashes the most dangerous fae on Earth: kelpies carrying the magic of the Horsemen of the Apocalypse.

Can Frank and the elves stop War, Famine, and Pestilence from decimating Alfheim and the world?

MAGIC SCORNED, Northern Creatures #8, available JANUARY 5, 2023!

GET FREE BOOKS

SUBSCRIBE TO KRIS AUSTEN RADCLIFFE'S NEWSLETTER

You will be notified when Kris Austen Radcliffe's next novel is released, as well as gain access to an occasional free bit of author-produced goodness. Your email address will never be shared and you can unsubscribe at any time.

WWW.SIXTALONSIGN.COM/MAILING-LIST-SIGN-UP/

ALSO BY KRIS AUSTEN RADCLIFFE

KRIS AUSTEN RADCLIFFE

Smart Urban Fantasy:

Northern Creatures

Monster Born

Vampire Cursed

Elf Raised

Wolf Hunted

Fae Touched

Death Kissed

God Forsaken

Magic Scorned

Witch Burned (*coming soon*)

* * *

Genre-bending Science Fiction about

love, family, and dragons:

WORLD ON FIRE

Series one

Fate Fire Shifter Dragon

Games of Fate

Flux of Skin

Fifth of Blood

Bonds Broken & Silent

All But Human

Men and Beasts

The Burning World

Dragon's Fate and Other Stories

Series Two

Witch of the Midnight Blade

Witch of the Midnight Blade Part One

Witch of the Midnight Blade Part Two

Witch of the Midnight Blade Part Three

Witch of the Midnight Blade: The Complete Series

Series Three

World on Fire

Call of the Dragonslayer (*coming soon*)

* * *

Hot Contemporary Romance:

The Quidell Brothers

Thomas's Muse

Daniel's Fire

Robert's Soul

Thomas's Need

Quidell Brothers Box Set

Includes:

Thomas's Muse

Daniel's Fire

Roberts's Soul

ABOUT THE AUTHOR

Kris's Science Fiction universe, **World on Fire**, brings her descriptive touch to the fantastic. Her Urban Fantasy series, **Northern Creatures**, sets her magic free. She's traversed many storytelling worlds including dabbles in film and comic books, spent time as a talent agent and a textbook photo coordinator, as well written nonfiction. But she craved narrative and richly-textured worlds—and unexpected, true love.

Kris lives in Minnesota with one husband, two daughters, and three cats.

For more information
www.krisaustenradcliffe.com